HIS SECOND CHANCE

HAMMOND FAMILY FARM ROMANCE, BOOK 2

LIZ ISAACSON

ISBN-13: 978-1-63876-023-8

HIS SECOND CHANCE

CHAPTER 1

*M*atthew Whettstein finished with his tie and went down the hall to the kitchen. Britt and Keith both sat at the tiny table pushed into a corner, each with a bowl of oatmeal in front of them. "How is it?" he asked his kids.

"Good," Keith said, getting up. He too wore his best Sunday suit, but his tie sat askew at his collar. Britt gave Matt a thumbs-up, her mouth full of her lunch.

Matt hated that he'd made oatmeal for lunch, but it was easy, and they had a long day ahead of them still. Not only that, but he'd been out in the fresh snow, fighting the tractor and then the barn doors for far too long.

If they didn't leave in the next five minutes, they'd be late to the wedding.

Matt did not want to be late for Hunter Hammond's marriage ceremony. He loved the kid—now a twenty-six-year-old man, Matt supposed—as if he were his own, and he'd been working for the Hammond's on their family farm for over fifteen years.

"Finish up, Britt," he said, turning to his son. "Let me fix your tie, bud."

Keith held still and let him do it, but he wore an edge in his eyes. Matt smiled at him anyway, because with a fifteen-year-old, it was either smile or snap. "It's crooked. I'm pretty sure Hunter was dating Molly when he was fifteen, and look at them now." Matt got the offending knot in just the right place and ran his hands over his son's shoulders.

He'd definitely put on some muscle since they'd moved to Ivory Peaks eighteen months ago. Keith had been working the farm too, earning money and learning the ins and outs of horse care from one of the best— Gloria Munson.

Matt thought he was a pretty decent groomsman too, and his pride in his work had only increased since he'd made the move permanent.

Keith loved working with the horses, though he'd never said so. Matt could just tell by the way the boy got up in the morning and took care of them before school, rain or shine. He could sometimes be found leaning against a fence, talking to a horse. He led them all to their therapy appointments, and he'd even agreed to participate in the equine therapy program that Hunter and his soon-to-be-wife, Molly, had started last year.

Pony Power had opened her doors to children with a variety of needs in May of last year, but Matt, Gloria,

Molly, and Hunter had been working on the program for almost a year before that. He loved watching the kids come and go on the farm, and he loved that his two children had been getting the help they needed too.

Behind him, a crash sounded, and Matt spun to find Britt on the floor, her bowl still skittering toward his boots. "You okay?" He stepped over the dish to his daughter, gently putting his hands under her arms and lifting her up.

Tears filled her precious blue eyes, and Matt hugged her, wishing with everything in him that he could take her weaknesses and illnesses from her. He couldn't, and most days, he accepted that. Sometimes, though, the ache in his father heart brought about a sense of injustice and sadness. He'd taken her to a half-dozen doctors, and none of them could give him an official diagnosis. With her stuttering and her poor muscle control, one had hypothesized she'd had a stroke at some point in her life.

Another had said her symptoms sometimes came from mental retardation, usually caused when the brain went without oxygen for too long. Another thought perhaps fetal alcohol syndrome. The real problem was, Brittany had not suffered any of those things, at least not that Matt knew of. No strokes. No time underwater or without oxygen. Her mother hadn't drunk while she was pregnant.

"You're okay," he whispered to his daughter, pressing his eyes closed for only a moment. "Did your legs just give out?"

She nodded against his shoulder, being very brave and

only sniffling. She suddenly pushed away from him, her eyes wide and afraid. "Is my ha-ha-hair okay, Dad-dad-daddy?" She reached up to touch her pretty hair, which Elise and Jane had come to braid that morning.

Jane was Hunter's half-sister, and she was only a couple of years older than Brittany. His daughter loved Jane with her whole heart and soul, and they'd been planning on matching hairstyles for the wedding for months now. Elise, Jane's mother, could plait hair into any number of braids, and she'd done one down to Britt's ear on each side, then pulled them back into a ponytail on the back of her head. The rest of her hair fell in soft curls to her shoulders, and Britt had stood in front of the mirror for ten minutes after Elise and Jane had left the cabin.

"It's still perfect, baby," he whispered, smoothing down a couple of errant curls. He touched his nose to hers, choking on his emotions. "You're beautiful." He lowered her to the ground and kept a firm grip on her forearm until she found her balance.

Just like that, she was back to her cheerful and positive self, and Matt wondered how she did it. He wanted to retreat down the hall and punch something while he growled about how unfair life was. After the anger subsided, he'd fall to his knees and beg God to help him with his daughter.

For a while there, Matt had begged God to cure Brittany, but after several months of pleading without any change in her condition, Matt realized he'd been asking for the wrong thing.

He didn't need Brittany to be cured; he needed to learn how to help her, take care of her, and protect her.

That was when Matt had decided he couldn't stay with his ex-wife. The road since then had been mostly uphill, with plenty of ruts and potholes, but Matt felt like he, Keith, and Brittany were almost to the top of their personal mountain.

"Ready?" he asked the kids. "We better get going. It snowed eight inches out there, and we've got to get to the gardens by one."

"I've got Britt," Keith said quietly, stepping around Matt in the small kitchen and taking his sister's hand. "You're bringing the saddle, right?"

"Stars and lights," Matt said, something his father used to say whenever he was surprised or scared. "I forgot." He jogged down the short hall to his bedroom, where the stained and polished saddle waited over the armchair. He gazed at it for a moment, then hefted it onto his shoulder and rejoined his children in the kitchen. "Got it. Let's go."

Matt had already cleared a path to his truck, and he'd already driven it that morning. They got to the vehicle, and Matt put the saddle in the backseat with Britt. "You keep an eye on that, now, okay?" He grinned at her as she pulled her seatbelt across her lap and clicked it into place.

He got in the front with Keith, and since he'd only been home for about forty-five minutes, the truck still held some heat. He got it fired up and the heater blowing again, and they set out for the Royal Chinese Gardens, which lay on the outskirts of Denver.

The drive took a while, but at least the snow plows had been out to clear the roads. Matt sang along with the radio, grinning at Britt as she added her sweet voice to the country songs she knew. Keith rolled his eyes a time or two, but Matt saw him tapping his foot to at least three tunes.

The gardens touted masterfully carved hedges, rare plants and trees from China, and the biggest flowering blossom festival in the state. All of that happened in the springtime, though, and as it as the middle of January, and everything existed under two feet of snow, Matt didn't think they'd be seeing any flowers today.

How wrong he was. The parking lot gate had blue and white flowers laced through it, telling people they'd reached the right destination if they were looking for the Hammond wedding.

Matt should've known. The Hammonds had more money than most people could comprehend, but they weren't stuck-up or pretentious. They were, however, public figures, and as such, there was an image to uphold. As he parked in an empty spot, Matt saw no less than three people with cameras, each doing something different, though he wasn't sure what.

"Come on." He got out, and while the temperature could steal a man's breath, he didn't mind it. He hailed from Montana, and he'd been working his father's farm for decades in weather much colder than this.

He retrieved the saddle from the backseat and listened to Keith tell Britt there might be icy spots on the sidewalk, so she needed to hold onto him tightly. She promised she would, and Matt led the way toward the huge, light, airy dome in the center of the gardens.

Molly had wanted a winter wedding, but she knew it would still have to take place indoors. She and Hunter had wanted to be married before Christmas, but the holidays had turned out to be a popular time for nuptials, and the Chinese Gardens had been booked. She'd taken the next available Saturday, and Matt had wondered what all the fuss was about.

Now, he knew. As he walked down the cleared and salted sidewalk, he understood why Molly had wanted this venue. Why she'd brought the pictures to the lunches she came to out at the farm, and why she and Gloria had poured over them for so long and so often.

Tall, alabaster pillars lined the walkway on both sides, a delicate white rope hanging down in a smile between them. Pink, red, orange, and yellow flowers ran the length of the supports, and on every other one, a large picture of Molly and Hunter had been nailed right at adult eye-level.

He couldn't help smiling at the photos. Molly and Hunter were some of his best friends, and he loved them both so much.

His breath steamed in front of him, and the saddle started to get heavy. He finally reached the dome and opened the door so his children could enter before him.

"There you are." A woman rushed toward him as if

she'd been lying in wait to accost him the moment he arrived. "Thank heavens. Bring that saddle right up front." She spun on her heel and marched away from him, moving fast for someone in a skirt so tight around the knees.

Matt nearly rolled his eyes, but he followed Jessa Thompson, the wedding planner. He couldn't even imagine what she'd have done had he forgotten the saddle.

"Find us a seat," he called over his shoulder to the kids. "Maybe up here by Elise." He passed her, and she got up to look behind him.

He continued all the way to the altar, where he and Jessa positioned the saddle in the exact right spot. "I knew it would fit," he said, pride in every syllable. He gazed at the saddle, which Jessa started decorating with flowers.

"The wedding starts in twenty minutes," she said, giving him a dirty look. "I thought you were never going to show up."

"I told you what time I'd be here," he said. "It takes five minutes to lace flowers through the leather." He knew, because he'd done it himself, and if he could get his thick fingers to tuck stems through the straps he'd purposefully created and looped to hold them, anyone could.

"Still."

Still what? he wanted to ask, but he didn't. He turned away from Jessa and retreated back to the first couple of rows. All of the Hammonds had already arrived, and Matt had a hard time telling some of Hunter's uncles apart. He did have a set of identical twins in there, so Matt didn't feel too badly about it.

He shook hands with Chris, Hunter's grandfather, and sat down next to him. "How are you?" he asked quietly. Quiet enough that no one nearby would overhear. He had a special relationship with the man, almost like Chris could channel the spirit of his father.

"It's been a busy morning already," Chris said with a smile. "Spilled juice all down the front of one of the flower girl's dresses, and then Ames got in a car accident on the way here."

"You're kidding." Matt stood up and looked around. "He's here, though, right?"

"He's here. He was driving over with Colton, so they didn't have any kids with them, thankfully."

Matt sat back down and looked at Chris. The man had eyes the color of fresh dirt, and he wore his eighty-four years of age really well. His dark hair was always trimmed, and Matt had learned that Elise had been doing that for him for years. Today, he wore an impressive suit—probably one very much like the ones he used to wear as CEO of the Hammond family company.

Hunter was the CEO now, and Matt had seen him in plenty of similar-looking suits, as he sometimes came straight to the farm from the office.

Matt would rather die a slow death than wear a suit to work each day. Just wearing one to church each week, sans jacket, was a chore for him. He always unknotted his tie and unbuttoned that top button on his shirt the moment he hit the driver's seat following the sermon, and he hoped he didn't choke today. After all, the wedding would be a lot longer than a Sabbath-day sermon.

"Matthew," a man said, and Matt turned toward the pastor himself.

"Hello, Pastor Benson." Matt stood up again, a smile dancing across his face. "Is she ready?"

"She seems to be." Pastor Benson shook his hand, his smile warm and his eyes filled with kindness. "She's actually asked me to find you. She wants you to come to the bride's room for a minute."

"Really?" Matt glanced around as if someone would tell him the pastor was lying.

"Do you see Gloria?" Pastor Benson asked. "She's supposed to go back too."

"I haven't seen her." Matt turned to survey the rows and rows of chairs, which had started to fill since he'd arrived. Jessa flitted from this item to that one, and the noise inside the dome increased as more and more people streamed through the doors in the back.

Matt swallowed at the sheer size of this place. It must hold five hundred people, and he suddenly very much wanted to escape.

"There she is," he said, a measure of relief filling him when he spotted Gloria's soft, wavy hair and freckled face. "I'll grab her, and we'll go back."

"Thank you," Pastor Benson said. "I need to get set up at the altar." He smiled and walked that way. Matt had listened to Molly detail how her father would walk her down the aisle first, then perform the ceremony. He supposed Pastor Benson did need to get some things organized before he went to join the wedding party.

Matt paused next to Elise and said, "Molly asked for me and Gloria to come back for a minute. Are you okay with the kids?" He looked at Keith, who nodded.

"We're fine, Dad."

"They're fine," Elise assured him.

He nodded at her, his gratitude for the woman reaching new heights. When she'd first come to Ivory Peaks, Matt had wondered what Gray Hammond had been thinking. She wasn't a city slicker, but she didn't understand farm life. Elise had learned, one day at a time, and she'd been fearless.

Matt admired that, and as he walked toward Gloria, he couldn't help admiring her too. Physically, she was downright gorgeous, with strong arms and shoulders that still looked feminine. Today, she wore a bright blue dress that hugged her curves and fell to her knee, along with a pair of black heels that put her closer to Matt's height. Maybe only a couple of inches shorter, in fact.

Since she'd arrived in Ivory Peaks, he hadn't been in a place to do much more than work with Gloria on the farm. They'd talked about their lives back in Montana, as she'd been born and raised in the same small town as him. They'd even dated for a while in Sugar Pond, and looking at her now, Matt wondered if he could have a second chance with the woman.

His heart boomed in a weird way, something it hadn't done in a long, long time. He nearly tripped over his own feet as he tried to figure out what was different now that hadn't been yesterday.

Maybe you're ready, he thought. He'd come to Ivory Peaks only a few months after his divorce, and he hadn't been thinking about getting a new girlfriend or wife.

Maybe now you are.

"Gloria," he said, his voice actually breaking as if he were the fifteen-year-old talking to the girl he had a crush on.

She turned from one of Hunter's aunts and looked at him. Her eyes slid right down to his polished and pristine cowboy boots and back to his face. Something glinted there, and Matt cocked his head.

"You look nice," she said, and for Gloria that was a huge compliment. She was task-oriented, always greeting him with something more like, "We have eight stalls to shovel this morning, and then I'm going to need your help with moving that stubborn bull out to the second pasture."

Matt was sure she'd never complimented him before. "Thank you," he managed to say, though he reached for his tie to adjust it. "You look amazing, as always." He glanced at Bree, who smiled at him. "Uh, Pastor Benson said Molly wanted to see us for a moment."

Gloria's eyebrows went up. "Oh. Okay."

For some reason, he offered her his arm, and for a reason wildly unbeknownst to him, she took it. Warmth spread through him, and his pulse increased until he could feel it fluttering in the vein in his neck. "I'm not sure why," he managed to say as they stepped away from Bree. "I was just tasked with finding you and taking you back."

"Let's go see what she wants," Gloria said in a soft voice he'd only heard her use a few times. Whispers from the past streamed through his mind, and Matt fantasized about a new future with Gloria. One where she didn't tell him he was blind to see his failing farm for what it was, and one where he didn't tell her she needed to grow up and realize the world was bigger than Sugar Pond.

Maybe she could forgive him for the things he'd said two decades ago.

Maybe he could ask her to dinner, and maybe she'd say yes.

A smile lit his soul as they left behind the burgeoning crowd and entered a private hallway. Gloria actually stepped closer to him, and Matt glanced at her as he tucked her arm into his body.

He wasn't sure if he was ready to move past his first failed marriage, but something in the back of his mind said, *Yes, you are, Matthew. It's time.*

CHAPTER 2

espite not being overly feminine or girly, Gloria Munson sure did love a good wedding. The Hammonds knew how to throw a party too, as she well knew from her time on the family farm. Every birthday, every holiday, every weekend it seemed, food, family, and fun could be found at the farmhouse where Gray Hammond lived with his wife and family.

Hunter Hammond came to the farm often enough for Gloria to know him well, and his almost-wife, Molly, came even more often than that. If Gloria had to put a label on Molly, she'd call the woman her best friend.

They worked together closely, along with Matt, on Pony Power, and besides Gloria, no one liked to see the horses and children in the program more than Molly.

"Did she say what she wanted?" Gloria asked, trying to tame the thrashing of her heart.

"If she did, I didn't get the message," Matt said, his

body so warm next to her forearm and hand. She had no idea why she'd linked her arm through his, only that it had felt natural and easy in the moment. Not only that, but he looked so dashing in his full, three-piece suit, and perhaps she'd imagined the two of them about to attend a high-society ball.

She did read a lot of historical romance novels, after all. She hadn't made it to the point where she'd bought any Regency dresses or anything. Gloria barely liked to wear a dress to church. In Montana, she'd been known to go in her jeans and cowgirl hat, but once she'd lost her father, the ranch, and every shred of dignity she had, Gloria had left the state in her rearview mirror.

In Colorado, she'd been reinventing herself one day at a time. Rebuilding her sanity one horse at a time. Restocking her savings one dollar at a time.

She probably had enough to splurge on a ballgown now, should she really want one. Gloria thought of the bright orange Post-it notes she'd scattered around her cabin. One on the bathroom mirror, one on the refrigerator, one above the front door.

Your own ranch.

Gloria wanted her own ranch with every fiber of her being. She'd thought she was set to inherit the one she'd worked with her father for so long, but that hadn't worked out.

"Here we are," Matt said, drawing her back to the hallway in the grand dome surrounded by snow-covered gardens. Gloria had found the landscape just as beautiful with flowers and vines wafting in the wind, the snow heaped on the sides of the sidewalk, and a cold, blue chill in the air as she had when she'd visited the Royal Chinese Gardens last spring.

He reached up and knocked on the door, and not two seconds later, a woman pulled it open. Her face softened as she took in Matt and Gloria, and Ingrid said, "Come on in," as she stepped back and opened the door. "Matt's here."

Matt swallowed visibly, and Gloria understood why. Every single person in the room was female, all of Molly's sisters, her mother, her cousins, and maybe even some friends. Gloria's life centered on the family ranch on the outskirts of Ivory Peaks, and she didn't know every person Molly associated with.

"Matt," Molly said, swishing forward in an enormous wedding gown. She radiated sunlight and joy, her smile broad on her perfectly made up face. "I have something for the two of you." She twisted but didn't try to turn in the dress. She'd probably fall down with a train that long and bushy. "Kara? Did you have those little boxes?"

"I have them," another woman said, and she too belonged to Molly. This sister had never been to the ranch, so she must be Lyra. She'd been living in Utah and going to school, and she'd gotten married this past spring.

She handed a pair of dark blue jewelry boxes to Molly, who extended them toward Matt and Gloria, her smile on double-high now. "Open them."

"You didn't have to get me a gift," Gloria said,

removing her hand from Matt's arm and reaching for the box. "In fact, I'm pretty sure people bring the bride and groom gifts." She met Molly's eye and smiled.

"I want you to wear these during the wedding," she said.

Gloria looked down at her box, and then at Matt. He gestured for her to go first, so she cracked the lid. A pair of gorgeous, dazzling diamond earrings sat nestled among black silk, and Gloria sucked in a breath. "Molly." She looked up at the woman. "I can't accept these."

"Yes, you can." Molly reached for the box and took it back. "You didn't even wear earrings, and I knew you wouldn't. You need these." She took them out and handed them to Gloria. "There's a mirror right over there if you need one." She turned expectantly to Matt.

"Here goes nothing," he said. "But my ears aren't even pierced." He grinned at Molly, who giggled, and opened his box.

Gloria caught sight of the shock on his face first and looked down into his jewelry box second. Cufflinks.

"These are amazing," he said, taking them out of the box. He stepped into Molly and hugged her tight, and Gloria wished she'd done that. She wasn't particularly touchy-feely, though she did feel things deeply. She just didn't know how to express them. Once, her grandmother had said she was stoic and strong-willed, because she'd been raised by a single father who knew how to communicate with horses and cattle better than humans.

Gloria had often found herself doing that too. She

could murmur the secrets of her heart to a horse, and it would simply close its eyes halfway as if in bliss and listen.

Matt turned to Gloria. "Help me put these on?" He wore hope and delight in his eyes, and Gloria nearly dropped her earrings at the sight of the boyish smile on his face. Her heart thumped in her chest as she handed her earrings to Ingrid to hold and reached to help Matt with his cufflinks.

He extended the first toward her, and her fingers touched his to take it from him. Sparks shot up her arm, and she steadfastly refused to look at him again. If she did, she had no idea what might happen. She'd probably spontaneously combust or something.

"I'm not sure...." She threaded the link through and popped out the back. "Oh. Got it." She smiled at him, her stomach swooping. At least she hadn't burst into flames. He didn't smile though, and she'd seen that look in his eyes before. Desire swam in those half-blue, half-gray depths, and she felt it move through her too.

She shifted her feet, which hurt in the heels, and she took the second cufflink. With that one in place, the cute little horse sparkling just like her earrings, she stepped back. She needed a lungful of air that wasn't scented like Matt's cologne and the woodsy, clean smell of his skin.

Her fingers twitched when she looked up and saw he had a lock of hair that had fallen onto his forehead. Before, when they'd dated, she'd swoop that back into place, lean into him, and kiss him.

Before, when Gloria had confidence and the whole world in front of her.

Now, she took another step back and bumped into Ingrid. "Sorry," she murmured. Ingrid handed her the earrings, and Gloria walked over to the mirror. It had been a long time since she'd dressed up with jewelry. She'd sold anything of any value before leaving Montana, and she certainly didn't need diamonds to teach a horse how to stay close to the rail.

With the gems in her ears, Gloria let her hands fall back to her sides. A distinct feeling cascaded over her, and she could only stare at her reflection. She felt beautiful, and Gloria never felt like that.

"They're lovely," Molly's mother said, and Gloria turned toward her.

Swallowing, she said, "Thank you." She turned and went back to Molly, whose sisters were now pinning her flower crown in place. "We should go, Matt." She stopped next to Molly and paused, trying to figure out which words to use.

"They complete that outfit," Molly said, holding very still. "You were gorgeous before, but now you're over the top." She grinned. "You're going to have so many men asking you to dance. Hunter has practically everyone from HMC here." Her eyes sparkled with mischief, and Gloria shook her head.

She sort of lunged at Molly and hugged her tight. So tight, Molly grunted. "Thank you." Gloria released her and walked past Matt, not able to look him in the eyes. Behind her, he said something to Molly, and before she knew it, he'd caught up to her.

He didn't offer his arm again, and they'd already started down the hall anyway. "Those earrings are stunning," he said.

"It's too much," she said. "I shouldn't have taken them."

"You know the Hammonds are billionaires, right?" he asked.

Gloria's step slowed, and she cut a look at Matt out of the corner of her eye. "I mean, I haven't asked, and I haven't seen their bank accounts."

"Every one of them," he said. "Hunter, all of his siblings, though they don't know it yet. His dad. All the uncles. The grandfather. Billions." He smiled in a soft, friendly way. "They can afford a pair of earrings."

Gloria wanted to argue with him that principles had to be maintained. At the same time, she didn't want to argue with him.

His fingers brushed hers, and Gloria pulled in a breath. On the next step, she inched closer to him, and this time his hand caught right on hers. He fumbled slightly but quickly aligned their fingers.

"Is this okay?" he asked, his voice a near-whisper as they approached the end of the hall. Beyond that doorway, the grand hall would arch above them, and they'd attend the wedding.

Gloria couldn't get her voice to work, so she simply nodded.

Matt squeezed her hand, and she wondered how she could tell him everything that had happened in the past twenty years. *One piece at a time,* she thought.

He increased his step and jumped in front of her right as they reached the doorway. "Are you staying for the whole thing?"

She had no choice but to look into those eyes. His curiosity lived there, shrouding something else she couldn't identify.

"The wedding, the dinner, the dance?" he asked. "All of it?"

"I was planning on it."

He took a step closer and looked down at the narrow space between their bodies. She had no choice but to breathe in the sexy, male scent of him, and while her brain screamed at her to back up, her feet didn't move a single centimeter.

"Are you really going to dance with anyone who asks?"

Gloria emitted a light scoff. "No one's going to ask."

"*I'm* asking," he said. "Right now." He took her other hand in his and met her gaze. "I don't want you to dance with anyone but me tonight."

She had no idea what to say. He wore his confidence well, and he always had. Well, he'd been a bit different than she remembered when they'd first reunited in Ivory Peaks. She'd learned he was only four months out of a marriage, and he'd seemed softer. Still strong and hard-working, but not so filled with bluster and laughter.

Months had passed since then. Over a year. Slowly,

she'd watched him heal into a new version of himself, and surprisingly, Gloria had done the same. Her attraction to Matt had never really left her; it had only been lying dormant.

Until now.

"What do you think?" he whispered. "Will you dance with me—and only me—at this wedding?"

CHAPTER 3

*M*att loved weddings. He'd take that admission to the grave with him, but he allowed himself to bask in the floral, somewhat earthy scent of the grand hall. He'd released Gloria's hand the moment they'd stepped out of the hallway, because he had two very big reasons to keep his hands to himself where others could see.

Two humans. Breathing bodies, who had brains and would definitely have some questions if they saw their father holding hands with Gloria. Both Keith and Britt knew her, of course. They'd spent the last year and a half with her at Ivory Peaks. Eating dinner with her at Chris's cabin was different than holding hands with her at a wedding, and his fifteen-year-old son would know that.

Matt knew it, and he felt the spaces between his fingers where Gloria's had been only a few minutes ago. He clasped his own hand, but it wasn't nearly the same as holding her long, cool, slender fingers and feeling his heart kick beats through his body the way a bronc did when he tried to get free from the strap around his belly.

"Daddy, look at Molly," Britt said from beside him, and he twisted to look behind him, the way she was. Britt had knelt up on the chair beside him, and he'd encouraged her to watch closely for the bride to make her entrance. That was how they knew the wedding was about to start.

Hunter didn't stand at the altar yet, so Matt added his low voice to the murmur marching through the crowd at the sight of Molly in all that white fabric. Her strawberry blonde-brown hair had been curled and pinned up, and she looked older than Matt had seen her around the farm.

Her father, the pastor, wore a smile that could paint masterpieces, his only rivaled by Molly's. Her electric green eyes seemed to zero in on every person, though such a feat would've been impossible with the number of guests in attendance.

Matt still felt her eyes meet his, and he grinned at her, one arm sliding around Britt to steady her as she now stood on the chair beside him. Molly blinked at her, and Britt giggled. "She did it, Daddy."

"Good," Matt whispered, noting the hush of reverence that had filled the hall. "We gotta be quiet, bug."

Britt nodded, and Pastor Benson positioned his daughter right in front of the gorgeous saddle Matt had brought for the altar. The flowers had indeed been woven through the straps and loops in plenty of time, and they spoke of a more casual event than the black tie one transpiring in front of him.

The frilly music faded, and the rhythm of a tambourine filled the hall. Matt actually looked up to the ceiling to make sure it wasn't a mistake. A bass guitar riff joined the beat, and a swell moved through the crowd when a group of men appeared way down at the other end of the aisle.

Gray Hammond led the dance—a legit dance—with shuffle steps and a pony. A for-real pony move with his toe on the ground and his other leg bouncing twice as he lifted his arms into the air.

His brothers came behind him as a drum joined the tambourine and the bass guitar. A smile bloomed across Matt's face, and Britt started to giggle again.

About fifteen seconds in, Wesley Hammond, the oldest of Hunter's uncles moved to the right of his brother, and another uncle—Colton—spread to the left. The twins made up the back part of the flying V, and they all danced in unison to the three instruments that promised something more to come.

This was lively, upbeat, and as Matt looked around, had brought a smile to every face in the hall. All five hundred of them. A couple of people clapped along, and Matt could admit that his cowboy boot was tapping with that tambourine.

A cry of "Yow!" filled the room, and it was Chris, Hunter's eighty-four-year-old grandfather. All the uncles dropped into a crouch, and Chris Hammond, the most proper of men Matt had ever known, the man who'd lost his wife last year, and the man who'd run a multi-billion dollar company for decades, played the air guitar like a professional—complete with him biting his lip like a rock star.

Whoops and hollers filled the hall, but the music was plenty loud enough to drown them out.

"So one, two, three, take my hand and come with me. Because you look so fine that I really wanna make you mine."

All the men jumped up into the air from a crouch, and that was a feat not easily done for men their age. Matt wasn't sure if he saw Wesley flinch or Colton's face grimace in pain, but it sure seemed like it.

They made a semi-circle around Chris, who walked through the middle of them, that air guitar still mighty busy. This hard rock song was classic Hunter, and Matt cast a quick glance at Molly, who laughed openly, her hands clapping right along with the beat of the drums.

Matt had heard this song plenty of times around the farm, as well as many others. Hunter loved a good electric guitar bridge in the middle of a drumbeat.

On the next lyric—"I say you look so fine that I really wanna make you mine,"—Hunter came running down the aisle toward his male family members. He carried a mic in his hand, and as he skidded on his knees in that deep, dark-as-midnight tuxedo, he tossed it up. His father caught it in mid-air, and Hunter either sang or mouthed the next words, Matt wasn't sure.

"Oh, four, five, six, c'mon and get your kicks. Now you

don't need the money, when you look like that do you honey?"

Hunter got to his feet, and the group of men started their synchronized dance down the aisle again as the guitars, drums, tambourine, and lyrics continued. They looked like suited bodyguards, all of them with perfectly pinned petals on their lapels and impeccable rhythm, as they jigged toward the altar.

Matt laughed, because this was the most fun he'd ever had at a wedding, and he kept his grin solidly in place while all of Hunter's younger half-siblings, his cousins, and his uncle's wives danced their way down the aisle too.

When he reached Molly, he wore so much joy that Matt thought it could fill the world ten times over. They danced together, and Molly had obviously been involved in the choreography, because she stepped in front of the row of Hammonds and did the same moves as they did.

The last person to come down the aisle was Elise Hammond, Hunter's step-mother. Matt had seen their special relationship, and Elise marched down the aisle in her stunning, glittering mother-in-law dress and took the mic from her husband.

"I said, are you gonna be his girl?" she sang right in time with the music. It immediately quieted to less-than-deafening, the guitar et al still providing the party atmosphere but not blowing out eardrums now.

Molly embraced Elise, and all of the uncles glommed onto Hunter. As quickly as that had happened, they separated and took up positions behind Pastor Benson, whose face looked like it had been taken off, permanently stretched wide, and then sewn back on.

Hunter's shoulders rose and fell in labored breaths, and he brushed off his knees before taking his position at Molly's side, all prim and proper and professional now.

The song had been less than four minutes, and everyone had found their spot. Energy ran through Matt like he'd never experienced, and he met Gloria's eyes. Hers too stretched round, and she mouthed, *Wow* to him, the delight and joy she felt not hard to find.

He laughed again and shook his head, especially when Hunter then accepted the cowboy hat from Pastor Benson and put it on his head. He wasn't really a cowboy, as the boy had gone to MIT and gotten one of the most complicated degrees Matt had ever heard of. He'd worked on some serious science stuff at his family company before becoming the CEO last year.

Still, he loved horses and dogs, and he loved the land out west from the city of Denver, and while his father still owned it on paper and they still lived there, Matt had a feeling that wouldn't be the case forever.

"Dearly Beloved," Pastor Benson said, his voice as loud as Hunter's had been screeching into the very same mic. "I don't think we need to do much else after that display of love and joy." He beamed at his daughter and then his very-near-future son-in-law. "I couldn't have chosen a better man for my daughter, and I think I'll skip the speech and get right to it. Hunter Gray Hammond, do you take unto yourself, to be your legally and lawfully wedded wife, Miss Molly Avery Benson? A man should cherish and love his wife, listen to her, and support her in all she does to build their life together. Will you do that?"

"I will," Hunter said, and Matt knew this part was off too. The woman usually pledged herself first.

"Miss Molly Avery Benson, do you give yourself to Hunter Gray Hammond, to be his legally and lawfully wedded wife, and take unto him to yourself as your legally and lawfully wedded husband? A woman should love and cherish her husband, listen to him, and support him in all he does to build their life together. Will you do this?"

"I will," Molly said.

Pastor Benson had likely married dozens and dozens of people, but Matt felt like this had to be the best union he'd ever done. Molly and Hunter were perfect for each other, and his heart took courage that he could find the same happiness they'd been able to. Their road hadn't been short, and it hadn't been easy, and that knowledge only gave him courage to take the next step.

It was more like the *first* step, but who was counting?

"I now pronounce you, Hunter, and you Molly, Mister and Missus Hammond, for now and for forever. Amen."

The cowboy hats came off then, and Matt thought he could hear the faint riff of that electric guitar just under the whoops and hollers and catcalls as Hunter dipped Molly back and kissed her.

Matt added his applause and cheering to the noise, and when the Jet song started up in earnest again, he joined in the dancing. It was too much of a bop to stay still, and he held onto Britt's hands while they tried to imitate the choreographed routine of the Hammond brothers.

Even Keith got into the spirit of things, and that warmed Matt's heart to the point of bursting. Maybe his kids had a chance of seeing what true love was. Maybe they wouldn't always be sad and silent about the loss of their mom. He'd known coming to Ivory Peaks a couple of years ago had been the right thing for him and his family, but the Lord had been a little slower to show him the blessings of the decision.

He could see so many now, and only one was the way Chris held Keith's hand above his head as Keith did a twirl in time to the music.

He turned, and Gloria stood there, jiving and jamming to the music. She was the most beautiful woman in the whole world, and Matt's vision went white for a moment. He got thrown into the past, to the first time he'd met her.

They'd been dancing just like this. Different place. Different occasion. Different time. Different song.

She lifted her head, those sandy curls swaying the same. Just like twenty years ago, Matt didn't waste a single second worrying about if he should grab onto her and dance.

He just did it.

CHAPTER 4

*G*loria laughed as she let Matt's strong arms hold her up and twirl her around. He'd matured a lot in the past twenty years, but the scent of his cologne hadn't changed at all. Still crisp and still clean, and she grinned at him as the music settled into something slower and more intimate.

His hand slipped away from hers and along her waist, and Gloria's lungs sucked at the air. She managed to mask the gasp into a simple inhalation, and her smile didn't slip at the sight of Matt's straight-teeth grin.

He'd asked her to dance only with him, and Gloria hadn't had time to answer him before his daughter had interrupted them. She loved the little girl with light green eyes and barely brown hair, as she'd gotten to know her pretty well over the past year and a half they'd lived next door to one another.

She made the mistake of looking into Matt's eyes, and

he brought her closer to his chest. She wasn't sure where he'd been the past many months, but she'd felt something plastic, rigid, and invisible between them.

It wasn't there anymore.

They hadn't talked much about personal things since she'd gotten the job at Ivory Peaks. They discussed farm business. Horse care. Tasks that needed to be accomplished. Now, she found her mind blank as to what to talk about at all.

Standing this close to him, with such warmth seeping into her skin from his touch, she didn't want to mention how they'd have to work once they got back from the wedding.

Every second that passed grew more awkward, and yet Gloria's vocal cords seemed to be growing rust.

"Earl Grey's gonna need new shoes this week," she finally said, immediately pressing her eyes closed in a tight blink.

"Nelson's already booked," Matt said, his voice back to the guarded one he'd used with her in the past. "I was thinking we should get away from the farm."

Around them, other couples danced and talked, laughed and genuinely seemed to be enjoying themselves. Gloria was too.

"I'm no good at talking," she admitted.

"That's not true," Matt said, plenty of playfulness in his voice. She knew, because that part of him hadn't changed at all. "We'll start easy. Do you still love cheese quesadillas?"

A smile touched her lips, and he'd always been so very good at making her feel comfortable, at making her feel like it didn't matter that her palate wasn't very refined, at making her feel like he was genuinely interested in what she thought.

"Completely," she admitted. "I've even been making them into double-deckers this winter. I put Colby jack on the bottom and on the top, I've been using pepper jack."

She needed someone to scratch the record and bring this dance to a halt. Cheese. She was talking about what *cheese* she used in making a snack for a five-year-old. The truth was, Gloria could eat quesadillas for breakfast, lunch, or dinner. She didn't care which. In her opinion, it was always a good time for bread and cheese.

Matt just grinned at her. "Keith would love that," he said.

Gloria wasn't sure if she should return the smile or excuse herself to the restroom and never come back. No one scratched a record, and she'd have to get her coat from the coat room before she could walk away from the wedding. Molly and Hunter hadn't served dinner yet, and Gloria had nothing and no one waiting for her back on the farm.

Not true, she told herself. She did have almost two dozen horses she could talk to. They were always glad to see her, especially if her pocket crinkled with sweets wrappers. She wished it was warm enough and clear enough to put on her rollerblades, grab a couple of the farm dogs, one of her therapy horses, and go for a run. The animals ran, at least. She bladed. She loved going in the morning, when the sun first crested the great Rocky Mountains. She loved going in the evening, when that same sun cast golden and pink rays on the mountains.

She could crank up her 80s rock music and just go. She didn't have to think about her father. She didn't have to wonder what had happened to Tailwind, the family ranch she'd thought she'd once inherit. She didn't have to try to interpret the look on a handsome cowboy's face.

"What?" she asked Matt.

"I asked if you wanted to try that new Pasta, Please place, and you didn't answer."

Gloria cleared her throat, wondering how bad this night could get. "I was thinking about something else," she admitted.

"What?" Matt asked.

"Rollerblading with Midnight Moon." She did allow a smile onto her face then. "He loves it, and I miss it."

A smile that could melt glaciers filled his face, reaching all the way up and touching his eyes. "It'll warm up soon."

"Yeah." Gloria sighed, half-glad and half-disappointed when the song ended. She stepped out of Matt's arms as a flurry of activity happened around them. People seemed to know what came next, as if there was a program announcement Gloria had missed. Maybe she had, in all honesty. She'd been pretty wrapped up in Matt's arms, and he'd always been able to keep the outside world and all its dangers from getting too close.

His fingers slipped down her arm and through hers,

sending shockwaves through all the fleshy parts of her body. That made the bones quake, and before she knew it, a smile tumbled onto her face. "Let's find the kids," he said. "It looks like we're moving into the ballroom for dinner."

"Everyone, please make your way to the Aspen Hall," a woman said in a crisp voice, the words amplified through the speaker system. "Dinner will be served in twenty minutes."

Gloria didn't want to be separated from Matt too badly, and she saw Travis Thatcher and Mission Redbay standing next to one another too. They looked a bit lost, to be honest, which Gloria understood. The cowboys from the farm west of the city didn't really know how to fit in with all the suits from the high-rise downtown. Hunter had a foot in both worlds, and he seemed to be able to move seamlessly from one to the other.

"Come on, gents," she said to the two cowboys standing there while people swarmed past them. "Come with us."

Travis flashed her a look of gratitude, and the two of them fell into step with Gloria and Matt.

"There's Britt," she said a moment later, pointing to her right. Matt released her hand and went to scoop his daughter into his arms. She clung to him with a smile that could make anyone's heart expand, and he said something to Keith too.

They returned to Gloria and the others, and Keith offered Gloria his arm. Surprise darted through her, but she quickly linked her arm in his. "Thank you." She felt like a queen as the lot of them joined the moving crowd on their pilgrimage to the Aspen Hall.

Gloria didn't think the view could get better than the living outdoors inside the grand hall where Hunter and Molly had been married. She'd been wrong. The Aspen Hall had huge, wall-to-wall murals of the woods one could find right here in the Rocky Mountains. Pines and shrubs and a big, blue sky.

And the aspens. They went around the entire place, which could easily hold twice as many people as Molly and Hunter had invited to their wedding. The aspens moved through their leaf cycle, from bright green leaves and those beautiful white trunks in the summer, into their fall foliage colors, to no leaves at all, back to their flowers and new leaf growth in the spring.

The power of life moved through Gloria looking at all those trees, and joy filled her soul. They'd had plenty of aspens on the ranch in Montana, and a keen sense of longing to see them pulled at her heart. The idea that she and Matt should return to Sugar Pond this summer entered her mind, but she remained sane enough to keep the suggestion to herself.

She and Matt weren't anything yet. Today had been the very first inkling that he even recognized she was a female and he was a male, and hey, they'd been together for a year.

A long time ago, she thought, quickly dismissing it. So what if it had been a long time ago? She was single; he was single. They'd gotten along great in the past, and they worked together well now.

She glanced at him as they all paused, trying to figure out if they had places to sit or could choose a table. With six of them, they'd need almost an entire table to themselves, and Gloria thought they better act fast to do that.

"Ladies and gentlemen," the same crisp female voice said. "There are no assigned seats. Please find a place that works for you and choose a card for your meal."

"I got the steak," Travis said, but Gloria couldn't remember what she'd chosen. She'd worked a cattle ranch in Montana, and she did love a good steak. Most people overcooked it, in her opinion, and she'd probably gotten the chicken. She wasn't even sure the second option was chicken, and she went with Matt and Keith as they started moving again.

"I'd like to be a little closer," Matt said. "Is that all right?"

"Anywhere's fine," Travis said, speaking for all of them.

Matt looked specifically at Gloria. She gave him a nod, and he moved toward the front third of the hall before selecting a table that would fit them all. He worked on getting Brittany settled, and Keith pulled out her chair for her. Gloria said, "Thank you," and took the seat. Keith went around the table to sit on the other side of his sister, leaving the spot beside Gloria open for his father.

She busied herself with reaching for the meal cards, but her mind fired questions at her about what Matt had said to Keith in the few seconds before they'd come back to her. She wondered what the fifteen-year-old thought about a relationship between Matt and Gloria. Maybe Matt had already spoken to his kids about it. Maybe he hadn't.

Worry leapt through her, because she'd never dated a man with children before. That situation had to be delicate, and she had no idea how much the kids knew about their mother. Heck, she had no idea what had happened to their mother, other than she wasn't around anymore. Matt hadn't said much about her at all. No one had.

With a start, Gloria wondered if she'd died. That would explain Matt's silence on the subject, as well as him taking a year and a half to even look her way. As Gloria found four options for her meal, she told herself she hadn't been waiting for Matthew Whettstein to look her way. She did not *need* a man in her life to be happy. In fact, the men she'd allowed into her life had brought her to her knees in *un*happiness, and she wasn't sure she wanted to go there again.

She sorted through the trout, steak, chicken, and pork options, not sure which one she'd chosen.

"We got a chicken," Matt said. "For Britt."

Gloria plucked out the card and handed it to the little girl.

"Steak for me and Keith."

She handed him the cards, and he passed one down to his son. She continued to read over the options, finally seeing the veggie-potato cake that had struck her taste buds when she'd selected the meal. "I think I got the fish."

She took the trout card and put the others back in the

middle of the table. Matt offered her a smile, and she must've returned it with enough vigor, because he lifted his arm and put it around the back of her chair. "Fish? I don't remember you eating a lot of fish."

"I do like trout," she said. "Dad and I used to go to trout fishing in the Missouri."

His eyes lit up. "We did that once, remember?" He leaned closer to her and drew in a deep breath. "You never answered about going out."

She hadn't meant to dodge the question. Every single one he asked seemed to get interrupted by something else. That wasn't her fault.

Right now, no one interrupted. Plenty of people were still trying to find their seats, and his kids seemed adequately entertained. Mission sat on her left, but he'd already turned away from her to talk to Travis. Both of them were good cowboys, and they shared a cabin a couple down from Gloria and then Matt, who lived on the end.

"I'll dance with you tonight," she said, her voice catching on itself. She cleared her throat. "I think it would be...fun to try that pasta place together." Heat filled her cheeks. She drew in a long breath, held it, and reached for the glass of pink lemonade that had already been poured. One sat at every place, and she hoped this one belonged to her.

As she took a drink of it, she supposed it did now even if it hadn't before. Once she felt cool enough, she looked at Matt.

Relief-joy had filled his eyes. "Let's look at our schedules when we get back to the farm." He ducked his head closer, ever closer. "And the weather. Okay?"

The weather had always played a part in planning outings in Montana too, and while Gloria knew her schedule—she'd had a date with a microwavable meal and her couch every night since arriving in Colorado—she only nodded.

She closed her eyes and sent up a prayer of gratitude for the microwave, the couch, and the ability to even purchase microwavable meals. When she'd very first come to Colorado, she hadn't had any of those things. There was no electricity in her truck, after all, and she'd been living out of it.

She raised her glass to her lips again, her eyes coming open. The cool, tart liquid had barely touched her tongue when someone jolted into her from behind. She moved so much, she hit the table, which also moved.

"Hey," Matt said, but all Gloria could process was that the taste of blood had infected her lemonade. Once that thought passed, the chilly feel of lemonade-in-all-the-wrong-places filled her entire awareness.

She looked down to see her entire chest had been covered in it. Both Matt and Mission stood up, the two of them talking. Gloria didn't hear what they said, because the rushing of panic in her ears made a very loud sound.

Her bright blue dress had quickly absorbed the pink lemonade, and it was now a splotchy mess of darker and lighter tones. As she took it in and wondered how bad it really was, blood started to drip from her mouth right onto the same spot where the lemonade had gone.

Drip, drip, drip.

She watched it, mesmerized for a moment, and then she lifted her head and searched for her napkin, pure humiliation filling her.

CHAPTER 5

*M*att's frustration felt abnormally high for some reason. He wasn't even sure why, only that his arm had been pinned and pushed the wrong way, and Gloria had made a startled, almost hurt, yelp when the man he now faced had stumbled into their table.

Mission stood closer to the businessman and said, "Go on, now," as if the man in the suit were an errant cow and not someone who'd already had too much to drink. Matt stood paralyzed, thrown back in time to all the instances where he'd looked at his wife in this exact situation. His heart pounded, taking all of the energy from him at the expense of his brain cells. Sweat broke out along his collar and across his forehead, moving quickly up his neck and down his arms. He needed to shed this jacket and tug at the tie at his throat just to get enough air.

"Sorry," the man slurred as a woman came rushing toward them.

"Troy, what are you doing?" She grabbed onto his arm and looked at Matt with wide, apologetic eyes. He knew how she felt too, and he wouldn't wish it on anyone. "I'm so sorry. I'm taking him home."

"Probably a good idea," Matt said in a wooden tone, suddenly coming back to the present. He wasn't stuck in that past anymore. He didn't have to find Janice in bed or passed out on the bathroom floor. She wouldn't be there when he brought the kids home, and he wouldn't have to protect them from seeing their mother that way.

"Sorry," she said again, pulling hard on Troy's arm to get him to move. He watched them go even after Mission sat back down, and it took so much effort to tear his eyes from them as the woman put her arm around the man's back to steady him further. Emotion stormed through his chest, and he couldn't make sense of it.

He shouldn't feel humiliated for what had just happened. A guy had stumbled into someone sitting at a table. Matt rotated his shoulder, which ached slightly from being hyper-extended in the wrong direction, but no one had really gotten hurt. He drew in a breath and tried to push against a tidal wave of memories.

"Daddy," Britt said, and Matt spun toward her. His children had been such a source of laser-focus for him since dropping Janice at the alcohol treatment facility in Salt Lake almost two years ago now.

"What, baby?" He returned to his chair and pulled it back into position between Britt and Gloria. His daughter pointed to Gloria, and when Matt looked at her, his heart leapt right back into his throat.

She held a napkin to her mouth, and it had several spots of blood on it already. White noise roared through his ears, and he jerked toward her. "Are you okay?"

"Yes," she said around the napkin. "The glass just jammed against my lip or something."

Utter helplessness filled him, something Matt was used to as he dealt with Britt's condition every day. He couldn't make her legs steadier. He couldn't even out her speech. All he could do was pray for strength and clarity of mind to know what to do when the episodes came. He did that now, taking in the stain on the front of Gloria's dress.

He saw his evening dancing with this woman and only this woman disappear in a single moment.

Instead of feeling sorry for himself, he stood and flagged down a waiter. "We had a little accident here," he said. "We need a couple of new napkins, and another glass of pink lemonade." He swept his hand toward Gloria and her wet place setting, and the man nodded.

"Yes, sir," he said. "Let me take your meal cards too, and I'll be right back."

He was too, and Gloria pushed herself away from the table while they switched out her plates, provided more napkins, and brought her a new glass. With all of that fixed, they sat up to the table again.

Her mouth had stopped bleeding, and she turned toward him with splotches of color on her face. "How

LIZ ISAACSON

does my lip look? Is it huge?" She tilted her face up toward his, almost the exact same way she had right before he'd kiss her when they'd been twenty-something and oh-so-in-love.

"No," he said, his voice filled with frogs. "Not huge."

She sighed and ran her fingers through her hair. "I should go home and get out of this ruined dress."

"I'm sure it'll come clean," he said, not looking at her chest. "It's only lemonade." He didn't want to make light of the situation, but it was over and done. He'd had plenty of experiences that he could've been bitter and frustrated about forever, but what good would it do? It would only ruin the wedding of two of his best friends, and he'd rather enjoy himself than stew in irritation for the night.

"And blood," she said, reaching for another napkin. "Maybe I'll run to the bathroom real quick and see if I can get some of it out now." She looked at him as if his opinion on this mattered.

Before she could move, the first plates of food arrived at their table, including her trout and his steak. Once everyone had been served, Gloria picked up her fork. "It's fine," she said. "Who's going to see me?"

Matt gave her a smile, because she was still the most beautiful woman in the world, stained dress or not. "Just me, sweetheart," he said. "And I don't care about a little blood on your dress."

48

"COME ON, GUYS," HE SAID HOURS LATER. HIS patience for being in public had worn way down, and he'd been at the Garden Center for hours. He'd not danced with Gloria past that initial twirl right after the ceremony, because she'd left immediately following dinner. She claimed she couldn't sit in a wet, stained dress for another moment, and Matt had simply stood with her, said good-bye, and watched her walk away in those black heels.

He had allowed himself to fume in frustration since then, and it was time to get away from people. He could never truly do that, because he usually had Keith and Britt with him everywhere he went.

Tonight, everyone seemed tired, and they made it out to his truck and on toward the farm without much talking. Back at the cabin, he said, "Let's get changed, and I'll make some popcorn. We can stay up and watch a movie until we fall asleep, okay?"

"Okay," his kids said together, and Keith went up the ladder to the loft where he slept. He could stand up fully up there, as the cabin had a high roof. It could've had a complete second floor, but it didn't. The huge, vaulted ceilings made the kitchen and living room seem twice as big as they really were, and the loft was a large area that took up half the house over the two bedrooms and two bathrooms that sat to the left of the kitchen, dining area, and living room.

Keith's bed had been pushed way into the quietest corner, and he'd told Matt at least a half-dozen times that he actually liked the loft. Matt had stopped feeling guilty about it, though the cabin they'd been given to live in at Ivory Peaks wasn't anything like the sprawling rambler they'd enjoyed back in Montana.

Matt followed Britt down the hall and into her room. "Pajamas, Britt," he said. "Hang up your dress like a big girl, okay? I'll take your hair out in a few minutes."

"I can do it, Daddy," she said, already reaching for the ties at the end of her braids.

"Okay." He crouched down behind her and unzipped her dress. "There you go, baby. Hang it up, okay?"

"Okay," she said, but he doubted she'd hang up her dress. He'd wander in here after he'd put her to bed and do it, just like he usually did on Sunday evenings, and pick up a little bit. He wasn't sure why he did it, other than to listen to his daughter breathe and know she was still alive before he went to bed himself.

He went into the last room at the end of the hall, his tie already loose from the drive home. He unlooped it from around his neck and tossed it on his bed, a sigh following it. He sat down, the tightness in his chest finally releasing as he undid the buttons on his shirt. He honestly wanted to step into the shower and wash his annoyance and disappointment down the drain.

Keith could make popcorn, and they'd watch what the boy wanted anyway, so Matt did exactly that. He could shower and re-dress in less than ten minutes, so they wouldn't be waiting long for him.

The hot water was exactly what he needed to unknot all of the things that had tangled that evening.

One, his feelings for Gloria, which he hadn't had to deal with until he'd seen her in that brilliant blue dress. Sure, he'd thought about her over the months they'd been working together. He'd ridden a horse with her once last year that had got his pulse pounding. But being attracted to someone and being ready to be in a relationship with them were two different things.

Two, his muscles, which had been so tight since the altercation with Troy.

Three, his thoughts, which hadn't seemed to quiet until he let them loose and then allowed them to go down the drain.

He wasn't married to Janice anymore. The kids were coping. He was coping. They loved one another fiercely, and Matt would do anything to keep them safe and healthy. He had a great job here, with great people. He'd started to break free from the gray clouds of his past and he could finally see a bright future for all of them. He wasn't going to revert back to the place he'd been just because someone stumbled into a table accidentally. He wasn't.

When he stepped out of the shower, the scent of buttery, hot popcorn met his nose, further buoying his spirits. He quickly pulled on a pair of joggers and a T-shirt and went into the kitchen.

Britt sat on the counter, stirring a spoon in rich, dark brown liquid. "Keith made me hot chocolate," she said.

"I hope you said thank you."

"Thank you, Keith," she called into the living room, where Keith had already claimed the loveseat. He stretched across it, lying against a couple of pillows he'd brought down from his loft.

"Sure thing," he said, and Matt blinked. His son sounded so much like Matt, and he'd never thought that before. His voice had dropped, and he used the same twang and accent and everything.

"There's enough for you, Daddy," Britt said, bringing his attention back to her. "It's hot milk. Keith lets you put in as much powder as you want."

"Yeah?" Matt turned to get down a mug. "How much did you put in?"

"Only two."

"Four," Keith called from the living room. He got up and walked toward them. "She put in four." He grinned at her, though his eyes challenged her to contradict him.

"They were small scoops," Britt said.

Matt chuckled and shook his head. "Put in as much as you want, baby," he said. "Just don't lie about it." He cocked his eyebrows at her. "Okay?"

"Okay." She ducked her head, her pretty hair falling between them, and kept stirring.

"I'll make another bag of popcorn," Keith said, opening the microwave.

Matt stirred in three scoops of hot chocolate mix and stirred his drink together while the popcorn popped. Once they all had a bowl and their drinks just the way they liked them, they went into the living room.

"I thought we'd watch *Monsters, Inc.* tonight," Keith said, the animated movie already paused on the screen. "Okay?"

"I love this one!" Britt said from her end of the couch.

Matt grinned at both of his kids and nodded. "Fine with me." He didn't much care what they watched. He just wanted to be with them, in a safe place, where they all felt comfortable.

Keith started the movie, which only held Matt's attention for about ten minutes. Then he found himself wandering to his phone and texting Gloria.

Did you get home okay? Did the hydrogen peroxide work on the bloodstain?

Yes and sort of, she said. *It's definitely not as noticeable, but I'm still going to have to take it to the dry cleaner.*

I can take it on Monday, he said. *When I go pick up the kids from school.* Elise Hammond took the kids to school in the morning, as she had three to get there for the day too. Matt did the afternoon pick-up, and he often ran several errands for a variety of people who lived out here at the farm.

They weren't terribly far from gas and groceries, as the little town of Ivory Peaks had a few stores like that. Three restaurants that served really great food. The population was only about twelve thousand in the immediate town, with lots of farms and ranches spreading out to the north, south, and west. To the east sat the mighty city of Denver, and the kids went to school in one of the suburban towns that butted up against the city.

In all, it took an hour to get to downtown Denver, but only twenty-five minutes to the children's schools, and only fifteen to the single Main Street in Ivory Peaks.

Matt loved being close to a city but not *in* the city. Colorado was similar to Montana, but completely different too, and he didn't mind the differences.

Gloria didn't respond to his offer to help, and that only caused another knot to form in the back of his throat. He tried swallowing it down, and it took a few times before it went. She'd always been so independent, even twenty years ago. Her mother had died when she was young, and her daddy hadn't treated her like a child. She'd worked their family ranch right alongside him, and Matt still didn't know what had happened to cause her to lose it.

She'd been in a right state of panic when she'd shown up at Ivory Peaks the first time, but she'd relaxed as time went on. She was strong and capable, and Hunter and Molly both said hiring her had been the best decision they'd ever made for Pony Power. She loved the therapy horses as if they were her own children, and he admired that about her.

We're watching a movie, eating popcorn, and drinking hot chocolate. You could come over if you wanted.

Feeling brave and slightly reckless, he sent the text.

Thanks, she responded. *I'm already in bed, so I'm going to pass. It's too late to put real pants back on.* She sent a smiling emoji that really did cause Matt to smile. *I have to go to town this week to get those meds for Lasso, so I'll take the dress then.*

Oh, right, he said, his hopes falling a little bit. He couldn't think of anything else to say, and he didn't want to be pushy, desperate, or fake. So he tucked his phone away and tried to focus on the movie. He couldn't, but at least he managed to keep his dignity with the pretty woman next door. For now.

He'd failed her in the past, and all he could do now was pray he wouldn't do it again.

A WEEK OR TEN DAYS LATER, MATT SET HIS phone on the kitchen counter while it rang and opened the fridge.

"Matthew," his brother answered, and he sounded happy. Matt suspected either the tone was forced or the texts his brother had been sending were blown out of proportion. Boone could do that without realizing it, and Matt needed to know which he was dealing with.

"Booney," he said in response, his grin wide and genuine though he hadn't been out with Gloria yet. He hadn't even brought it up again. Neither had she. Winter around a farm with almost thirty horses, stables, barns, and therapy appointments was no laughing matter, and they didn't just sneak away for an hour without someone knowing and a major production made of it.

Since neither Matt nor Gloria liked to make a fuss or

have much attention on them, he wondered if they should try to get together here on the farm instead. He could make lunch for her one day and call it a date. Heck, they'd eaten together with Elise and Chris twice since the wedding. Matt packed up a bin of food and took it to the generational house where Chris lived, and they spent an hour together in the middle of the day. It was nice for everyone, and Matt liked the familial culture that had come from it.

"What's up?" Boone asked.

"I'm callin' to see how things are," Matt said, pulling out a package of bacon. He could make sandwiches from this. He loved a BLT, and Keith would smear peanut butter on untoasted bread and add the bacon to that. Britt liked a grilled cheese with bacon in it, and none of those required a whole lot of actual cooking.

"You sounded a little down in your texts." He put a pan on the stove, not encouraged by Boone's silence. He paused and tilted his head toward the phone. "Boone? How are things at Saffron Lake?"

His brother owned about ten acres that included a private lake. He and his wife had named it Saffron Lake after Boone and Matt's grandmother, and leaving Montana had been hard for Matt in that he wouldn't get to go visit his brother, take his kids to see their cousins, and feel connected to his grandmother, whose spirit lived in that lake.

"They're...they've been better," Boone said.

Matt abandoned his quest to make dinner while he

checked on his younger brother. "So the texts weren't hyped up."

"Not really," Boone said, his voice lowering. He was moving, Matt could tell, and he heard the rush of wind across the speaker next. "I think I made things out to be better than they are, actually."

"I don't know what to say."

"It's fine," Boone said. "Gerty loves Karley, and we'll work through it."

"Boone...." Matt let his name hang there, not sure how to give his brother this advice. He hadn't asked for it, and the words hadn't lined up in Matt's head yet anyway.

"I love her," Boone said. "We're just goin' through a rough patch. All relationships do."

"True." Matt cleared his throat. "Is it you or her?"

"Her," he admitted. "I think she's feeling guilty because of Nikki, which makes no sense. She's been gone for six years, and Karley and I have been officially dating for one."

"What changed then?"

"I mentioned getting married." He sighed as if tying the knot was the worst thing a man could want. "She... she's not sure she can do that."

"She's practically done it," Matt said. "I don't get that."

"She's here a lot, yes," Boone said. "Not as much as you think, though. She still works in town, and I go pick Gerty up from her office every day." He sighed again. "I don't know. I've been thinkin' about comin' down there for the summer."

"Come," Matt said instantly. "I know Gray would let you work, and he's got a daughter the same age as Gerty. They'll work too, and with Britt, they'll never be alone. It'll be great." He could just see it in his mind, and he wanted his brother and his niece to come to Ivory Peaks so badly. Maybe then Matt could ask him how to date after the loss of a spouse and how to protect his kids from any heartache that might come from that.

Boone had lost his wife to a rare blood disease years ago, so it wasn't quite the same as Matt's situation, but they'd both found themselves single fathers. Boone hadn't started dating until a couple of years ago, and he'd struck out until he'd stuck close to home—Nikki's best friend, Karley.

"I'm going to think about it. Can you text me Gray's number?"

"Sure thing," Matt said, reaching for his phone. "Maybe you just need a break, and you'll get it here, Boone. There are lots of people to help with Gerty, and she'll have friends. Things become clear when you're here in Ivory Peaks."

"Okay, okay," Boone said. "Just send me the number."

"Okay." Matt tapped to do that and added, "I love you, brother. I'm selfish in that I want to see you and Gerty again."

Boone chuckled, and Matt could just see him shaking his head as he looked over the lake. "You just want to show off your farm."

"That too," Matt admitted, hitting *send* on the phone

number. "Okay, I sent that number. If you're okay, I have something I want to talk about for three minutes." He turned back to the stove and set the phone on the slim counter between it and the fridge, where the package of bacon lay. "It's not something. It's someone...."

"Ooh," Boone said, his voice pitching up. "I'm done. I'm starting the timer. Start talking."

Matt took a deep breath and opened the drawer to pull out the scissors. As he exhaled and sliced open the top of the bacon package, he said, "Remember Gloria Munson? The woman I dated a long time ago in Sugar Pond?"

"Yeah." Boone drew the word out for far too long, making Matt roll his eyes.

"She works here now," Matt said. "I maybe asked her out, and she said yes, but we've never been able to get together."

Silence came through the line, and as Matt laid the first piece of bacon in the cold pan, he said, "That's it."

"That was ten seconds," Boone said. "Not three minutes."

"Tell me what to do," Matt said, exasperated and now embarrassed he'd brought up Gloria. "I'm bad at this, obviously."

"This one is easy, brother," Boone said. "You hang up with me and you call her. Find out what she's doing for dinner tonight."

"I'm making sandwiches already," Matt said, looking down into the pan.

"Invite her over for sandwiches then," Boone said.

"That sounds too...easy."

"All right," Boone said. "*I'm* hanging up now so you can do this really easy thing. Report later."

It took a few seconds for Matt to say, "Yeah, okay," but Boone had already ended the call.

CHAPTER 6

*G*loria clapped her gloves together as she went up the steps to the deck off the back of the farmhouse. A few weeks had melted by since Molly and Hunter's wedding, and the snow was doing the same right now. She didn't believe for a single minute that winter had ended in Colorado. It had been February for a few days, and they still had a few months where it could snow at any time.

It was just a warm snap, that was all.

Kind of like the hot spell Matt had put on her at the wedding. Nothing had come of that either, and she tried not to feel disappointed that they hadn't gone on a date. She saw him every day around the farm. They ate lunch together with Chris or Gray, as well as a couple of other cowboys, several times each week. It wasn't like she wasn't speaking to him.

But it wasn't that same, heated voice he'd used to ask her to dance with him at the wedding.

She reached for the handle on the sliding glass door at the same time she saw all the people. Hesitating, but in the middle of the motion, she still opened the door. A blast of heat hit her first, but the noise wasn't that far behind.

Gloria wasn't sure she was up for a huge, family dinner tonight. Elise had invited her to "come by about six and have tacos."

At least four pans of tacos sat on the kitchen counter in long, aluminum foil containers. The entire Hammond family was there—Gray, Elise, and their three children, Jane, Deacon, and Tucker. Chris, Gray's father, already sat at the table.

The front door opened, sending a whoosh of cold air through the house, and Gloria stepped inside and slid the door closed behind her. Wesley Hammond came down the hall, laughing in his loud, cowboy voice, his son grinning at his side. Michael had grown up a lot, and Gloria smiled at the two of them.

She'd forgotten they'd be in town for the weekend, which only doubled her desire to head back to her own cabin and whip up something easy for dinner. It was hard to cook for just one person, and Gloria had learned that the hard way. She'd thrown away a lot of food over the years until she'd learned all she needed was a few convenience foods. Cans of soup and boxes of Rice-A-Roni. Freezer meals or the smallest bag of pasta and the smallest can of spaghetti sauce.

Gray stepped over to greet his brother, and the noise level increased. Gloria found Hunter and Molly in the living room, seated on the couch, practically fused together at the hip. Hunter had his arm around his new wife, and they were the picture of perfection.

They spoke to her parents, and Gloria's mind ran away from her then. This was truly a family dinner, and she didn't belong here.

"How are you, Gloria?" Elise asked, stepping in front of her. She wore a smile that could warm souls, and Gloria had liked her from the moment she met her.

"Just fine," Gloria said. "You?"

"Great." Elise turned as the crinkling of aluminum foil sounded, and she darted back into the kitchen to get her youngest son away from the food.

Gloria wondered if she could just slip back out the door. No one would mind, and she could claim she had a headache and hurry through the darkness to her cabin.

"Come sit," Chris said, beckoning to her.

"Oh, I think I'm going to go." She moved toward him anyway, because she had a real soft spot for the older gentleman. Ten years older than her father, Chris had been a balm to her weary soul when she'd arrived in Ivory Peaks. He and his wife had taken her under their wing, and she'd loved Bea to pieces.

"How are you feeling?" she asked. "Matt texted to say that his stomach was a little sick after lunch today."

"Just fine," Chris said. "He told me the same thing. I

hope he's okay." He twisted in his seat. "Where did he get to?"

Gloria's pulse betrayed her by bounding along like a rabbit trying to get away from a hungry dog. "He's here?"

"Yes, I just saw him...." He twisted left and right, but he didn't find Matt.

She'd started scanning for him too, but Gloria couldn't find him either.

"His son called," Chris said. "He's probably out front talkin' to him." He patted the table at the seat next to him. "Sit. Matt can sit by you."

"Uh, his kids will want to sit by him." Gloria had eaten dinner with the Hammonds plenty of times in the nearly two years since coming to their farm. They always left their doors open, and lots of people walked through them. For some reason, tonight felt like a bigger deal than normal.

For one, Pastor Benson and his wife had come. Wes was in town with his son. Hunter and Molly, who maintained a residence in a high-rise in downtown Denver due to Hunter's position in the family company, were here.

It felt like Gloria shouldn't be.

"I'm not feeling that great," she said. "I think I'm going to head home."

"No, don't go," Elise said, arriving at the table with a couple of rolls of paper towels. "I got the sweet pork tacos just for you."

Guilt slicked through Gloria. "It's just that Pastor Benson is here...." She let the sentence hang there, because she wasn't sure why that mattered, other than she felt uncomfortable intruding on a family affair.

"It's a celebration," Gray said, joining his wife. "You have to stay, Gloria."

How he'd heard that she wanted to leave, she didn't know. She glanced back toward the living room, where Hunter, Molly, and her parents were starting to stand. As she swept her gaze back over Wes and Michael, now talking to Jane and Deacon, she spotted Matt.

The world narrowed to just him, though the farmhouse was large and easily accommodated everyone who'd come to dinner tonight. He held Britt's hand as they entered the room, and his eyes latched onto hers too.

He wasn't family. If he stayed, maybe she could too.

Somewhere in the back of her mind, her memories stirred. The two of them—Matt and Gloria—had eaten plenty of family meals with Molly and Hunter, and Gray and Elise. Why was this different?

Because you want it to be different, Gloria told herself.

Keith came in the back door, and Gray held up both hands. Gloria stepped away from him, because he was about to get loud.

"All right, everyone," he yelled, which did get everyone to settle down. "It's a fiesta tonight." He beamed around at the group, though Wes and the kids had moved behind him, into the kitchen. "That's why we've got the balloons and the tacos. I'll let the Bensons say what we're celebrating."

The attention shifted from Gray to Pastor Benson, who wore the widest smile Gloria had ever seen on the man's face. She liked his sermons, because he spoke about real things. Actual challenges people faced and how to overcome them, not hypothetical things or grand hyperboles about loving everyone, everywhere, all the time. He used real-life examples about how to love someone who'd caused hurt, someone who'd stolen something, or someone who wouldn't forgive.

She needed those smaller lessons over the bigger ones, and she liked that Pastor Benson took his congregation down the road toward perfection in small steps. She believed God wanted that too, that He didn't expect her to be all-loving, all-forgiving, and all-righteous immediately. But that every step she took in the right direction counted, and then she'd be ready to take the next one.

Her thoughts flew back to Matt, and she realized she was ready to take the next step with him. Maybe he wasn't with her—at least not as ready as he'd once thought he was. Maybe something at the wedding had just bitten him, and he regretted talking in that low, husky voice and asking her to dance with him, and only him.

She looked at him again, but he'd focused on Pastor Benson. Gloria did too, finding the pastor's arm around his wife. "We're celebrating, because Margie here has officially gone into remission."

Joy filled Gloria as a smile popped onto her face.

Cheering and applause lifted the roof on the farmhouse, and Molly's mother could've lit whole cities with the beaming light coming from her face.

"What a blessing," Chris said from beside Gloria. She agreed, but she just clapped along with a few other people.

"Okay," Gray said. "We're so happy for Margie, obviously. We're glad they could come out to the farm to celebrate with us. Elise has tacos for miles, and there's chips and salsa, guacamole, and salad." He reached up and ran his hand through his hair. "Let's pray. Hunt, would you?"

"Sure," Hunter said from the living room. He folded his arms and dropped his head toward his chest, taking a moment to just breathe.

Time froze for Gloria then, because she'd always appreciated Hunter Hammond and his maturity. The whole room hung in the silence, and he let it. She needed to take more moments like this to just breathe, and then allow the silence into her life. She could feel the Lord easier when it was calm and quiet, and she was so grateful Hunter had allowed that time for Him to enter all of their lives.

"Dear Lord," he finally started, his voice strong and yet subtle at the same time. "We're so grateful to be gathered here tonight as family. We're grateful for modern medicine and all it can do to give us more time together here on earth. Please be with any who are suffering tonight, because they're not with the ones they miss, who've already gone home to Thee."

Gloria's eyes burned as tears rushed into them. She

missed her father so very much when it got too quiet, but she knew she needed to let herself feel the things she did. The regret. The hurt. The longing to speak to him just one more time.

"Bless the food," Hunter said. "Please continue to bless each of us here with good health, and bless any who come here seeking better mental and physical health that they'll find it with our counselors and horses. Amen."

"Amen," chorused through the farmhouse, but Gloria could barely push the word out of her mouth.

Activity happened then, but Gloria stood right next to Chris, who didn't move. "What do you want?" she asked him. "I'll get it for you."

"I think she got chicken, dear," Chris said, his voice higher than normal. Gloria caught him wiping his face. "I'll take a few of those."

"Chips and salsa?"

"Always." He gave her a watery smile, and Gloria patted his shoulder before she jumped into the fray. She chatted with Jane, who'd gotten in line in front of her, about the junior high musical coming up in the spring, and she took the plate of chicken tacos and chips and salsa to Chris.

When she turned to get in line again, she met Matt's eyes. He reached his hand toward her, and Gloria had to tell herself not to fly to him. She stepped in what she hoped looked like a normal gait and slid her fingers through his.

"I feel dumb being here," she admitted, her voice getting swallowed up by the noise of people chatting and laughing as they sat down or continued to get food.

"I feel that," he said. "But Hunter insisted I come."

"Elise told me the same thing."

He glanced toward the table, where his daughter sat next to Jane. His fingers in hers tightened, and he said, "I feel bad we haven't been able to get together."

Gloria didn't know what to say, but she came up with, "We see each other every day."

"Yeah, but...." He inched forward and released her hand to pick up a plate. He looked back at her, their eyes locking. "It's work. I want to see you outside of work."

Heat shot through Gloria, making her stomach roar and tighten. Or maybe that was the sight of the sweet pork tacos.

"How about we plan on going to the Spring Wing Fling," he said. "It's not for a couple of months, but at the rate we're going, that might be perfect." He gave her a bright smile filled with hope, and Gloria didn't think there was a female alive who could resist that grin.

"The Spring Wing Fling?" she repeated. "Isn't that in April?"

"Yes, and you love buffalo wings. They have a dozen different flavors at the fling. Have you been?"

"I didn't even know such a thing existed."

"It does, and it's great," Hunter said, leaning over the island from the wrong side and grabbing the spoon for the guacamole. He put more on his plate, grinned at them, and turned back to the dining room table.

"HMC is sponsoring it this year," Wes said from behind Gloria. "I'm here helping Hunt through what a sponsorship looks like."

They moved through the line, putting food on their plates, the weight of her non-answer in her head. She'd done this at the wedding too. He'd asked her to dance with him, and they'd been interrupted. She'd never said yes or no.

Tonight, as he left the bar to head to the table, she said, "Matt."

He turned back to her, questions in those dark, dreamy eyes. "Yeah?"

Gloria cleared her throat and added a quick dollop of sour cream to her tacos. She moved out of the way too and pressed closer to him. "I'd love to go to the Spring Wing Fling with you."

A smile spread across his face. "It's a date."

Her throat felt like she'd swallowed sand, but she asked, "How about you come to my cabin for lunch tomorrow too?"

His eyes widened, but there was no hesitation when he said, "I can do that."

"Just the two of us," Gloria said, a sudden rush of power and satisfaction driving through her. She'd felt like this with him before, over the year they'd dated in Montana.

"It's a date," he said again, and they joined the

Hammonds at the dining room table. Gloria laughed at the story Wes told about Michael's first junior high dance, and she helped Britt get up to get more salsa for her remaining chips. Through it all, what she could serve for lunch tomorrow on her first date with Matt swirled through her mind.

CHAPTER 7

*M*att needed another shower, and he'd taken one only a few hours ago. He went up Gloria's back steps anyway and knocked. He didn't want to postpone this date, and she knew what conditions currently existed on the farm.

Several seconds passed before she opened the door, and she stood there with a towel in one hand, fresh from the shower. Her eyes scanned him from hat to boot, and he could admit he did the same to her. She had wet hair that made his chest tighten with desire and bare feet that made him smile, along with a comfortable pair of jeans and a sweater the color of the sky that hugged her body.

"You showered."

"You found the mud out there."

"It's impossible to miss," he said. "Do I have ten minutes to shower?"

"Seeing as how I haven't even started lunch yet, I'd say

so." Gloria toweled the ends of her hair, and Matt wanted to step into her and smell the scent of her shampoo in the few moments before he kissed her.

"Ten minutes," ground through his throat, and he turned to head next door to his house. He hurried through the chore of getting clean, and he did his best to leave his grimy clothes in the washing machine without turning it on. In the end, he couldn't do it, and he started the machine before he ran back to Gloria's.

The back door had been left open a crack, and he took that to mean he could enter without knocking. Music filtered out of the cabin, and when he entered, he found Gloria standing with her back to him, singing along with the song.

He grinned and closed the door, which brought her around to him. "You and your eighties rock," he said.

"I love it," she said, reaching for the device on the countertop that played the music. "It's what I listen to when I rollerblade too."

"Who are you going to take out first with you this spring?" he asked, taking a seat at the bar. Gloria worked with all of the therapy horses for Pony Power. She got them comfortable with people; she trained them to stand as still as statues while they got saddled, brushed, and mounted. She taught them to push balls with their legs, and she taught them not to get spooked by anything, ever.

Part of that training included her taking a horse running with her, except she didn't run. She rollerbladed, her earbuds in and the eighties rock loud. The horse ran with her, usually in the grass alongside the road, and it had to deal with whatever came their way. Cars, trucks, other animals, fences, whatever.

Matt had seen her do it a time or two, and it was impressive.

"I think Earl Grey," she said. "He's ready, though Midnight Moon is too."

"Could you take them both?"

"No," Gloria said. "I want them to look to me as the leader of the herd. If you put two of them together, they look to each other."

"Ah, I see." Matt knew a lot about horses, ranches, and farms, but he'd been learning how to train horses to be therapy animals, something Gloria had done for a few years in Montana before coming here.

"You know who else wants to come?" Gloria asked, turning back to the stove. The scent of something browning and crisping met his nose, but he couldn't place what she'd made for lunch.

"Who?" he asked.

"Your daughter." Gloria reached to turn off the stove, and then to get down plates. She put them on the counter while Matt tried to process what she'd said. She met his eyes, but he was blinking so fast that she came and went every other half-second.

"What?"

"She wants me to take her blading."

Matt shook his head, immediately rejecting the idea. "She can't even stay steady walking."

"I know," Gloria said, her voice pitching up. "I've been thinking about it all the same. I read this article about a mother who ran the Boston Marathon with her three kids in a jogging stroller."

"You're kidding."

"She set a Guinness World Record," Gloria continued, clearly not kidding. "With the three kids, plus the stroller, she pushed one-hundred-eighty pounds. Britt's what? Sixty-five pounds if she's dripping wet."

"Gloria."

"The stroller wouldn't be as big as a three-person stroller," she said. "We'd just need a single. I could do it." She flexed for him, a smile made of pure sunshine on her face. "I'm strong, Matt."

He licked his lips, because the woman didn't have an ounce of body fat on her. Everything about Gloria was lean, long, and strong, and he had no doubt she could push his daughter in a stroller while she rollerbladed.

Then why can't she? he wondered. Because he was afraid Britt would get hurt? They'd probably both love it, and Matt wasn't going to take anything from his daughter if she could have it.

He grinned and chuckled. "All right."

"All right?" Gloria's eyebrows went straight up. "Wow, I did not expect you to agree to that."

"Oh, come on," he said, laughing now. "I'm not Mister Says-No-To-His-Kids."

She turned back to the stove, grinning too, and collected the pan. "I made chimichangas from the tacos from last night. Elise gave me a whole bunch of them, and I had these uncooked flour tortillas in my fridge. So I just scooped the filling out of the tacos, rolled it up in the tortillas, and fried them."

She took them out of the pan one by one and put them on a plate with paper towels. After replacing the pan on the stove, she got out sour cream and ranch dressing. "I don't have guac, so this will have to do."

"This is great," Matt said, admiring the perfectly golden brown chimichangas. "It's fried food, Gloria. It can't be bad."

She grinned at him again and held up a bottle of water and one of lemonade, her eyebrows up.

"Lemonade," he said, and she put it in front of him. She collected one for herself too before finally joining him at the bar.

He looked at her, a new thrill moving through him. He reached over and took her hand in his. "I'm glad we were finally able to do this. I've been next door, trying to figure out how to see you without it being weird or just you hanging out with me and the kids."

"I like your kids," she said.

"They like you too," he said, reaching for a plate. "I just want you to myself for a real date." He flashed a smile in her direction, but he didn't dare look at her fully. He'd just said, "real date," and he didn't want to know if that surprised her or not.

She surprised him when she said, "I want that too; that's why I invited you for lunch." She used the tongs to serve him two chimichangas, and Matt spooned sour cream over them, his face warming and then heating past the point of comfortable.

That only made him want to keep his face down for longer, until the redness he was sure had crept into it had dissipated.

"Tell me how you met your wife," Gloria said, and that brought Matt's head up.

He looked fully at her as she spooned sour cream onto her plate. "My wife?"

She glanced at him, something playful in her gaze. "Yeah, your wife. I'm assuming you had a wife. Maybe you didn't."

"I did," he said, his heartbeat bouncing in a weird way he hadn't experienced before. Sort of like a double-dribble with a *bump-ba-bump* that repeated in a loop.

Gloria seemed utterly at-ease, and Matt sliced into his chimichanga so he could take a bite and buy himself some time.

"I haven't dated a whole lot," she said. "The last guy I went out with—his name was Ender Nunez—had worked for us at Tailwind for years. We dated for two maybe? My father loved him."

Matt cut a normal bite and put it in his mouth, listening intently.

"He asked me to marry him; I said yes. Then Daddy got sick." She took her own bite and chewed it. She exhaled and sat up straighter. "I didn't know until the will was read that Daddy had given Tailwind to Ender."

"You're kidding."

"He was close to Daddy, and I thought that was so sweet and so wonderful." She sighed and shook her head. "I didn't know he'd gotten Daddy to change the will."

"Was there anything you could do?"

"I sued him," Gloria said. "Cost me everything, and the judge *was* sympathetic. He said he wanted to give me the ranch, but legally, Ender was in the right. He counseled Ender to give me a job and pay me really well."

"Did he?"

"He offered me a job, and I can admit it had a decent salary. I didn't take it." She offered him a quick smile. "I couldn't. Maybe that makes me weak. It was easier to pack up everything I owned in my truck and leave, honestly. So I did that."

"It doesn't make you weak," Matt said.

"You weren't the only one taking the last two years to heal." She took another bite, and Matt realized he'd eaten an entire chimichanga while she'd been talking.

"I'm so sorry," he said. "I didn't know."

"You've been a very good friend," she said, keeping her eyes on her plate now. "When I showed up on this farm and saw you, I was devastated and hopeful at the same time." She gave a light laugh. "I was just so embarrassed. I didn't want to explain how I'd lost Tailwind, and I didn't want to admit how I'd been living out of my truck for a couple of weeks, and that I cried like a baby the first night I got to stay here."

Sadness tugged through Matt, and he put his fork down and his arm around Gloria. "I would've helped you."

"You did help me," she said, snuggling into his side for a moment before straightening again. Matt let his arm drop back to the counter. "You didn't ask me any questions, and that was exactly what I needed. You simply became my friend again after twenty years, and I didn't have any friends at that time."

"Well, I'm glad about that, then," he said, though he felt like he could've done so much more if he'd only known. At the same time, maybe he would've failed at being her support, as he'd barely been functioning as an adult himself. "You've been a very good friend for me too."

She allowed the silence to come between them, and Matt searched the cracks in his heart and found them mostly sealed.

"Janice and I met at church, if you can believe that," Matt said. "I'd say it was love at first sight, but it was more like love at first note. She was a phenomenal singer. She'd come to our congregation as part of a traveling choir, and she was an angel inserted into my life, straight from heaven."

"It sounds like you really loved her," Gloria said.

"I did," Matt said. "We got married only six months later, and Keith came along a couple of years after that."

"You stayed in Montana?"

"Mm hm, yep," he said. "She worked as an insurance agent in Billings, and I ran a small farm. When that went under, I started hiring out to other farms. I'd been coming down here for years before I made the move permanent."

"Did Janice and the kids come?"

"No, I'd come live down here myself," he said. "Gray needed the help in the busy season, and then he started going to Coral Canyon, Wyoming every summer. I ran the farm for him in his absence."

"You run the farm now."

"In a way," Matt said.

"You're the foreman."

"Yes," Matt said.

"Do you want a place of your own?"

Matt shook his head. "You know what? I don't. I did that in Montana, and it's a lot of work—back-end work that regular cowboys don't necessarily see. I'm happy to let Hunt and Gray handle all of that, especially with Britt's health issues and Keith's teenager...issues."

Gloria giggled, and Matt joined her, bumping her shoulder with his. "Admit it. He's hard sometimes."

"He has a certain attitude," Gloria said. "But he does everything around the farm required of him. He doesn't complain to me, and I've never heard you say he gives you a hard time with his chores."

"No, just his homework. Doing the dishes. Not being able to drive, despite him not being sixteen years old. Did you know it's *embarrassing* to be picked up by your father in ninth grade? I'm surprised he's made it this many months, honestly."

Gloria laughed with him, and Matt sure did like this

relaxing, casual conversation. "Anyway," he said, blowing out his breath and looking at his second chimichanga. He wanted it, but his stomach rioted around the one he'd already eaten. "Janice started drinking after work. It was just a little bit, only on the weekends…until it wasn't. Then it was every night, and then every morning, and then all the time." He stared at the window across the counter and stovetop, getting thrown back into the past, where he didn't want to be.

"Britt's condition was worsening, and when Janice nearly killed the two of them in a car accident, I decided I had to step up and be the father and protector my kids needed and deserved." His voice dropped into a monotone, but he couldn't correct it. "I called an alcohol treatment center in Salt Lake City. The best one in the west, though we couldn't afford it. I filed for divorce, and I dropped off Janice the day after that was final, and the kids and I continued on to Ivory Peaks. We'd been here for a month or so before you showed up at Keith's birthday party."

He drew in a deep breath, held it in his lungs, and then blew it all out. "It was hard, those first few months. Keith was *so* angry with me. He didn't want to leave all of his friends in Montana, and I couldn't go back. I needed a fresh start, and I believed he did too."

"Mm."

Matt tucked into his second chimichanga, the silence between him and Gloria still charged, but with a different kind of energy. No nerves, and no awkwardness. This tension felt very much like desire and attraction, and Matt couldn't help the way it flowed through him as it if had attached itself to all of his red blood cells.

His mind slowed as he finished his last bite, and after he'd swallowed, he said, "I think I need to take Britt back to the doctor. Janice swears up and down she wasn't drinking when she was pregnant, but one of the causes of symptoms like hers is fetal alcohol syndrome." His voice could've splintered it was so wooden.

Gloria didn't say anything; she simply slid her hand over Matt's and squeezed. She had been a very, very good friend over the past couple of years, and Matt felt strong with her at his side. If he had to take his daughter to the doctor and hear hard truths, he wanted a woman like Gloria there with him...and providing a safe place to fall afterward.

.

CHAPTER 8

$\mathcal{H}$unter Hammond frowned at the screen in front of him, and then down to the open binder on his desk. Uncle Wes sat on the other side of it, looking at something on his phone. Michael, Hunter's cousin and Uncle Wes's son, stood at the wall of windows which overlooked the city.

"Why can't I just give them a bunch of money and be like, 'have a great time'?" His voice came out as a grumble, as it often did when he had to spend all day in this office. Hunt had no idea how his father and uncles had done this. He too itched to be outside, under the blue sky though it was still cold in Colorado, his thoughts revolving around the upcoming planting season and whether or not the runt kitten in the barn would survive the night.

Molly, his wife, had texted him that she didn't think the runt would survive. She'd been in the barn for hours since the kittens had been born, along with Jane, Deacon, and Tucker—Hunter's half-siblings. They all lived at the farm together, though technically, Molly and Hunter lived in the high-rise penthouse next to this one.

They'd been married for about two months now, and Hunter had never experienced anything half as magical as coming home to his wife. Molly liked to bake and cook, but that wasn't why Hunt loved her so much. Her presence in his life calmed him and provided an anchor that had been in the wind since his mother abandoned him at school and then left him and Dad in Ivory Peaks while she moved on to bigger and better things.

Hunt had not invited his mother to his wedding, a decision he'd labored over with Molly, Dad, and his therapist. They'd all told him the same thing: This was his wedding, and he should have people there who cared about him.

Sheila didn't, not really.

Not only that, but Hunter had invited hundreds of people he barely knew, simply because they worked for HMC, the family manufacturing company he now sat at the head of. He'd talked to Wes and Dad about the guest list extensively, and in the end, the name that gleamed from at least a dozen buildings around downtown Denver had to be honored.

It wasn't like they couldn't afford to have a massive wedding; they could. And they had. Hunter had loved every minute of it too, and a smile touched his lips despite his uncle's silence and Michael's hefty sigh.

"I don't want to go to all of their meetings," Hunt said, once again trying to get Uncle Wes's attention.

"Then don't," Wes said. "I only did to maintain relationships, Hunt. Remember, a lot of what you do is to keep a relationship that took us years to get, or years to build. Sara Richmond is the activities director for the Rhodes Mansion. They have an image to maintain in the community, and they want the Spring Wing Fling to be the best it can be, because they only get to host it once every five years."

Hunt listened to Uncle Wes talk, trying to absorb what he really meant. "She doesn't really care what my opinion is."

"I doubt it," Uncle Wes said. "But she has to invite you, because you have the checkbook. She'll do her best to make you happy, no doubt about that." He looked up from his phone, and while he had turned sixty this year and had plenty of gray in his beard and hair, his eyes still seemed as young as Hunt had ever remembered.

His oldest would be thirteen this year, and his youngest would turn eight. Hunter was definitely glad he'd gotten married earlier in his life than Uncle Wes, though he and Molly didn't want to have children right away.

Hunt had to work on a daily—sometimes hourly—basis to make sure he kept his commitments to Molly. He wanted to be home when he said he would be. He wanted to call her when he said he would. He wanted to take the time off he needed to be with her and work on their relationship. She'd been very worried that his job would consume him—and he was too, truth be told.

The weight of the world started to press on his shoulders, and Hunter dodged and let it fall to the floor. He'd learned that over the past year of working in the top-floor corner office. If he didn't do something today, there was always tomorrow.

"So I need to show up and act interested," Hunt said. "But let her do what she'd like to do."

"Basically," Uncle Wes said. "And if you can't stand to go to a meeting, Hunt, don't go. Just text her in the morning that 'something came up,' and you trust her decisions, and to let you know if she needs anything from you."

Hunter nodded, appreciating his uncle so much. "Thanks, Uncle Wes." He got to his feet. "I think I'm going to say something like that for the stuff in this binder." He tapped it and turned to his cousin. "Come on, Mikey. Let's go get something to eat."

The near-teen turned from the window. He'd matured a lot in the past several months, and when Wes and his family had shown up for the wedding in January, Hunter had been stunned to hear his cousin's voice had dropped and his legs had lengthened. Aunt Bree had proclaimed that Mike had grown six inches in as many months, and he'd definitely turned into a lankier version of the boy Hunter had once known.

"Can we go to that place that will put gravy on the

fried cheese curds?" He gave Hunt a smile, his braces now with blue bands.

"Yeah, sure," Hunter said, lifting his arm to put it around his cousin's shoulders. "And you can tell me all about this girl you danced with at the junior high."

Mike cast a quick glance at his dad. "No, thanks."

"Oh, come on," Uncle Wes said, chuckling. He groaned as he stood.

"Dad, you told everyone in the whole family—*and* Matt and Gloria and Aunt Molly's parents—about the last dance. You're cut off."

Hunter burst out laughing, and he paused to reach for his jacket, which he'd hung on the coat rack beside the door. Uncle Wes stood in the doorway for several long moments every time he came to Denver. He'd made the trip with Michael twice in the past two months, and apparently the schools up in Coral Canyon, Wyoming kept the kids after schools one Friday a month, and they hosted dances.

Mike had been going every month, and Hunt had heard all about a girl named Kacie Wright. The texts about six p.m. on the second Friday of the month had kept Hunt and Molly entertained for hours, and Hunt didn't want to do anything that would jeopardize his relationship with his cousin.

Everyone needed someone to confide in, and Hunter knew Mike didn't want it to be his father...at least right now. Hunter could be that person—he *wanted* to be that person—and he'd told Mike he would keep his secrets as long as he didn't think his cousin was in any danger.

"I won't tell a soul about this one," Uncle Wes said, bringing his son to his side and grinning at him. "I promise."

"Nothing to tell anyway," Mike said, though he met Hunter's gaze with plenty of meaning in his. "I danced with some girls. One of them mentioned that I should run for student council next year, and I'm thinking about doing that."

"Can you do that in junior high?" Hunt asked, shrugging into his jacket.

"Yeah, in Coral Canyon you can," Mike said. "It's eighth and ninth graders, because remember, we don't go to the high school until tenth grade."

"Oh, right," Hunt said. "I always forget that."

"Would that require summer stuff?" Uncle Wes asked. "Remember, you're coming here this summer to work."

"I haven't forgotten, Dad," Mike said, rolling his eyes and leading the way out of the office. Hunter watched him go, and Uncle Wes crowded into the doorway beside him.

"He thinks I'm on him all the time," Uncle Wes said. "He has no idea what that even looks like."

"He just doesn't want to leave his friends and come work the farm this summer," Hunter said. "I get that, Uncle Wes. It's not that fun."

"I don't need details." Uncle Wes's voice dropped in volume by half. "Just tell me if he's talking to you about Kacie or Ella."

"Kacie," Hunter said, his lips barely moving. "He danced with her four times. She's the one who suggested he run for student council, because she's going to."

"Hmm." Uncle Wes stepped out into the hall and started after his son. "He better not be kissing both of them."

"Don't worry," Hunt said, following him and keeping the kissing talk to himself. "He's thirteen. This is all normal for a boy his age." Uncle Wes hadn't been thirteen for a long, long time, and times had been different. But Hunt had been about thirteen about the time his father had started taking him away from his friends in the summer and driving them north to Coral Canyon. He and Elise still took the family up there for four months out of the year, and since Jane hadn't started high school yet, the kids often missed the last month of school here in Colorado.

They owned a home up there, and they spent summers in a cooler environment, closer to all of their family. Hunt could admit he'd thought about doing the same thing and trying to manage HMC remotely. Molly loved Coral Canyon, and she loved it when Hunter didn't work all the time.

The idea kicked around in his head, but he knew it wouldn't happen this summer. This would be the first full summer season that Pony Power would be open, and Molly had big plans to expand their children's therapeutic riding center, and Hunter wanted to be right in the thick of that with her.

"Besides, you're the one who told me to kiss as many girls as I could, and I wasn't much older than your son."

"I still hear about that from your dad," Uncle Wes said as he joined his son in front of the elevator. He grinned at Hunter and then his son. "I didn't know you were going to do it—and I stand by my advice." He looked at his phone as if he didn't care about anything in the world. "Have you been kissin' Kacie, Mikey?"

"I'm not answering that," Mike said, his voice even and cool. Hunter knew he had, and he marveled at the boy's resolve to keep it to himself.

"Why wouldn't I do it?" Hunter grinned at his uncle. "I idolize you, Uncle Wes." They laughed together, though Hunter hadn't exactly lied. Uncle Wes *was* one of his heroes, and he did take every piece of advice given to him seriously.

His phone chimed as he joined his family on the elevator, and he glanced at it after meeting Mike's eyes and offering him a confident smile. "Oh, no," he said when he saw the text from Matt.

"What?" Mike asked.

"Our runt kitten just died." Hunt held up his phone, knowing his wife would be upset. "I'm going to need to make a detour to Willows and Petals," he said. "Get some flowers for my wife. She's been working hard to keep that baby alive."

"I'm sorry, Hunt," Uncle Wes and Mike said together, their voices almost the same now. It was as freaky as it was cute, and Hunter nodded at the two of them.

He quickly started tapping out a message to her, sending his condolences and love and telling her he'd bring dinner to the farm that night too.

Thank you, baby, Molly sent back. *Your dad says to order bacon cheeseburgers from The Burger Babe. Get Wes to work his charm. I want the salad and lots of the Hammond fries.*

Hunter grinned and tilted his phone toward his uncle so he could read it. "Done deal," Uncle Wes said. "I'll call it in right now."

CHAPTER 9

*G*loria entered the barn with a couple of bottles of milk in her hand. "Molly?" she asked, her eyes taking forever to adjust to the dimmer light inside. If the sun wasn't quite so glinting off the last remaining snow on the farm, she wouldn't be nearly as blind. "Matt?"

"She ran over to Chris's to get a heating pad," Matt said, rising from the crate where he'd been sitting. Gloria blinked, his handsomeness filling her sight. A smile came quickly, and sudden shyness overcame her.

"Are you going to eat at the farmhouse?" she asked. "Wes and Hunter just arrived with the food."

Matt sighed and pushed his hand up the back of his head, dislodging his cowboy hat. "I need to shower." He removed the hat completely and scrubbed his hand through his hair. "I feel dirty from head to toe." He met her eye. "The kids will want to eat with the Hammonds."

"I'm sure they will," she said. "They can, right? Keith is fifteen. He knows how to get from the farmhouse to your cabin." She let the words hang there, waiting for him to say they should take their burgers and fries back to his cabin and eat together.

He stepped toward her and ran his rough fingertips down the side of her face. "Would you wait for me to shower? We could eat at my place tonight, just the two of us."

Happiness flowed through Gloria with the strength of river rapids. "I've seen you shower. You're like lightning. I can wait."

His eyebrows shot up. "You've seen me shower? I thought that glass was frosted." The teasing quality of his voice made her feel feminine and well, sexy.

She put one hand against his chest as she laughed. "Of course I haven't *seen* you shower. I just meant you're fast."

"If we take our food and sneak off, everyone's going to know." Matt's eyebrows stayed high, silently asking her if she was ready for that.

Gloria wasn't sure if she was or not. She felt every year of her age then, and she drew in a breath. "Who cares if they know?"

"You don't? Chris will have questions. Elise. Molly."

"Your kids," Gloria said, and she hit the bullseye with that. "It's you who'll have to answer some real questions for your kids. I don't want to put you in that situation if you're not ready to have those conversations with Keith."

Matt let a sigh leak out of his mouth. "I don't know what I'm ready for."

"Are you done with the horses?" she asked.

"Yeah."

"Why don't you go shower and think about it?" she asked. "If you want, you could just text me, and I'll bring the food. You could easily just say you're tired. It wouldn't be a lie, and it wouldn't be a big deal."

She turned as the barn door opened behind her, and Molly came inside. Gloria automatically fell back a step, her self-consciousness rearing up and rendering her silent.

"Got it," she said, relief in her tone. "I'm just going to slide it under the horse blanket. Hunt's back with the food."

"Yeah," Matt said, his voice as calm and cool as ever. "That's what Gloria came to tell us."

"Howdy, Molly." Gloria followed her over to the horse stall where Molly had put a whelping box and the eight kittens. The mother cat had given birth in the toolbox in the neighboring equipment shed, but Molly had moved them over here. The barn was warmer, closer, and more comfortable for everyone. The mother had accepted the kittens after the move, something Molly had worried about, and Gloria admired her for working so hard around the equine therapy center and with these kittens. She had a heart as big as the ocean, and she wasn't afraid to love with it.

Gloria envied her that, and she cut a glance at Matt, who she'd told about her disastrous relationship with

Ender. He'd been kind and non-judgmental, and Gloria hadn't known how badly she'd needed that until he'd given it to her.

"How's Supernova?" Molly asked. "Is he taming his attitude any?"

"Slowly," Gloria said, giving her a smile. "How are the kittens?"

"Noisy," Molly said as she sat back on the crate and started shoving the heating pad under the horse blanket. "If the mama is around, they're yelping for her."

Gloria looked down into the box Molly had set up for the kittens, and they were cute.

"I don't think I'm going to the farmhouse for dinner," Matt said. "I'm exhausted from wrestling with those goats, and I need to shower."

"If the kids want to stay, I'll keep an eye on them." Molly got to her feet and dusted her hands together.

"Would you?" Matt asked hopefully. "I know Keith will want to stay with Michael and Hunter."

Molly gave him a smile and then turned to hug Gloria. "Of course. Are you going to come up to the house, Gloria?"

She held onto Molly's shoulders while she met Matt's eyes. "Maybe I'll just take Matt his food, and then eat mine in my pajamas." She pulled away and grinned at Molly. "It's been a long day already."

Molly blew her breath out. "You're telling me." She did look utterly exhausted. "I'm going to see if Hunt will let us take our food and go too." If she had any inkling that

Matt and Gloria would then eat their food together, she didn't indicate it. "I'll walk with you back to the house."

"Thanks, Mols," Matt said. "And Gloria? If it's too hard to bring the food, don't worry about it. Keith can bring it when he's done."

"Okay," she said, and she left the barn with Molly. They headed toward the brightly lit farmhouse, the energy pulsing from it infusing right into Gloria's chest.

"You should take some time off," Molly said.

"How am I going to do that?" Gloria asked.

"We have plenty of horses that are trained and working now," Molly said, glancing at her. "I mean it, Gloria. You work too hard, and I can see the exhaustion in your face."

Gloria ducked her head, but she didn't deny it. "I haven't been sleeping super well. That has nothing to do with the work here."

"I run Pony Power," Molly said. "I'm going to force you to take two weeks off if you don't take a day this week, and one next week."

"You can't do that." She brought her head up, disbelief coursing through her.

"I can," Molly said firmly, though she smiled. Gloria had loved working with her for the past several months, and she knew Molly was one of the biggest reasons she was already ready to move on with her life.

"I don't know what to do on days off," she said.

"You pack a picnic," Molly said. "And you go hike in the mountains for a while. Eat. Enjoy the peace and quiet. Camp if you want. Then come back."

"That does sound nice," she hedged, but she didn't want to go alone. Matt had kids he couldn't just leave behind, and Gloria couldn't even imagine the questions then. Her mind started down a path that showed all four of them camping in the Rocky Mountains, a clear stream bubbling in front of them. Matt stood there with Keith, the two of them fishing, while Gloria braided Brittany's hair and then made pancakes over the propane-powered portable stove.

She cleared her mind as she went up the few steps to the wide deck and saw people moving around inside the house through the open-blind windows.

"Then take tomorrow off," Molly said. "Or the next day if you're in the middle of something. I'm only going to tend these kittens for one more day, and then I'll be back downtown." She paused as she put her hand on the doorknob. "That doesn't mean I won't know if you don't take a day off."

"I could take my rollerblades and head south," Gloria said. "Just blade during the sunrise and sunset and take naps in between." She didn't really have money for a hotel or anything, but she kept that to herself. All of the Hammonds, of which Molly was now one, had plenty of money. Money upon money, and while they paid well, Gloria wasn't rolling in cash.

"That sounds like a fun trip for you," Molly said, grinning at Gloria. "Really, Gloria. I don't want you burning out. You know what the center needs and how it's running. You can have Travis or Cody do your chores. Matt can come over from the farm side. We can cover for you."

"I know you can," Gloria said, her stomach grumbling for something to eat.

Molly brightened the night with her smile and entered the house. Chatter spilled out of the house, as did the scent of fried food and warm hamburgers. Gloria normally loved eating in the farmhouse with all the Hammonds, but with the prospect of a quiet dinner with Matt in lieu of this, she found she wanted that more.

Keith turned toward the two women as they entered, and he held out a bag for Gloria. "Dad texted me to say you were going to take him dinner, and that Britt and I could stay here."

"Oh." She took the bag and watched Molly practically skip over to her husband. Hunter scooped her right into his arms, his smile wide but his eyes concerned for his wife. They spoke, and Molly nodded as she tipped up into his arms and kissed him.

"Are we okay to stay?" Keith asked, drawing her attention back to the teen.

"Yes," Gloria said. "Did you put something in here for me?"

"Yep, two burgers, two fries. Wes said there's salad if you want that."

"I'm good with burgers and fries," Gloria said with a smile. "What should I tell your dad about when you'll be home?"

"An hour?" Keith asked, turning toward Michael Hammond as the boy called for Keith. "Is that okay?"

"Text your dad," Gloria said. "I'll tell him too."

"Okay." Keith had already turned away, and Gloria stood on the outskirts of the crowd, drinking in their energy. Then she turned and slipped out of the farmhouse and began the quick walk to the cabin where Matt lived.

She'd be surprised if Matt wasn't already showered and waiting for dinner, and she barely felt the cold by the time she climbed the steps to his cabin, which sat at the end of the row and right next to hers.

Her fingers shook as she fisted them and knocked.

"Coming," Matt called from within the cabin, and he opened the door a few seconds later, holding a pillow to his chest. "Hey." He tossed the pillow to the right and focused on her again. "Everything go okay with the kids?"

"I didn't even see Britt," Gloria said, her pulse skipping. She hadn't even looked for the girl, though she'd surely been there. "Keith gave me the food and said they'd be about an hour."

"C'mon in," Matt said, and he smelled like spicy soap. His hair curled along the ends, and a certain dampness still clung to it. He wore gym shorts and a T-shirt the color of blueberry skin with a simple pocket on the chest.

Gloria stepped into the house, finding it far too warm. She said nothing as she walked through his living room to the kitchen. "Your cabin really is huge." She'd been inside before, but compared to her cabin, his seemed twice as big.

HIS SECOND CHANCE

The foreman's cabin usually was, because he often lived in it with his family. It could serve as a second family dwelling, but Hunter and Molly lived in the city.

"When Hunt takes over the farm, he'll probably live in the farmhouse. Gray and his family will move in the generational house. I'm probably safe here."

"You think so?" Gloria put the paper bag on the counter and faced him. "I think when Hunter and Molly come back to the farm, they'll live in the generational house. Gray still has a family to raise, and it's bigger than Hunter's right now."

"Very true." Matt had closed the door and followed her into the kitchen. He opened the bag and took out all of the food. "I'm so hungry."

"Me too."

"Are we using plates?" Matt asked. "I was just going to go in." He grinned as Gloria reached for a burger and started to unwrap it.

"We can just go in." She wrapped the ends of her paper around the burger and took a big bite. The juicy, meaty burger made her moan, along with the salty bacon and creamy cheese. "Oh, yeah," she said around the mouthful of food. "This is great."

Matt started to chuckle, and he didn't sit down as he took a bite of his burger. "Mm, yeah."

Gloria sure did like this easy-going version of Matt, though she'd seen him be tough with horses, and bark commands at the other cowboys around the equine therapy center. She'd seen him hug his children in one moment and protect them fiercely in the next.

So much about him had changed, but even as she thought that, she knew that wasn't right. What she knew about him from long ago had grown into something new. It spoke of the man he'd been then, and the man he was now.

They didn't say much as they ate, though they both found a seat. They worked on their feet too much to eat there too. It didn't take long to eat a hamburger and fries, not as hungry as they both were, and Matt got out drinks for the two of them.

He sat on the couch with his Diet Coke, a sigh coming out of his mouth. "Do you want to watch something?"

"Only if it's a romantic comedy," Gloria said, getting up and stepping toward the living room. He had a long couch, a loveseat, and a wingback chair. He sat on one end of the three-seat couch, and Gloria hesitated before she took a spot on the other end.

"You and your romantic comedies," he said, pointing the remote control at the television.

"I could say the same about you and your action-adventure superhero movies."

"At least they're entertaining."

"The romcoms are entertaining," Gloria said with a falsely wounded voice. "It's about character, Matty, not blowing something up."

He turned to look at her. "No one's called me Matty in a long time."

"Sorry," she said. "I know you hate that."

He looked back at the TV, but Gloria wasn't sure if he was really watching it. The channel guide flipped so fast he surely couldn't be reading it. "It just reminds me of something I'd rather not be reminded of."

"I know. I'm sorry." She tucked her legs underneath herself and reached up to let her ponytail out. "When's the last time you talked to your dad?"

"A while," he admitted. "Listen, I made an appointment for Britt next Monday. Can you cover for me with the goats and chickens? I can get Travis and Cody to do my horse chores."

"Sure," she said. "Molly told me I have to take a day off this week, and one next week. I could go with you on Monday."

He turned toward her again. "Could you?"

"Sure."

"Sometimes, when I'm at the doctor, I can't absorb everything they say in the moment. It gets overwhelming really fast. Having another set of ears would be nice."

"I'll talk to Travis and make sure he won't be too overwhelmed with both of us gone. I could just go in the morning or afternoon, whenever the appointment is."

"It's in the morning."

"I'll talk to him tomorrow. Well, probably on Wednesday. I'm going to drive south tomorrow. Maybe find somewhere I can blade and watch the sunset. Then I'll be back."

"That sounds fun," he said. "I wish I could come."

"I'll send you a video," she said. "I'm thinking I'll go to Garden of the Gods. There's usually not a lot of snow there."

"That sounds amazing." He patted the couch next to him. "Why don't you come sit by me?"

Gloria let her eyes drop to his mouth, which had curved up into that sexy smile that had completely undone her last time. She'd just started to move, because she did want to hold his hand and snuggle into his side, when the front door opened.

"Daddy," Britt chirped as she entered the house and stole Matt's attention. "Guess what? Molly said I could stay and help her with the kittens tomorrow if it's okay with you." She hurried toward Matt, her eyes wide and hopeful.

"It's school tomorrow, baby," he said.

"Just a Tuesday," Britt said. "We don't do *anything* on Tuesdays."

Gloria turned her sliding-over motion into a stand and went into the kitchen.

"Did you walk here yourself?" Matt asked, getting up to go look outside the front door.

"I'm here," Molly said from somewhere outside. "Sorry, Matt."

Gloria cleaned up their wrappers and boxes, one ear on the conversation. She knew Matt had a hard time saying no to his children, and that if Britt gave him one more plea, she'd be missing school tomorrow.

"I'll keep her with me the whole time," Molly said. "I

just couldn't tell her no."

"Join the club," Matt said. "All right, Britt. You can miss school tomorrow. You have to miss on Monday too. I got a doctor's appointment."

"No," Britt said, and Gloria caught her frown. "Daddy, I hate the doctor."

"He's going to help us this time," he said, barely turning toward her. He looked back at Molly. "I'll talk to Gray, but I'm not going to be around the farm that day."

"I'm sure it'll be fine." Molly entered the house, and Gloria knew the moment she saw her. "Oh, hey, Gloria."

"Hey." She turned and put the trash in the garbage can. Molly watched her long enough to meet her eyes after Gloria turned back to her. She watched her connect all the dots, and Gloria just wanted to disappear.

Molly crouched down in front of Britt. "Ask your daddy if you can come sleep with me in the farmhouse. Uncle Hunter is going back to the city, and I'll be all alone."

"Can I, Daddy?" Britt turned to him with such hope, and Matt grinned and nodded at her.

"Go get your pj's and clothes for tomorrow. I'll get your toothbrush and stuff." The little girl started to wobble-step down the hall, half-skipping in a way that made Gloria think she was about to fall down. "Clean underwear!" Matt yelled after her.

Molly giggled and smoothed her hair back. "I can keep Keith too. I'm sure he'd love to sleep in the bunk beds with Mike." She threw a glance into the kitchen, where Gloria sipped from her can of diet cola. She had no idea what to say to Molly, who sure seemed to be working hard to give Matt and Gloria some alone-time.

How embarrassing.

"Whatever he wants," Matt said. "I'm in no shape to put up much of a fight tonight."

"You need time off too," Molly said. "I told Gloria the same thing."

"It's just been a rough couple of days," Matt said.

"I told him I was taking tomorrow off, I'll have you know." Gloria pushed away from the counter. "Thanks for letting me eat with you, Matt. I'm going to head to bed too."

He looked at her with surprise, clearing wanting her to stay. He said nothing, and Gloria reached for her jacket.

"I didn't mean to interrupt," Molly said.

"You didn't." Gloria gave her a smile. "Matt somehow convinced me to eat my hamburger in my jeans, and that was a miracle."

"Ready," Britt said, and she came running down the hall.

"Whoa, slow down," Matt said, moving toward her. He reached her just as she tripped, and he managed to catch her as he dropped to his knees. "See, baby? Slow down."

Britt put both of her hands on his cheeks and squished them together. "I'm just so excited, Daddy. Did you know there are eight kittens in the barn?"

Matt grinned at her. "I know, Britt. I was out there with them tonight."

"Why didn't you tell me?"

"Because then you'd want to miss school." He got to his feet and passed her to Molly.

"I'll take good care of her," Molly promised.

"She falls sometimes," Matt said, clearly concerned.

Molly nodded, her eyes round. "She will go slow with me, right, Britt?"

"Yes, ma'am," she said, and Gloria would've done anything for the girl in that moment. Both Molly and Matt laughed, and then Molly left the cabin.

The moment the door closed, Gloria zipped up her jacket, though her walk would only take twenty seconds. "I really am going to go."

Matt spun back to her. "Do you have to?"

"Yes," she said. "I'm tired too, cowboy, and you look like you're about to drop."

He gathered her into his arms and drew in a deep breath. "Mm, okay," he said. "You'll find me before you go tomorrow?" His lips landed on the side of her neck, just below her ear.

Gloria shivered though his cabin was too warm, and she'd just put on her jacket. Everything with Matt seemed made of chills, thrills, and big, warm hands. She wanted more, more, more, but she stepped back and tucked her hands in her pockets. She wasn't sure where they'd been before, but the shape of his shoulders seemed to have imprinted into her fingertips.

"I'll see you tomorrow," she said. "Sweet dreams, Matt."

"Sweet dreams, Gloria."

CHAPTER 10

*T*he thunder woke Matt in the middle of the night, and he knew his bed wouldn't be empty for long. Britt disliked storms, though she'd try to be brave for a little while. He couldn't hear rain against the roof or window, which meant it would be snow, and Matt was so glad he didn't have to get up early and get to work on the ranch.

At the same time, guilt stole through him. Gloria would need help getting the paths cleared. Gray would be out before first light checking on the animals.

"Daddy?"

"Yeah, baby?" He turned toward his open door and saw Britt's silhouette.

She held a blanket in one hand. "Can I sleep with you?"

"Of course, baby. Come get in." He flapped the blanket back on his left for her.

"Keith says I'm too hot to sleep with him all night," Britt whispered when she reached the bed.

"I said she could stay," Keith said from the doorway.

"It's okay," Matt said. "Come pile in." He was sure his fifteen-year-old wouldn't crawl into bed with his younger sister and his daddy, but he did.

Matt smiled into the darkness as the thunder hit the sky outside again. Keith and Britt settled into stillness, and Matt thanked the Lord that they were all safe, dry, and warm from the storm outside. He wanted to keep them right here with him forever, so they'd never experience the hard things in life.

"Daddy?"

"Yeah, baby?"

"I don't wanna go to the doctor."

"I know, baby." He reached over and patted her leg. "We have to go."

"They take too much blood."

"We're going to figure out what to do to help you," Matt said. "This time, I'm going to have them do all the tests, baby. It's time we stopped ignoring it. Okay, baby?"

A couple seconds of silence passed, and then his daughter cuddled into his side. "Okay, Daddy."

"You can do it," he whispered into her hair. "You're a brave girl, and you can let them take some blood."

"Okay, Daddy." She took a breath. "Do you think Molly could come with us?"

"No, baby," Matt said gently. "Molly has loads to do." He took a breath, because perhaps he could whisper to his kids that he liked Gloria Munson. He cleared his throat. "I think Gloria might come. Would that be okay?"

"Oh, yeah, I like Gloria," Britt said. Her grip on him lessened and lessened, her breathing evened and evened, and she fell asleep a few minutes later. Matt kept his eyes closed too, but his mind moved through so many questions and fears that he couldn't allow himself to fall asleep.

"Daddy?" Keith asked, his voice barely loud enough to be heard.

"Yeah, bud?"

"You and Mom aren't going to get back together, are you?"

Matt turned his head toward his son, but he couldn't see him through the darkness. "No, bud, I don't think so."

"I don't think so either," Keith said. "She could've come here, and she didn't."

"She...." Matt didn't want to paint Janice in any colors at all. "She—"

"She knows where we are, and she didn't come," Keith said, his voice cracking.

Matt pressed his eyes closed, but he didn't know what to say. "I did leave the address of the farm with her in Salt Lake."

"I looked up the program," Keith said. "It was only twelve weeks, and she could've come. She didn't."

"Your mother has her own demons to fight," Matt said. "I...wanted to help her. I tried. Lord knows I tried. In the end, I had to protect you and Britt. I failed a few too many times before I realized that, and I'm sorry, Keith. I'm sorry."

"It's not your fault, Dad."

"I loved her with everything I had," Matt said, his own anguish rising up and coloring his voice. "It wasn't enough, bud. I wanted it to be, but it wasn't enough."

"I emailed her last fall, and she gave me her number," Keith said. "I told her again where we were. She didn't come."

"I—I'm so sorry, son." Matt wanted to tell him he was never going to leave Keith's side. He'd always be there for him. He said nothing, because his actions had already told his son that.

Keith sniffled, and Matt just let him. When he quieted, Matt whispered, "Keith, I love you."

"I know, Daddy. I love you too."

Matt reached across Britt and put his hand on Keith's shoulder. His son put his hand over his and said, "I'm tryin', Dad. I'm trying to work hard. I do everything you ask."

"I know you do. You're amazing."

"Sometimes, I lay up in the loft, and I look up at the ceiling, and I think—there's literally three feet between me and the universe. What if I just went through the roof? No one would even know until morning."

"Maybe we need to get a proper house," Matt said. "So you can have a real bedroom. I'd like a garage to park out of the snow."

"I'm not saying we need to move."

"But maybe we do." He pulled his hand back to his own side. "I've got some money. We could get a little place of our own, maybe in Ivory Peaks so it's not too far from the ranch and you'll be closer to the high school."

"Jordan did say that if I lived closer to town, his mom would let him come pick me up for school."

"Then we'll start looking," Matt said. "What's school like for you today? Could you skip? We could drive around and look after Britt's appointment."

"I've got a chemistry test," Keith said.

Matt nodded into the darkness. "I'll find a realtor." They fell into silence, and when Matt closed his eyes this time, his mind did settle.

"Daddy?"

"Yeah, bud?"

"Are you dating Gloria?"

"I want to," Matt said, letting the first thing he thought come out of his mouth. His pulse bumped, and he pulled in a breath. "I mean…yeah…I want to." He turned to look at Keith again, and once again, only got darkness. "What do you think of that?"

"I think you deserve to be happy too."

"You are my number one," Matt whispered, and he closed his eyes and saw his son as the little boy he'd once been. He'd been so chubby as a baby, and Matt smiled into the silent darkness. He could see him grinning at the camera with red popsicle staining his face. He watched him walk across a miniature stage to graduate from kindergarten, and he wondered when the tall, lanky, quiet teenager had stolen his little boy from him.

In that moment, Matt knew he hadn't lost that little boy. Keith would always, always be his little boy, and he would always, always need his dad. Matt wanted to be there to be that father for his son, and he said, "Always, Keith."

"Thanks, Daddy," Keith whispered. He turned over then, and Matt listened to his son breathe deep, blow it out, and then fall asleep.

"Thank you for these children," Matt whispered to the room. "Please help me to take care of them the way they need me to take care of them. Please, *please* don't let me fail them again."

HOURS LATER, MATT STOOD NEXT TO BRITT, HER hand gripped tightly in his. He watched the nurse prep the needle, knowing his daughter was eyeing it too.

"Just a little poke," she said.

"We'll get ice cream after," Matt said.

"The p-p-pink p-p-pony kind?" Britt asked as the nurse moved to her other side.

"Yes," Matt said, looking past his daughter. Gloria sat in the chair behind him, and he'd enjoyed her steadiness through the drive here and the appointment. She'd told him and Britt about her day off last week, though Matt had heard most of it already.

Britt loved stories, and Gloria had indulged her by telling her about the red rocks, the bluest sky she'd ever seen, and a new horse she'd ridden up in the mountains. She'd then told Britt that as soon as it was warm enough and the fields weren't made of mud, she was going to run Earl Grey while she rollerbladed.

Britt flinched, and Matt blinked. The needle had gone in her arm, and he watched her blood flow out and into a vial, praying that the red liquid had the answers he needed. Even as he begged the Lord for that, he knew he wouldn't get it.

The distinct thought came into his mind that he'd already gotten the answer to his daughter's health problems.

"All done," the nurse said a moment later. She finished up, capped the vial, and pressed a piece of cotton to the crook of Britt's elbow. She wrapped a heart-stamped piece of tape across it and gave them a smile. "Doctor Kitt will be in soon." She ducked out of the room, and Matt switched to Britt's other side.

"Okay, baby?"

"Okay," she said, but her big, light green eyes held tears, and she wrapped her skinny arms around Matt's neck and clung to him.

"The pink pony ice cream is going to be so delicious today," he whispered. "I think Miss Rose will give you extra bubble gum too."

"You think so?" Britt sniffled, her voice so perfect and yet so tinny.

"Yeah, I think so," he said, glancing over to Gloria. She offered him a kind smile, and Matt returned it. "I'm sure Gloria wants to get one of those special grilled cheese sandwiches too."

Her eyebrows went up, but Britt pulled away, her face lit with wonder. "The kind with p-p-pulled pork?"

Matt grinned and touched his nose to his daughter's. "Yep, that kind."

"There's a grilled cheese sandwich with pulled pork?" Gloria asked.

"They have this amazing pizza one too," Matt said. "Have you ever been to Great Cheeses?"

"I didn't know such a place existed."

"Gloria," Britt said, twisting toward her. "You will love it. *Love* it. Th-th-they have this one with m-m-mac and cheese on it."

Gloria rose to her feet, her smile singular on Britt. "Mac and cheese *on* the grilled cheese?"

"Mm hm," she said. "Daddy gets that one alm-m-most every time."

"It is delicious." Matt was glad he'd thought to bring up Great Cheeses, and he'd drive any distance to make his daughter happy. He thought about what Keith had asked him last night, and he wondered if Britt thought about her mother coming back.

"Hello," a man said as he entered the room. He carried a chart with him, and Matt straightened to shake the doctor's hand. "I'm Doctor Kitt."

"Matt," he said. "My daughter, Brittany."

"Brittany is such a great name," Dr. Kitt said. "My wife's name is Brittany."

"Wow," Britt said, beaming up at him, and Matt was glad he'd brought her to this new doctor. He hated these kinds of offices and visits too, but he was determined to get answers and learn how to take care of his daughter properly.

Like he'd told her last night, it was time.

"This is Gloria," Matt said, indicating her, and she raised her hand in a half-wave.

"Very nice to meet you all." Dr. Kitt sighed as he sat on the rolling stool. "I've looked over her records you sent from Montana," he said, tapping on the computer. "We've got the bloodwork you did last year. I know Jessica took some more." He looked up, his eyes kind and wide open. He was going to tell the truth, and Matt braced himself.

"Britt, can you do a couple of things for me?"

"Sure," she said, and Matt smiled at her though his pulse waved like a flag in a stiff breeze.

Dr. Kitt stood up, and he was a big man. He held out his hand. "Can you shake my hand?"

Britt looked at Matt, who nodded. She did, and Dr. Kitt smiled. "Can you squeeze harder?"

Britt looked like she was trying. Her forearm shook, but her fingers didn't make a dent in Dr. Kitt's flesh whatsoever.

"Perfect," he said anyway. "Can you tell me what five plus five is?"

Britt held up both hands. "Ten."

He grinned at her like she was the most charming child in the world. "What about seven plus nine?"

Britt was near the end of third grade. Matt had met with her teacher four times this year about Britt's math grade. Others her age were passing off multiplication facts. Britt still counted on her fingers.

His immediate reaction was to jump in and prompt her. If he sat with her in the evenings, she could get her math right. She even looked at him, but Dr. Kitt held up his hand, low and to the side, so only Matt could see it.

He fought against his desire to help her, protect her. He nodded and said, "You can do it."

"Nine is almost ten," Britt said slowly. "Um, N-n-nine is alm-m-most ten. Eleven?" She looked at Dr. Kitt while Matt's heart shattered. At home, he would've asked her how many more seven was than six. She knew that. She could take that one from seven, give it to the nine, and make sixteen. He'd done that with her at home.

Dr. Kitt said, "Perfect. Britt, can you get down from there?"

Matt once again wanted to jump forward to help her. Going down steps made her unsteady, and this was one of those high patient beds with a wide step several inches below where her feet dangled.

"Daddy?" she asked, scooting all the way to the edge.

"You can help her," Dr. Kitt said, and Matt steadied his daughter with one hand in his while she dropped to her feet. She pitched forward, but he was there to catch her, and then she stepped to the ground.

"Ta-da." She put up her free arm and grinned at the doctor.

He laughed like she was his grandchild, and he took his seat behind the computer screen again. "Very good, Britt. Do you have to search for words sometimes?"

"Yes," she said.

"Do you stutter sometimes?"

"Yes," she said.

"A lot?"

She looked at Matt, who nodded. He hadn't asked his daughter questions like this, and the last doctor he'd taken Britt to had asked *him* all these questions, in front of her. He liked Dr. Kitt so much more, as he treated his daughter like a human being.

"More when I'm n-n-nervous," she said. "Or excited. When I try to talk too fast."

"When you're scared?"

"Yes."

Dr. Kitt scooted out from behind the screen. "What is your favorite thing in the whole world?"

"Horses," Britt said, her face brightening. "Wait. K-k-kittens. The barn cat just had k-k-kittens. I love them."

Dr. Kitt laughed, a big, booming sound that filled the small exam room. "Horses and kittens. Yes, you would love my daughter. She loves horses and kittens too." He glanced at Matt and then back to Britt. "You climb back up there, okay?"

She did, and Matt just hovered nearby to help her should she need it. She wobbled on the turn, but she managed to get back on the patient bed, her legs dangling off the front of it. Dr. Kitt scooted right in front of her. "Do you want to know what I think?"

"Yes," Britt said somberly.

Dr. Kitt smiled, and he kept those wise, friendly, dark eyes trained on Britt. "I think you're a wonderful little girl. You're not as big as other girls your age, and you struggle with some things, like talking and doing math and even walking sometimes. Right?"

"Yes, sir," she said.

"We can't really diagnose what I think you have, because it's impossible to measure. We won't see it in your blood. We see it in the symptoms you show—like the stutter, the trouble with math, the stumbling." He put both hands on her knees. "I think you have partial fetal alcohol syndrome. It happened when you were growing inside your momma, so it's not your fault. Not only that, but there's so much we can do to help you be as strong as possible, and so much you can do to learn how to talk even when you're scared or nervous or really excited about the new kittens in the barn."

He grinned at her, but Matt felt like the world had been dropped onto his back.

"Like what?" he asked, clearing his throat. "What can we do to help her?"

"Physical therapy," Dr. Kitt said. "Yoga, exercise, and specific movements that will help her legs and feet be stronger. She can do auditory therapies that help with her ability to memorize things, especially math facts. She loves horses, and there are equine therapy programs for kids that can help build friendships, core strength, and communication skills."

"We run an equine therapy center for kids," Matt said, nodding to Gloria. "Well, Gloria does. Britt does that already."

"Oh, wonderful," Dr. Kitt said. "There's art therapy that helps with memory, and it sure seems like you're a kind, loving father. Consistency is key with children with pFAS." He met Matt's gaze head-on. "Do you know if your wife drank while she was pregnant?"

Matt felt backed into a corner, and he got thrown eight years into the past, where he'd stood in front of Janice and demanded to know when she'd started drinking. He was outside his body, and he could see everything so clearly.

"She said she hadn't," he heard himself say now, reliving that scene in the kitchen in the house in Montana. "But I think she lied to me. I think she drank while she was pregnant with her."

He came back to himself, and he hung his head, his own failures crashing over him in huge, heaving waves. Gloria stepped to his side and put her hand in his, and the world righted. Not only that, but he didn't have to bear the weight of it by himself anymore, and he glanced at her, hoping he could convey to her how grateful he was she'd come along.

"If it's any consolation," Dr. Kitt said, sitting back down on his rolling stool. "I don't think she drank in the first trimester, which is when the vast majority of brain development is happening. That's why she doesn't have the typical facial abnormalities we see with kids with FAS. But the fetus develops throughout the pregnancy, and I'm going to look at the blood for liver function and other organ function, which is where we see damage from later trimester drinking."

Matt just kept nodding and nodding. He threw in an, "Okay," but he seriously couldn't handle much more.

Dr. Kitt kept talking, and Gloria took the paperwork he handed over, and she asked him a few questions. Matt simply kept his hand in hers, hoping he could thank her properly later.

CHAPTER 11

*G*loria knew the moment Matt had zoned out. "Yes, he can make it work," Gloria said when Dr. Kitt asked if they could make it to a physical therapy appointment on Friday afternoon. "He's committed to her health. I'll make sure he knows."

"It's a lot to take in," Dr. Kitt said, glancing at Matt. "Go over everything with him—and Britt. See what makes the most sense." He grinned at the little girl, and she smiled right on back. "I can make referrals for specialists, therapists, and even help get her into educational programs that will help her thrive instead of make her feel like she can't keep up."

"It all sounds great," Gloria said, feeling like a little slice of heaven had been opened up, and brilliant white light poured into the exam room. "Thank you, Doctor Kitt."

"Yes," Matt said, his fingers tightening in hers. "Thank you, Doctor Kitt."

"You can stay in the room as long as you'd like. Call with anything." He beamed around the room and then walked out.

Gloria looked down at Britt and took a big breath. "Wow. What did you think of all of that?"

"He had a big laugh," Britt said, grinning like a fool.

Gloria giggled. "Yes, he did."

"You were so brave, baby." Matt released Gloria's hand and scooped his daughter into his arms. "Pink pony ice cream, and all the grilled cheese sandwiches you want."

"Yay!" Britt cheered as Matt headed for the door. Gloria watched as two of the people she admired most opened the door and walked into the hall. Matt needed some time to process, and Gloria folded the papers and pamphlets into her purse to deal with later.

"Thank you for giving him an answer," she murmured as she followed the two of them out of the doctor's office.

An hour later, she stared at the grilled cheese sandwich in front of her while Britt giggled. "I t-t-told you, Gloria," she said with glee. Then she picked up her sandwich—laden with cheese and pulled pork—and took a big bite. Half the sandwich spilled out of its bread borders, but Britt didn't seem to mind at all.

Gloria picked up knife and cut her sandwich in half, some of the ooey gooey mac and cheese falling out too. They'd eaten dessert first in the form of ice cream, and then Matt had driven them to this hole-in-the-wall place with the strangest and yet most amazing grilled cheese sandwiches in the world.

Matt looked up from the papers he'd asked to see, his face full of worry and words. He cleared it quickly and smiled at his daughter, Gloria, and then his sandwich. "I'm starving." He tucked the pages about speech therapy under his basket and grinned at the two of them.

"Daddy?"

"Yeah, baby?"

"I'm gonna work so hard to get stronger." She took another big bite of her sandwich while Matt blinked.

Gloria watched him for a moment, and when his eyes met hers, the familiar lightning crackled between them, as well as a new bond that she hoped would last a long time.

"I know you are, baby," he said. "I am too, okay? It might be hard for both of us, but I think we can do it."

"Gloria can help." Britt looked at her with wide-eyed innocence. "Right, Gloria?"

"Definitely," she said. "Before you know it, you'll be the one with the rollerblades on, with a horse running at your side."

Britt's eyes got really wide. "Really? Do you think so?"

"I think…." Gloria cleared her throat. "I think we're only limited by our own expectations for ourselves." She glanced at Matt again. "It might take a long time, but I think you can do anything you want to do, Britt."

She didn't want to give the girl any false promises, and she certainly wouldn't do that with Matt as a witness. She knew him quite well, and he'd seemed a couple of breaths away from a complete breakdown a few times in the past hour. Then he'd smooth everything away, and he'd laugh and tell Britt he'd help her get caught up with what she'd missed at school that day.

Right now, his façade was falling, and Gloria offered him a smile he couldn't return. They finished eating, and he drove them all back to the farm.

"Daddy, can I watch cartoons on the couch?" Britt asked as he got her out of the truck.

"Absolutely," he said. 'Then I can take a nap." He grinned at her and held her hand in his as they went up his front sidewalk. "I just need to run over to the stable with Gloria real quick, and then I'll be back."

He glanced at her, and though them going to the stable was news to her, she nodded.

"You'll be okay?" he asked, going up the steps.

"Yes, Daddy."

"I'll be a minute," Matt said to Gloria. "You can come in."

"I'll run home for a minute," she said. "Come grab me when you're ready to go."

"Will do."

Gloria sighed as she turned away, the stress of the morning finally over. She enjoyed spending time with Matt and Britt, that was for sure, but she couldn't even imagine the burden Matt carried, and so silently too.

He couldn't break down, and he couldn't act afraid or worried, though he was probably both. She wanted to be the person he could come to when he needed a release, the woman he could trust to shoulder hard things with him, the woman who could be strong when he needed to be weak.

Inside her cabin, she paused and took a deep breath of the stillness and silence. She couldn't believe it had snowed again, just when the Earth was starting to thaw out. She wanted spring to come, and then summer. Gloria craved a sunrise with rollerblades on her feet and a horse at her side.

She closed her eyes, and in that dream, there was always a dog too. The farm had a few dogs, and they'd stay with her if she took them. She hadn't last year, but this year, she was going to take a dog or two with her while she bladed.

Gloria collected a bottle of mango lemonade from the fridge and had just popped the lid to take a drink when Matt knocked on the front door. "Gloria?"

"Come in," she said, and he entered. She held up her bottle. "Lemonade?"

"Yes, please." He approached, and she stepped out of the way. "Strawberry...or mango." He reached for a bottle and said, "Mango." He twisted the lid, the *pop!* filling the space between them.

He took a long drink and then sighed. "Thank you."

"Of course."

He finally met her eye, and standing as close as they were, fireworks exploded through her system. "Thank you for coming today. Thank you for being so non-judgmental. Thank you for being...here."

Gloria ducked her head and said, "You're welcome." She looked up at him again. "What are we doing? Do we really need to go to the stable?"

Matt took another drink of his lemonade and set the bottle on the counter. "I just want to walk for a bit. Will you walk with me?" He took her hand and lifted it to his lips.

"Sure," she said.

"I don't want to talk about anything."

"No problem." Gloria tugged him toward the front door. "We do need to talk about something," she said. "At some point."

"Oh? What would that be?"

Gloria stepped out onto the front porch. "Why we broke up last time, and how we're going to make sure that doesn't happen again."

He dropped her hand, and Gloria turned back to him. He wore an angry expression on his face, and Gloria hadn't been expecting that. "Why did we break up last time, Gloria?"

"Because...." She didn't want to say anything that sounded like an accusation, though she did want to have this conversation.

"I was more immature than you," he said. "I distinctly remember you telling me to grow up."

"That was...because you started dating someone else without even breaking up with me first."

Matt's eyes blazed with defiance, and she really didn't want to have a two-decades-old argument.

"I'm sorry," she said. "I shouldn't have brought it up. Let's just walk." She started for the steps, but his boots didn't follow her.

"It's obviously bothering you, if you brought it up," he said.

Gloria turned back to him, her mind racing. "I just want us to be really honest with each other this time."

"I was honest with you last time," he said. "I was not dating Keri. Not even close. We danced a couple of times while I was waiting for you to show up."

He *had* said that last time, and Gloria didn't know what to say.

"I'm not saying I did everything right," he said. "But you didn't either. I'm not saying I wasn't immature, because I was." He came down the steps, slowing as he reached her, as the fight left him. "I did not cheat on you. We broke up, because neither of us were ready for the type of relationship two people like us have."

Gloria swallowed, trying to get her heart to go back to the right place in her chest. "What kind of relationship is that?"

"The kind where it's serious and long-term. The kind where we're our worst selves with the other, and it's okay, because they love us and forgive us." He cleared his throat and ducked his head, the brim of his cowboy hat concealing his face from her for a moment. "The kind where we recognize that who we were twenty years ago is not who we are now. We accept that, and we can leave the past where it belongs."

He reached up and trailed his fingers down the side of her face. "I talked to Keith about us. He said I deserve to be happy too, and right now, Gloria, I only have one thing that makes me all that happy."

"Your kids."

"One thing I'm not related to." He gave her a smile. "I'll give you a hint: It's a person, and she's got this gorgeous blonde hair, and these greenish-blue eyes that drink a man up and swallow him whole." He inched closer to her, but there was no way Gloria was kissing him on her front sidewalk, with his daughter watching cartoons in the next cabin over.

Today didn't feel like a day she wanted to remember forever and ever, and kissing Matt Whettstein had a way of lodging in her brain and never letting go.

"I want to leave the past where it belongs too," she said. "I apologize for bringing it up."

"I don't want to be judged for something I did twenty years ago," he said. "Especially if it's not true, and especially because I'm not that man anymore." He slid his hand down her arm to her waist and stepped right into her personal space.

"I don't want that either," she said.

"So we agree that we're not going to revert to who the other person was back then," he said.

"Yes. And we agree that we'll be honest with each other. If you're not feeling things with me, Matt, just tell me."

He bent his head closer to hers, his breath warm and

welcome against her cheek as he said, "I feel all kinds of things when I'm with you, Gloria."

She giggled, and she pressed her cheek into his. "Come on, now. If you want your walk—your no-talking walk—we better get going. By my watch, your son is going to be home soon."

CHAPTER 12

*W*esley Hammond glanced out the passenger window and said, "It's right there about half a block down."

His nephew, Hunter, drove down the Denver street, close to downtown, but not right in the thick of all the tall buildings.

"I see it," Hunter said. "The Funky Chicken?"

"Yep." Wes relaxed in his seat, though he didn't particularly enjoy field trips like this. They'd been fine when he took them himself, or when his brother Gray came along. He didn't have to explain anything then.

But with his thirteen-year-old in the backseat, and Hunter driving, heat ran under Wes's collar and all along his forehead.

"This looks like your kind of place, Dad," Mikey said from the back, and Wes nodded.

"It's great. You'll love it. They have the most amazing

sauce. Better than what I had in California, but don't tell Uncle Cy that." He grinned over his shoulder, glad when Mikey reciprocated.

Wes loved the trips to Colorado with his son, because it gave him time to truly talk to the boy. There was something about not having his mother around that made Mikey open up, and without the distractions of his younger siblings, Mikey got to be front and center.

Not only that, but Wes had a strong suspicion that Mikey would be the next CEO of Hammond Manufacturing Company. Hunter had taken on the role for now, but he'd been very clear that he didn't want to do it forever, not the way Wes had.

"They look busy," Hunter said, easing past the fried chicken restaurant because there was nowhere to park out front.

"The owner is Cora Richfield," Wes said, clearing his throat. "We met about twenty years ago, only a few years before I left HMC. She was the recipient of the HMC business grant that year."

Hunter swung his attention toward Wes. "The HMC business grant?"

"Laura may have discontinued it," Wes said, though he knew full well that Laura had stopped donating to the small businesses around Denver and in the surrounding area. Wes had founded the program in his first five years as CEO, and he'd funded the first business grant with his personal money to show the board of directors that investing big business money into small businesses in the

136

area only improved their bottom line. It only strengthened the economy in the area, and a thriving economy helped everyone.

"What is it?" Hunter asked.

"You've been to The Burger Babe," Wes said, shifting in his seat. "That was my first investment in small businesses around the city. Once that was a success, I was able to institute the program, where people would send in applications for small businesses they wanted to start around the area. And, uh, HMC funded them."

"You own The Burger Babe," Mikey said as Hunter made a right turn.

"No," Wes said. "We're business partners. I'm an investor in Hillie and the restaurant. After her, HMC became the investor, and I, as the CEO, managed the portfolios."

"The Funky Chicken is one of your investments," Hunter said.

"They won the HMC small business grant," Wes said, gently correcting him. "You must have paperwork on them somewhere."

"Maybe accounting is managing things now," Hunter said. "I haven't heard anything about restaurants or a small business grant." He pulled into an available parking spot around the corner from the restaurant and came to a stop.

Looking at Wes now, Hunter looked like he was trying hard to figure out what Wes's motivation was. He was one of the smartest men Wes had ever known, and he offered him a smile. "I did it, because we all got—*get* —such a huge break. You don't think about money. You don't think about how to start a business. You just start it—and then you leave it back east to be run by a friend."

Hunter looked like Wes had slapped him, and he hastened to add, "Which is fine. It's great. I'm not saying you should've done anything different than you've done. Our lives are amazing, and I felt like there are so many opportunities to give others that same amazing...ness."

"Is this going to delve into a lecture?" Mikey asked, and Wes twisted in his seat to look at his son.

He grinned. "I guess if it did, that was it."

Mikey smiled back. "I liked the use of 'amazingness,' though my English teacher would dock me points and say that wasn't a word." He unbuckled his seatbelt and reached for the door handle. "I'm starving. Let's go see this chicken palace of Dad's."

"It's chicken *funkiness*," Wes said, following his son onto the sidewalk.

"So let me get this straight," Hunter said, joining them. "You bought the businesses for these people. They must give you some percentage of their profits."

"Yes," Wes said.

"This is what you did with the community outreach program."

"Yes," Wes said again. "It's far better than sitting in meetings and continuing to pad the pockets of businesses already thriving in the city." In his opinion. Not everyone felt the same as him, obviously, but he hoped Hunter would consider bringing the program back.

"You have a huge corporate budget at your disposal," Wes said, turning the corner first. He adjusted his cowboy hat, feeling a bit out of place wearing it in the city. At the same time, he sure did like wearing it in the city. "It's just like everything else at HMC. You have to be responsible for the distribution of those funds, and give them to places and people you believe in. It's one of the easiest way to be able to sleep at night."

"I hate having a huge corporate budget at my disposal," Hunter grumbled. "No one ever told me to take classes about 'how to manage huge corporate budgets' at MIT, and it's a *really* good school."

Mikey started to laugh, and even Wes smiled. He knew Hunter wasn't joking, and he slung his arm around his nephew. "It isn't something you can learn in a class anyway, Hunt. It's something you manage with your heart."

"I suck at that too," Hunt said miserably. "You realize I've been in therapy for over a decade, right, Uncle Wes? Because my heart's broken."

"That is so not true," Wes said with a laugh. "I've seen you with your wife, Hunt. You know exactly how to use that thing." He reached for the door, enjoying the ding as he opened it and stepped inside.

Plenty of people stood inside, and it looked like at least a twenty-minute wait. He joined the line, though he could've easily gone to the front of it.

"How do you decide who gets the grant and who doesn't?" Mikey asked.

"It's a gut thing," Wes said. "Believe it or not, Mikey, I used to be a people-person. I could meet them and get a feeling for who they are and what they really want. How hard they were willing to work. That kind of thing." He glanced at his son but looked away quickly. "I still know that about a person after a few minutes of conversation."

"That's why you won't let me get anything but an A in algebra," Mikey said.

"You don't even try in that class," Wes said with a grin. "Look at Hunter. He didn't have to try with that kind of thing either. Now he's an MIT grad, running a multi-billion-dollar company."

"Don't remind me," Hunt said sarcastically.

"Wesley Hammond," a woman said, and the next thing he knew, strong, wiry arms got flung around his neck, pulling him down to her height. "I've missed our semi-annual chats, young man."

Cora Richfield pulled back, and she'd definitely aged too. She had the same gray in her hair that Wes sported in his, though not an ounce of life had disappeared from those vibrant, hazel eyes.

Wes laughed and swept his cowboy hat off his head so she could see he was definitely not a young man anymore. "Cora, you look exactly as I remember." He hugged her again, drawing the attention of the people standing in front of them.

"Come into the back," she said. "We can eat in my

office." She flicked her gaze toward Hunter and then Mikey. "Oh, these fine men belong to you. I can see the Hammond in them."

"Hunter," Wes said, indicating the boy who now stood taller than him. "He runs HMC now, Cora." He beamed at his nephew. "He does a fantastic job of it too."

Hunter stuck out his hand, his pleasant, professional smile on his face. "Nice to meet you, ma'am."

"Definitely a Hammond with those manners." Cora grinned at him and shook his hand before turning to Mikey.

"My son." Wes had never felt prouder than he did in that moment. He put his arm around his son's shoulders again, smiling at him with all the love and hope and pride a father could have. "Michael. He's thirteen, but tryin' hard to be thirty."

Mikey rolled his eyes and extended his hand too. "Nice to meet you, Cora. My dad says he's a people-person, but he's still working on not letting embarrassing things come out of his mouth."

Wes chuckled, but Cora burst out into a peal of laughter. Mikey looked at her and then Wes, cocking his eyebrows as if to say, *See? I'm right.*

Wes let him have his moment of victory, because maybe Wes did say things before thinking about them. Bree, his wife, sometimes told him that, especially as the kids had started becoming teens.

"It's a life-long endeavor," Cora said through her giggles.

"None of us are perfect," Wes said, glancing around. "Though this place still looks absolutely fantastic." He'd always liked the bright colors on the walls in red, green, and blue party shapes, with a nearly-neon yellow chicken dancing among the confetti. "He still looks as funky as ever."

"And not a single person has complained about the color." She patted his chest and stepped away from him. "Come on. I'll put down a fresh batch of tenders. If I remember right, you like the sweet potato fries. Shoestring."

"Your memory is iron-clad," Wes said, gesturing for Hunter and Mikey to follow her in front of him.

"WE'RE LEAVING IN AN HOUR," WES CALLED AS Mikey's boots thundered past the office in the farmhouse where he sat visiting with his brother.

"I know!" Only a moment later, the front door slammed, and his son needed a few seconds to run down the steps and make a right turn. Wes caught sight of him sprinting across the front lawn, his goal obviously that barn on the other side of the pasture.

Sure enough, the teen ran toward the fence and then along it, his long legs moving him at a decent clip.

"He's in a hurry," Gray said.

"Gerty's in the barn," Wes said. "It's amazing what he thinks I don't know."

Gray chuckled and shuffled something on his desk. He wasn't wearing his slacks and button-up white shirt, and Wes didn't wear his suit. Not to hang out in their childhood farmhouse, in the office their father had dominated for so many years.

"We didn't think our parents knew anything either," Gray said, sitting back in his chair with a sigh. "He's a good boy. He'll be fine."

"He has a girlfriend in Coral Canyon," Wes said. "Two of 'em, I think."

"Not true," Hunter said as he walked by the office, his voice sounding like he'd just put something in his mouth. Probably toast. That man could eat toast at any given time, even just after the huge lunch they'd just had.

"It is true," Wes called.

"Not in his mind." Hunter's voice continued to move away from him, and Wes was too lazy to get up and continue the conversation.

"I'm not sure teenagers have actual minds that work," Gray said. "At least that's what I'm seeing."

"Don't tell me that."

"Hunt was one of the best, that's for sure," Gray said.

"That's because he didn't have siblings, and his two favorite things to do he could do one alone and one with you."

"I don't regret giving him that crossword puzzle book, not even a little bit," Gray said. "And it's rare that I can get him to go fishing with me these days."

"Not by choice," Hunter said, framing himself in the

doorway. "And I'm here now. The whole rest of the day off. Why are we standing here, lamenting our lack of fishing time?"

"Because your wife is waiting for you in the stable, and you already promised her your afternoon off." Gray gave his son a kind, fatherly smile. "We'll go this weekend."

"We'll be back in two weeks for the Spring Wing Fling." Wes groaned as he got to his feet. "Maybe Mikey and I could go with you."

"Trout Lake will be thawed by then," Hunter said, lifting his last bite of toast to his mouth. His dark eyes glinted with mischief, and Wes wondered what that was about. "I can talk to Mikey about it."

"Better you than me at this point," Wes said. He met Hunter's eye. "What's he sayin' about Gerty?"

"You know I'm not going to tell you," Hunter said with a smile. "If it's dangerous for him or I think he's getting himself in too deep somewhere he can't get out, I tell you. Otherwise." He shrugged.

"She's a cute girl," Gray said, moving to the window.

"Close to his age," Hunter said, and Wes felt ganged up on in that moment.

"She lives in Montana," Wes said.

"I don't think we need to talk about long-distance relationships," Gray said, turning to smile at his brother. "People make them work."

"He's *thirteen*." Did Gray seriously just compare Mikey and Gerty—who was only twelve—with him and Elise? Seriously?

Hunter chuckled, but Wes didn't really see what was funny. "Uncle Wes, you need to chill. He's got a long way to go before you're done with him liking cute girls close to his age."

"I think Boone will move here with Gerty, besides," Gray said.

"Really?" Wes asked.

"Yes," Gray said. "He's been here a week. He's a great worker, and he wants to make a move. I offered him a job."

"Did he take it?" Wes asked.

"He said he wanted to talk to Matt, and he has some things to tie up in Montana if he does." Gray returned his gaze out the window. "I think he will. His brother's here. They're both single dads. They need one another."

"I hope he does," Hunter said. "Boone's a hoot. Takes the pressure off me to be funny at family parties."

"Oh, my word," Gray said at the same time Wes said, "Hunter, you're never as funny as you think you are."

He stepped next to his brother and watched the breeze blow into the blooming trees in the front yard. "I don't know how you survived this."

"It was not easy," Gray whispered. "And Jane is only twelve, but goodness, you'd think we've doomed her to a friendless life by saying that yes, we're going to Coral Canyon for the summer, just like we have for the past dozen summers."

"Bring a friend with you," Wes said.

"And what? She'll abandon Opal and the twins? Ava

and Ella adore Jane."

"She's getting older than them," Wes said. "Things change." That was exactly what he didn't like about time continuing to march forward, but he'd spoken true.

"Jane can stay with me and Molly," Hunter said, and he still hadn't taken a step out of the doorway.

"No," Gray said firmly, turning back to his son. "No, that's not how it works. I appreciate you offering, but no." He held up one finger, and the lawyer inside Gray Hammond came out. "Do not mention this to her either, Hunt. She doesn't get to think she has options. She's part of our family, and our family goes to Coral Canyon in the summer."

"Okay, okay." Hunter held up both hands in surrender, and he wasn't bothered by his father's attitude.

"Can I leave my annoying teenager with you?" Wes joked as he approached Hunter.

"Sure," Hunter said easily. "You'll be back in two weeks. I'll put him to work here."

Wes considered it for a couple of heartbeats, and then he shook his head. "I'd do it, but Bree would probably put my stuff out on the porch if I did." He chuckled, shook his head, and reached for his suitcase, which he'd set just inside the office door.

"If he's not back on time, though, I might just leave him. See how he likes that." He stepped past Hunter, who still wore a form of a devilish smile on his face.

"He'd like it just fine," Hunter said. "Gerty's staying through next weekend."

CHAPTER 13

*M*att straightened his bow tie while Britt sat cross-legged on his bed, her tablet in her hand. "Shoot," she said, her voice full of disdain. "That stupid rabbit got me again."

"Time to put it away, baby," he said, turning from the mirror. The tie wasn't going to stay straight anyway. "And listen to you. No stutter on the 'rabbit.'" He grinned at his daughter and sat on the bed with her. "How's speech therapy going?"

Britt's face lit up. "Good. Miss Byrant brought her baby to class the other day, and we all got to give her a kiss."

"Wow," Matt said, pushing his daughter's white-blonde hair back off her forehead. "You said her name was Chloe."

"Chloe Louise," Britt said, scooting to the edge of the bed. "She is so cute, Daddy. You would love her." He watched her steady herself for a moment, and then Britt skipped toward the door, leaving the tablet behind on the bed.

Since the doctor's appointment, Matt had taken the bull by the horns and dug in to get his daughter the help she needed. She went to speech therapy twice a week now, getting pulled from her regular class to work with someone to help her form the right sounds and gain confidence in her words.

She had an educational plan now for math, and she went to a special education classroom during that hour her teacher taught the stuff to the rest of Britt's class and got the one-on-one help she needed. Matt didn't let a single evening slide without asking her about her math, as he'd done in the past.

Being a parent was simply exhausting, and he sometimes didn't have the brain bandwidth to follow up on everything. Molly, who'd once taught elementary school, had found out about Britt's condition and offered to help her in the afternoons, and that had been a direct answer to one of Matt's prayers.

His heart swelled with gratitude for the Hammonds—all of them. Gray, Elise, and their kids, who were so kind to his. Hunter, Molly, and Chris, who'd brought Britt a jump rope when he'd learned that her physical therapist wanted her to have one.

Tears choked in his throat, and he got to his feet. "Thank you, God," he murmured. "For leading me to this place, with so many people willing to help." All he had to do was send a text, and Elise would have dinner on his table in under an hour. He hoped that at some point when he wasn't barely holding his own head above water, he could be the Lord's hands for someone else.

"Wow, Dad," Keith said when Matt walked into the kitchen. "Look at that jacket."

The theme for tonight's Spring Wing Fling was "old-fashioned," and Matt had no idea what that meant. He knew Hunter had raided his grandfather's closet and pulled out one of his suit coats from yesteryear.

He'd modeled the jacket a couple of days ago, and Hunt looked striking with his dark hair and eyes and that burnt red suit coat. It definitely looked vintage, and Chris had teared up seeing his grandson wearing his clothes.

On his clothes, Matt had consulted with Gloria, as the two of them were attending the Spring Wing Fling together. Hunter had provided tickets for them, and Matt couldn't wait to see Gloria's fifties fit-and-flare dress.

The best he could come up with was one of his father's old corduroy jackets with patches on the elbows. Boone had brought the jacket a couple of weeks ago when he'd come to Ivory Peaks to visit and talk to Gray Hammond about a job.

"It's nice enough, right?" Matt tugged on the ends of his sleeves. "I think my father had shorter arms than I do."

"Can Uncle Boone bring more of granddad's old clothes when he moves here?" Keith asked, resetting the electric kettle on the burner. "Those are so on-trend now." He stirred the cup of hot chocolate and slid it over to Britt.

"I don't know if Uncle Boone is going to move here permanently."

"Yes, he is," Keith said, meeting Matt's eyes. "Gerty texted me this afternoon that they'd be here for permanent once school got out in Montana."

Matt's eyebrows stretched up. "Wow. I hadn't heard that." Of course, Matt knew Boone wanted to leave Montana. They'd talked about it a lot. Boone had arrived at Ivory Peaks Farm last night for the second time in three weeks. They'd planned to take the kids into the mountains for spring break, and while Matt couldn't be gone for the whole week, he had taken three days off.

Before Matt could get his phone out of the oversized pocket of his corduroy jacket, his front door opened, letting in the wind. It was early April, but nowhere near what Matt would label springtime. At least not yet. The weather in Colorado could change on a dime, and he'd already checked the weather for next week—sunny and high sixties. He could practically taste the tulips and budding trees.

"There he is," Matt said, smiling at his brother. "Keith said you decided to move here 'for permanent.'"

Boone grinned as his larger-than-life personality filled the cabin from top to bottom. "That I did. Just this afternoon. Right, Gerty?" His daughter entered the cabin behind him, and she looked as cowgirl as they came. Blue jeans, red cowgirl boots, a plaid shirt in pink, black, and white.

"Yep," she said, giving her dad a look that didn't exactly convey happiness.

"What are y'all planning for tonight?" Matt asked. "Besides the hot chocolate, obviously."

"Can I have the hazelnut kind, Keith?" Gerty asked, beelining for the barstool right next to Britt. "Look at your hair, Britt. You cut it."

"Daddy took me to Miss Priss," Britt said with pride etched in every word. "She bobbed it."

"I love it," Gerty said with a genuine smile. She always wore her blonde hair long, and today, it had been braided into a single strand that fell down her back. She'd obviously been wearing a cowgirl hat at some point, because the braid didn't start until way down by her neck.

"I ordered pizza," Boone said. "Gerty has three movies to choose from. Britt promised us we could see the kittens."

"Oh, my *meow*," Britt said, her voice more animated than Matt had heard in a long time.

"Meow?" he asked, but his daughter forged forward.

"You would not *believe* how big they are, Gerty. Boots is huge now, and Molly says she's gonna sell them as mousers."

"How'd you get someone to deliver pizza out here?" Matt asked.

"Aren't you late to pick up your date?" Boone asked without looking at him. "Pretty sure I saw Gloria pacing in the front window as we came by."

Matt's heartbeat spiked, and he spun toward the clock

glowing on the microwave. He was late. "Shoot," he said, reaching for his wallet on the side table. It went in his back pocket while his keys got swiped up and his cowboy hat came off the hook and got smashed on his head.

"I'll be back late."

"We'll be here," Boone said, clearly enjoying Matt's panic.

He dashed out of the house, then paused, and went right back in. He hurried over to Keith and gave him a hug. "Love you, bud. Help out tonight, okay?"

"I will, Dad."

Matt moved over to Britt and planted a big kiss on her forehead. "Be careful on the path to the barn, Britt. It's already dark outside."

"Okay, Daddy."

"Love you, baby."

"Love you too," Keith and Britt chorused back to him. Then Matt could leave, and he ignored his brother's statement that he knew how to get Britt to the barn and back safely. It was okay to remind her she needed to be careful.

He flew next door, went up the steps, and pounded on the door. "Calm down," he coached himself, reaching for that blasted bowtie again. It sat completely sideways, and he yanked it back into place as Gloria opened the door.

"Sorry I'm late," he blurted. "And for the pounding."

"I did think it was the Big Bad Wolf for a moment." She wore a teasing glint in her eye, and she scanned him down to his boots and back. "I love the jacket. It totally fits the theme."

He looked down at himself and back at her. "You think so?"

"It's perfect."

He let his eyes move down her dress too, drank in those black and white Mary Janes. The heel on those brought her closer to his height and made his mouth water. "Wow, you look stunning."

"It's a really bright pink," she said, tugging on the sleeves that hugged her upper arms, showing off those muscles she used around the farm.

"It's amazing." So amazing, he couldn't stop himself from touching the dress. He slid his hand right along her waist, right where the skirt flared out and where she had a black and white belt cinched. The wide collar on the dress reminded him of the driven snow in Montana, and the buttons down the front of the dress lay perfectly flat. The dress fit her like a glove, and Matt leaned all the way into her to take a deep breath.

"I can't wait to dance with you tonight."

"Let's hope this doesn't jinx it," she said. "Last time you asked me to dance, we didn't really get to."

"Right, I forgot I wasn't going to mention the dancing." He pulled away and got control of himself. For all he knew, his kids and brother could be watching through the living room window. "Ready?"

"Ready." Gloria linked her arm through his, and they went down her front steps and to his truck. He played all the Perfect Gentleman cards and opened the door for her, helped her up, and adjusted the air once he'd gotten behind the wheel.

"Tell me something that's happened in the past twenty years I would never guess," he said, cutting a glance in her direction as they drove off the farm.

"Ooh, that's a tough one. Are you going to do the same?"

"I can." He gave her a smile, glad things between them were so easy and so casual.

She thought for a few minutes, and he'd just turned onto the highway when she said, "I've got one. Remember how I used to hate guacamole?"

"Oh, that I remember," he said, chuckling. "All avocados, I believe, even though those fried ones at Archie's are to die for."

"You'll never guess what one of my favorite foods is now."

Matt swung his whole head toward her. "Guacamole?"

She beamed at him with all the power of the sun. "Love it."

"Wow." He chuckled and shook his head. "Who'd have guessed?"

"Taste buds can actually change," Gloria said. "Some people who never liked mushrooms before will find they like them. That kind of thing."

"I had no idea."

"I looked it up online, so it could be false." She laughed too, and Matt sure did like the sound of that. He wanted to go on a drive with this woman every single day, and as they reached the outer lights of the city, he kneaded the wheel, trying to think of the next time they could get off the farm together.

"I heard Boone's moving here," Gloria said.

"Yeah, he is," Matt said.

"Happy or not?"

"Happy," Matt said, playing the old game they'd once shared.

"You never told me something that's changed about you," she said.

"Uh, let's see...." Matt wasn't sure what she remembered about him, or everything he'd once told her. "Did you know I got a technology certificate for agriculture?"

"No, sir, I did not," she drawled. "Where'd you do that?"

"Montana State. It was an outreach program. Sixteen weeks. We learned all kinds of different technologies to aid in more productive agriculture. It's why we have the sprinkling systems we do at Ivory Peaks." He pushed the pride out of his chest. He'd suggested that it would save time, money, and water, and Gray had purchased the expensive equipment.

Yes, Matt knew how to run it, but anyone could figure it out.

"That's great," Gloria said, and the next thing Matt knew, her cool, slender fingers had coaxed his away from the wheel. She held his hand in her lap, and Matt looked over at her. There were enough street lamps now to see her face, and she wore a blissful look of happiness there, her lips curved just-so in a sexy-sweet smile.

"I've heard this place is amazing," Gloria said. "Have you ever been to Rhodes Mansion?"

"No, ma'am," he said. "You?"

"Never. I've only been in Colorado for a year and a half, and I think I've left the farm about twelve times."

Matt laughed, really tipping his head back and laughed. "That's not true."

"Maybe not," Gloria said with a giggle. "But I definitely don't get off the farm to go to mansions."

"Hunter said it would be a good time. It's chicken wings and dancing. Sounds like a rip-roaring good time to me."

"I probably should've worn a black dress," Gloria said. "To hide all the sauce stains."

Matt made a turn according to his maps program on his phone, and he knew instantly which huge house on this historic Denver street was the Rhodes Mansion.

"Ho-ly cow," Gloria breathed, because she'd obviously spotted the house with all the pillars and bright lights.

Oh, and the limousine easing up to the curb. Matt was sure his beat-up pick-up truck should never touch the same asphalt as a car like that, but he got in line anyway.

"This is amazing," he said, taking in the vines, the trees, and the lights that had been embedded into the grass leading up the sidewalk to that huge front porch that spanned the entire front of the house.

Gloria rolled down her window, and Matt got the spicy, sweet heat of barbecue sauce straight in his nose.

"Smells amazing too." She turned back to him, her eyes lit from within. "I can't wait to try all sixteen sauces."

"Even the one with the ghost peppers?" he asked, incredulous. Gloria had not liked super-spicy foods twenty years ago.

"Even that," she said. "That's our mission tonight, cowboy. Try all sixteen sauces."

Matt chuckled, his stomach tightening as he inched forward. "All right, sweetheart. You got yourself a deal."

CHAPTER 14

*G*loria sure did like the red carpet treatment. She hardly ever got treated like a queen, though every time Matt looked her way, she felt like royalty.

He pulled up to the valet and handed him their VIP tickets, courtesy of the CEO at HMC. "Right this way, sir," the man said, and someone opened Gloria's door too. She put her hand in the tuxedo'ed man's and let him help her from the truck. She faced the house and drew the energy it exuded straight into her very soul.

Matt arrived at her side, tucking something in his inside jacket pocket. Then he took her hand and they stepped onto that red carpet that extended up the sidewalk toward the entrance to the Rhodes Mansion.

"This is insane," Gloria whispered, glancing around like the paparazzi would jump out from behind a bush or a tree and start snapping pictures. Why anyone would care about her and Matt, she wasn't sure. It simply felt like something that would happen, because celebrities made walks like this.

"Kind of out of my wheelhouse," Matt admitted. "That's for sure."

"Mine too," Gloria said.

"I would love to get off the farm with you again," he said. "This is exciting." He glanced at her as they took the first step up the wide staircase that led to that pillared porch. "I mean, not that I don't love eating lunch with you. That's fun too. I just—" He cut off, and Gloria glanced at him.

"I've noticed Hunter comes out to the farm early in the week," she said, placing her feet deliberately on the steps, as this was an old house and they weren't even. "Maybe he and Molly would take your kids for an evening while we go to dinner."

Matt nodded, his eyes also glued to the stones at his feet. She loved a man in cowboy boots, and Matt wore his well. Everything he wore seemed rimmed with gold, and Gloria felt like the luckiest woman in the world as she walked with her arm in his. "I'll talk to him and Molly," he said. "That pasta place is callin' our names." He lit up the night with his smile, and Gloria basked in the warmth of it.

A woman met them at the door with a tray of drinks, but Matt waved away the alcohol. "I'm driving," he said. "Do you have soda?"

"James does," she said with a smile, nodding to the

right. Another man stood there with stout glasses of soda, and Gloria followed Matt's lead and took a diet cola. She wasn't one for much alcohol, and she didn't want to drink in front of him anyway. His ex-wife had gone to an alcohol treatment facility, and she suspected he didn't drink at all, ever, not just when he was driving.

The walls stretched up to vaulted ceilings, and Gloria craned her head back to take in the rich, patterned wallpaper. "Feels old," she said.

"This room is too narrow," Matt said as he led her through a set of arched double doors and into the main room of the party. This space opened up in a way that did make it easier for Gloria to breathe, and two walls held tables with the different chicken wings and their unique sauces.

Men and women dressed in their old-fashioned finest milled about, drinking, laughing, chatting, and of course, noshing on the wings. She spotted a couple of tall men in cowboy hats and knew instantly she'd found the Hammonds.

"Chris didn't need a ride, did he?" she asked when she saw Wes and Hunter and not the older gentleman. She'd grown quite attached to him over the months, and regret tugged at her that she hadn't checked with him.

"Gray and Elise are bringing him," Matt said, moving toward Wes and Hunter. Molly arrived about the same time, and she carried a plate with three different varieties of chicken wings.

"This one is honey mustard," she said, indicating the

creamy yellow sauce. "This one is your standard buffalo, but I've heard people talking about how amazing it is. That there's something a bit different about it." Molly smiled around at the group, her eyes catching on Gloria's. "The last one is a maple smoky sauce. It's actually quite good."

"You tasted them already?" Hunter asked, reaching for one of the honey mustard ones. Gloria could not imagine a worse food to eat while standing up, in a dress and heels. A quick glance around showed that no one else seemed to be having a problem, and she told herself not to be so self-conscious.

"I couldn't help it," Molly said, grinning at her husband. "You know my weakness for all things mapley."

Hunter stuck the whole wing in his mouth. One bite. There, then gone. He chewed and took a wet-nap from a man passing by, a pile of them on his tray. "That I do, sweetheart. That one's *good*. It's sweet and tart and a little spicy."

Wes took one of the maple smoky ones, and Molly extended the plate toward Matt and Gloria. He looked at her. "What do you think? Start traditional?"

"Start us off traditional," she said with a smile, and they both took one of those wings. Gloria followed Hunter's lead and popped the whole thing into her mouth, but she licked her fingers clean, because that sauce was to die for.

A moan came out of her mouth, and her knees went a little weak.

"Holy frijoles," Matt said around his mouthful of food. "I need this in my life every day."

Molly giggled and let Hunter take another wing.

"I got the Tex-Mex blend," Michael Hammond said, edging into the group. "This one is a lemon pepper sauce. And then a Carolina heat. It's the one with the ghost peppers."

"Hold onto your cowboy hats," Wes said with a grin. "Where's my drink?" He looked around and located his fizzy, clear soda on the chest-high table nearby. "I'm going in."

He picked up the bright red wing while his son watched, a glowing smile on his face. "The whole thing?" Wes asked, looking to his son for confirmation.

Gloria loved all the Hammonds, and her gratitude for Hunter especially knew no bounds.

"All in, Dad." Michael's grin was a little too wide, and Gloria switched her attention back to the oldest Hammond.

Wes stuck the whole wing in his mouth, and it took less than a single heartbeat for the heat to register in his eyes. "Holy—" He chewed fast, his drink hovering near his mouth. He gulped the liquid and signaled for more.

Michael tipped his head back and laughed, as did everyone else in the group. Gloria clapped for Wes once he finally got the wing down, because his face had turned about as bright red as the sauce.

"I wish to amend our goal for the night," Gloria said, reaching for one of the milder honey mustard wings on

Molly's plate. "I think we should taste fifteen out of sixteen of the sauces."

Matt grinned at her with all the heat of the Carolina ghost pepper sauce, and that was enough for Gloria.

ABOUT AN HOUR LATER, HER BELLY FULL AND her goal for the night accomplished, she looked up as Matt got to his feet. They'd found a table in the corner of the room, reserved for VIPs, and she'd enjoyed the conversation with Elise, Molly, Gray, Wes, and Chris. Matt too, of course. They all got along so well, and they all seemed excited to have Boone coming to Ivory Peaks once summer hit.

"Can I have this dance?" Matt asked, those dark eyes glittering at her like so many stars in the midnight sky.

"I want to dance too, baby," Hunter said, pushing his drink further from him and standing.

Gloria put her hand in Matt's and went with him out to the dance floor. A few people still lingered near the tables, sampling the wings, but the dancing part of the evening had definitely begun. In the background, Patsy Cline's iconic voice sang, "I...fall...to pieces," as the old-fashioned ballad played.

In front of her, the sexiest man alive only had eyes for her, a fact that made Gloria squirm a little bit beneath her skin. Matt easily took her into his arms, one hand firmly on her waist and holding her close to him,

and one taking hers out to the side. He moved effort-
lessly for a man his size, and she felt the whole world
disappear.

He sighed and shifted them to the music, perfectly in
sync with the rhythm. "Keith and I have been talking," he
said, his voice low as his mouth sat fairly close to her ear.
One breath in, and she got his cologne, the scent of his
skin, and the hint of dryer sheets from the jacket too.

"About what?" she asked.

"Getting a place of our own," he said. "Off the farm. A
real house, in town."

Surprise moved through Gloria, and she was glad they
weren't looking at each other face-to-face. The room
around her swirled, because whenever she'd danced with
Matt, he was all she could focus on.

"Interesting," she said.

"He'd like a bedroom of his own," Matt said. "His
friends all live in town. It's ten minutes to the farm. Easier
to get the kids to school. All of that."

"Your cabin comes with your salary at Ivory Peaks,"
she said. "Will the cash be enough for a house?"

"Probably not," he said. "But I—" He cleared his throat
and kneaded her closer. Her chest touched his, and she
sank into his warmth. He ducked his head, the brim of his
cowboy hat touching her ear, and Gloria closed her eyes.

She liked this man, probably far too much, but she
couldn't pull back on the reins and get herself to slow
down. They'd not been moving fast in the first place.
Hunter and Molly's wedding was nearly three months old

now, and Matt had not even come close to acting like he wanted to kiss her.

Gloria sure did want to kiss him, and the fantasy played out behind her closed eyelids.

"I sold Janice's insurance agency before we left Montana," he said. "She had a lot of clients, and it was worth a lot. It was how I paid for her treatment, and we split the rest. It's enough for a good down payment on a house in Ivory Peaks."

"Oh," Gloria said, opening her eyes and letting her hand drift up the back of his neck, touching the short hair there.

He shivered in front of her, and Gloria smiled to herself. She removed her hand from his out to the side and raised it to the back of his neck too, and the delicious weight of his second hand on her hip would have her smiling for days.

Hopefully, he'd get the hint that she'd really like to repeat this night very soon, and hey, maybe he could kiss her tonight. Not right there on the dance floor, in front of so many people, but maybe out on the farm. Maybe her front porch.

She tried not to think too hard about where the kiss might take place, especially because it might not happen tonight at all.

"I'll miss living next door to you," she said, her mind blanking for other topics of conversation.

"It's months out," he said. "We haven't looked or

anything yet. But it's something Keith would like, and it's something I can give him."

"You're a good dad, Matt," she whispered.

"I'm doing what everyone else is doing," he said. "Their best."

Gloria pressed her cheek to his, bumping his hat slightly. He smiled, and so did he, and he reached up to re-seat his hat. The song ended, and Frank Sinatra came on.

"Do you want to go look at the gardens?" Matt asked. "They're supposed to be stunning."

"More so than where Hunter and Molly got married?"

"I doubt that," Matt said. "But they're doing tours, if you want to step outside."

"Sure."

He took her hand and led the way toward the wide windows along the back wall. She followed him outside into the tea lights and torches and topiaries. It was as if the Lord had sprinkled magic on the land here, and delight filled Gloria.

"Would you two like a tour?" a woman asked, and Matt answered in the affirmative. "When we do weddings here at Rhodes Mansion, there's the option to get married inside the hall where you just were, as well as outside if the weather permits." She turned back to them and walked backward between two hedges. "Do you two have a date set?"

Gloria dang near fell down, but Matt continued on with an easy stride. "Not yet," he said as easily as he breathed.

"We offer garden nuptials until usually October," she said. "It really just depends on how early Mother Nature sends the snow."

"I'll bet," Matt said, his grip on Gloria's hand intensifying.

She almost burst out laughing, but she managed to hold it in. The gardens were lovely, and she could see billowing ribbons and bountiful baskets of blooms out here for the perfect summer wedding.

"Thank you so much," Matt gushed at her as they made their way back to the mansion. She told them they could stay out in the garden and "enjoy the beauty" for as long as they wanted, and Matt led her over to a bench beside a dwarf tree that would probably bloom in the very near future.

"What do you think?" he asked. "Would you want to get married here?"

Gloria wasn't sure if he was being serious or not. Perhaps the guide lingered within earshot, and she glanced over her shoulder. The guide wasn't anywhere to be seen.

"Have you thought about getting married?" he asked gently. "Maybe you haven't."

"Have you?"

He took a few long seconds to search the hedges in front of her. "I think I'd like to get married again, yes," he said. "I think it would be nice to have a partner. Someone who can help me with the kids, who I can be my best self with and my worst self with. Someone who I can help when they need it. It's nice, being married."

Gloria nodded, her thoughts flying back to her previous engagement. "Yeah, I think it would be too."

Matt exhaled. "So, summertime for you? Spring? When were you and Ender going to get married? Can't have been winter in Montana. Everyone knows better than that." He grinned at her, and Gloria returned the gesture.

"Summer," she admitted. "Montana in the summer is my favorite time and place."

"It's pretty nice here in the summertime too," he said.

"It is," she said, weighing her next words. "I don't think I'll be getting married this summer or anything."

"Definitely not," he said.

"Why do you say that?" she asked, turning to look at him. Her eyes dropped from his to his mouth. "We could fall madly in love and have a shotgun wedding in a few months."

His eyebrows went up as he said, "I can't decide if you're teasing or not."

She reached up and ran her hand down the side of his face. "It's hard to know if I'm falling in love with you again when you haven't kissed me."

His eyes widened slightly, and the movement in his throat testified of his nerves. "I've kissed you before."

"It's been a while," Gloria murmured. "A woman forgets."

"I find that...surprising," Matt whispered, and then both of his hands cradled her face and guided her mouth to his. Her eyes drifted closed, and the moment his lips touched hers, Gloria remembered.

She remembered the way he always breathed in at the beginning of a kiss.

She remembered how he started slow, almost exploratory, in his movement.

She remembered how wonderful it was to be kissed by this man, as he made it an experience they could both enjoy. He took, and he gave, and Gloria had missed kissing him for twenty long, long years.

CHAPTER 15

*M*att's first reaction to kissing Gloria sent him on a high. Then, panic streamed through him for a moment, because Gloria wasn't his wife, and he shouldn't be kissing her. Thankfully, his brain caught up to the fact that he and Janice had been divorced for a while now, and he wasn't being unfaithful by starting to fall in love with someone else.

Gloria reminded him of everything he wanted to be—strong, capable, smart, powerful, kind, caring, and loving. The way she kissed him back told him she *needed* him, and he hadn't felt needed by a woman in a long time.

His blood temperature rose along with the pounding in his chest, and he finally got up the willpower to pull away. They breathed in together, and just like the first time they'd kissed, over twenty years ago, neither of them said anything.

He supposed the kiss had said it all, and he hoped it

was all good for her. He lifted his arm and wrapped it around her, enjoying the way she curled into his chest. They sat on the bench for a few minutes, the scent of earth from the garden mingling with barbecue sauce from the party still going on behind them.

"I have no reason to go back to Montana to get married," Gloria finally said. "My life is here now. So I suppose a spring or autumn wedding in Colorado would be acceptable." She straightened and looked at Matt, and he could get lost in eyes like hers, and hair the color of rich honey, and a smile so beautiful and kind.

"Outdoors, of course," he said, his voice a little froggy. "I don't see you getting married inside."

"Outside would be ideal, yes." She nudged him playfully. "For you too. You don't exactly thrive behind walls."

He grinned and chuckled. "That I don't."

"And if Boone is moving here, you wouldn't go back to Montana for a wedding."

Matt paused for a moment, his life in Montana flashing through his head. "I don't suppose I would," he said. "My mom's not there anymore. Dad went north to Canada. Boone'll be here...." He trailed off, lost in the past and spiraling. "I can't believe Boone is coming here. My grandmother would roll over in her grave."

He smiled all the same, because Boone couldn't dedicate his life to Saffron Lake, the ten acres in Montana that Boone had taken care of since their grandmother's death.

"Is he selling Saffron Lake?"

"I don't know," Matt said. "I doubt he knows. I just...

he needs a change. He knows it; I know it. Everyone knows it."

"I know what that feels like," Gloria said, getting to her feet. "It's still hard."

Matt joined her, easily taking her into his arms again, though the music couldn't be heard out here. "Change is always hard."

"You'd think the Lord would've made us more adaptable," Gloria said, smiling up at him. "Why are humans such creatures of habit? Why do little things in our schedules freak us out so much? Hardly seems fair."

Matt bent down and touched his cheek to hers. "I think that's just you, sweetheart. You live and die by the schedule."

"It makes life very neat," she whispered.

"It sure does." He swayed with her, creating their own private dance in the garden behind Rhodes Mansion, and Matt couldn't remember a more perfect moment, or a more perfect night. Mentally, he reached out to grab onto it, but it slipped through his fingers like smoke, leaving him frustrated and wanting.

"Let's go back inside," she said, stepping out of his embrace. "I need another drink, and you promised me more dancing."

He wasn't going to say no to her, especially with that sexy smile on her face. He only hoped he could keep this woman in his life for as long as possible, and that she too didn't grow bored with him and start looking for something better someplace else.

❀

A COUPLE OF WEEKS LATER, MATT CHECKED THE time on his phone and looked back at Mrs. Rigby, Britt's third grade teacher. She pointed to something on a paper that Matt would have Molly go over with him and said, "She's improved so much, Mister Whettstein," with a bright smile. "She works so hard, and we're starting to see it in her scores."

"That's great," Matt said, though he didn't care about the numbers Britt produced. "She gets the math, right? She can do it?" He looked from her classroom teacher to her special education teacher, Mrs. Brown.

"She can do it," Mrs. Brown said.

"She's not getting in trouble?"

"I don't think Britt knows how to be trouble," Mrs. Rigby said with a grin.

"The other kids aren't teasing her because she leaves all the time, right?" Matt had worried about this the most. Britt got pulled out of her classroom several times a week now, and while she was generally a positive ray of sunshine, even she knew she was different. For a kid, different rarely meant good.

"Not at all," Mrs. Rigby said. "Several of our students take advantage of the programs and services the school offers. Everyone is very familiar with it."

Matt nodded, his worry subsiding for a few moments. It would come roaring back in his quiet moments, because he couldn't help the constant thought that he needed to make sure Keith and Britt were well-cared for. "Okay." He reached for the paper. "I can keep this?" The clock ticked dangerously close to the time the high school would let out, and he needed to pick up Keith in just a few minutes.

"Yes, sir," Mrs. Rigby said. "I'm so glad Britt's doing better. She just needed a little extra help."

"Me too," Matt said, speaking the truth. He couldn't believe he'd ignored the issues for so long, but he told himself to be kind to himself. He could only handle so much, and moving to Colorado, starting over, getting divorced, and taking care of the kids had taken everything from him.

He had more mental bandwidth now, and he'd taken the next step when he could. No one could expect more from him.

He shook hands with the teachers, thanked them, and bustled out of the elementary school. In the truck, he quickly sent a text to Keith that he was a few minutes late, and his son responded that it was no big deal.

When Matt pulled into the circle drive at the high school, he didn't see his son. "Come on," he grumbled, reaching for his phone again. *We have that appointment with the realtor in ten minutes. I'm here.*

With some of his extra mental space, Matt had called a realtor to help him start looking at houses. He'd specifically said he wanted at least three bedrooms, a bit of land for a couple of horses, and a garage. Those were his must-haves, and he was grateful he wasn't a picky man. He also didn't think he was asking too much of the Lord with a list that included a garage and a bedroom for each of them.

Coming, Keith said, and Matt looked up from his phone just as the front doors of the school opened. Keith and a pretty brunette exited together, both of them smiling. They weren't holding hands, but they sure looked like they could at any moment.

Matt's eyes narrowed at the same time his heartbeat started gonging in his chest. "Who is that?" he murmured to himself, studying his son's face for any signs of how he felt about this girl. Then she turned fully toward him, looked over her shoulder as she said something, and when she faced him again, she hugged him.

Keith hugged her right on back, which sent Matt's eyebrows sky high. Of course his son would know girls. He'd likely been talking to them for months. Perhaps even as long as they'd lived here in Ivory Peaks. For some reason, the thought had literally never occurred to Matt to ask him about girls.

He only ever mentioned a few friends, and they all had boys' names. Matt had met all of them, as they'd come to the farm last summer. There had been no females.

A sense of betrayal moved through Matt, but he couldn't name why. His son and the girl parted, she waved, and Keith continued toward the truck. He opened the door and climbed in while Matt was still watching the girl walk away.

"Who was that?" he asked, realizing after he'd spoken that the words sounded like a demand.

Keith looked at him, his expression already guarded. "Kassidy."

"Kassidy who?" Matt made no move to put the truck in gear. "Why haven't you mentioned her?"

"Nothing to mention," Keith said, looking out the windshield.

"I disagree," Matt said, finally reaching for the gear shift. "She hugged you. You looked so...happy about it."

"Am I not allowed to be happy?" Keith asked.

"Of course you are," Matt said. He eased away from the curb and made the right turn. "So we like this girl? Or...?"

"Dad, I don't want to talk about girls."

"Too bad." He glanced at his son, his eyes sweeping his phone to know where to turn next as he returned his attention to the road. "We talk about stuff, Keith. It's what we do."

"It's painful sometimes."

"Yeah, well, life is."

Keith huffed into the silence, but Matt didn't press him again. He'd asked, and Keith knew he had to answer. In fact, the longer the silence went on, the guiltier his son would feel, until he'd finally spill his guts.

Sure enough, not two minutes later, Keith said, "Yes, fine, okay? I like her. She's in my forensics class—which by the way, we get to do fingerprinting next week, and I'm stoked about that—and my Math Nine class, and I don't know. She's nice. She's pretty. She's smart."

"Ah, the dangerous trifecta," Matt said with a smile. "And? Does she like you?"

"I don't know," Keith said. "Maybe? Jordy's talking about going to prom, and he said I should ask her."

Matt swallowed all of his fears. He didn't have a son old enough to go to a prom. The very idea was *ridiculous.*

"Yeah, sure," he said, and the words only sounded slightly strangled. "Prom. That sounds fun."

"I have enough money to pay for it," Keith said. "I haven't spent a dime since we moved here."

"I thought you were saving for a truck."

"I am," Keith said. "Prom will be like a hundred bucks. I can afford it."

"I can too," Matt said.

"So you think I should ask her?"

"If you want to go with her," Matt said, eyeing his son again. "Which you obviously do."

Keith pulled his phone from his backpack. "Yeah. I'm gonna text Jordy now and see if he's really gonna go. He sometimes just says stuff."

Matt let his son have his time to text his friend, and he navigated them to the first house they'd see that afternoon. "Look, Keith," he said as it came into view.

Together, they looked at the gray-brick house, a rambler that could've been taken from their neighborhood in Montana and dropped here. The front yard was still yellow, but greening in the spring temperatures, and someone had cleared all the beds around the house, the three trees in the front, and along the sidewalk.

The shutters adorning the windows smiled out at him in bright white, and Matt sure did like the look of this place. The driveway didn't have a single crack in it, and the roof was brand new. He knew that last bit from the listing Ben had sent him, and he saw the realtor come out of the front door—which had been painted a darker gray than the brick—before he could put the truck in park.

"It has a garage," Keith said, still peering at the house.

"It's really nice," Matt said.

"We haven't gone inside."

"I sent you the listing."

"I didn't look at it." His son turned to face him with a devilish glint in his eye. "I wanted to be surprised."

Matt grinned back at his son. "Come on. We only have time to see two places today before Britt is done."

They got out of the truck in near tandem, and Matt shook Ben's hand, introduced Keith, and they all started for the house. Ben talked and talked about the features— the garage door opener, the heated driveway, the upscale landscaping—before they even reached the front door.

"I don't know," Matt said with his hand on the knob. "A heated driveway? Feels like too much for us. We're simple country folk."

"It's in your budget," Ben said. "It's the very best thing in your budget right now, and I honestly don't think it'll last long."

Matt nodded, a lump forming in his throat. He wasn't sure he was ready to pull the trigger on buying a house.

One look at his son's hopeful face, and Matt knew he'd do whatever he had to in order to make Keith happy.

"If it's in the budget…." He followed Ben into the house, and with the wood-laminate floors, the high ceilings, and the upgraded appliance package that came with the house, Matt couldn't believe this place was within his budget.

It had four bedrooms, not just three, and the paddock was fenced and big enough for five horses.

"The owners found themselves in a situation that required an immediate move," Ben said. "They've been back east in Washington D.C. for about four months now. The wife just barely managed to find some time to come clean everything up here and get it listed."

"Why is it so cheap?" Matt asked. "For real."

"It's not cheap for Ivory Peaks," Ben said. "It's farther out than a lot of people want to be for their life in the city. The next closest listing—the one we're headed to now—is a hundred thousand less than this one. It's definitely on the upper end of the budget in Ivory Peaks."

"Then why will it go fast?" Keith asked.

Ben looked at him, a measure of surprise in his gaze. Matt smiled at his son, nodding as if to say, *Good question.*

"The market is volatile right now," Ben said. "We honestly can't predict what will sell quickly and what won't."

"Okay," Matt said, glancing around the kitchen-dining room-living room combination space. He did like how open it was. He loved the vaulted ceilings. His kids would have their own bedrooms upstairs, and the master suite was probably bigger than his whole cabin right now. "Let's go see the other place."

"It was terrible," Keith said with a laugh. He got up from the dinner table and took his plate into the kitchen. "Dad, can I get out the cake we bought?"

"You bought a cake?" Gloria's greenish-blue eyes twinkled at him. "What kind of cake?"

"Red velvet," Matt said. "It's Keith's favorite." He turned toward his son. "Sure, get it out. Get out the ice cream too."

"Did you get the cookie kind?" Britt asked, leaning up onto her knees as she took another bite of her taco. She didn't eat a whole lot, that girl, but she did love it when Matt made tacos. Gloria had brought all the toppings, so he hadn't even had to spend time chopping or dicing tonight.

He sure did like her seated next to him, on his side of the table, with the two kids opposite them. He gave her a smile and then looked at Britt. "You don't eat cookies and cream with red velvet."

Britt blinked as she finished chewing. "Why not?"

"Because," Keith said. "It's weird. We got vanilla."

"But vanilla is so boring." Britt pouted and watched Keith in the kitchen. If Matt knew his son, he'd bring over the cookies and cream for his sister, because neither of them could stand to see her unhappy.

"Kind of like that second house," Matt said, bringing them back to the topic they'd been discussing. "It was a real fixer-upper."

"You like a good project," Gloria said.

"Not that big of one," Matt said. "Plus, with the commute, and Keith finishing up his driving, and then starting high school." He shook his head. "I just want a house we can move into."

"Are you going to get the first one then?" Gloria faced him, smiling in that kind, supportive way she had.

Matt exhaled heavily, turning to see what had happened when the clacking of plates nearly deafened him. "You okay in there?"

Gloria got to her feet and went to help, leaving Matt to watch. Keith looked up at her, and she offered him that same kind smile. She straightened the plates and held one while Keith put a slice of cake on it. They worked together well, and Matt's heart warmed at the sight of them in the kitchen together.

Once everyone had cake, and Britt had her cookies and cream, Keith said, "I think there are more houses to look at, right, Dad?"

"I'm sure there are," Matt said, the flavor of the cream cheese frosting sending his taste buds straight to heaven. "But if we like that one...." He shrugged. "I don't know. I don't know what the right thing to do is."

"We'll pray about it," Britt said. "Now, Daddy, Gloria

and I would like to talk to you about something." She sounded so grown up and so proper, and Matt's eyebrows rose toward the loft.

"You would?"

"That's right," she said, meeting Gloria's eye. Neither of them said anything, and Matt waited, glancing between them every few seconds.

"Is anyone going to say anything?" he finally asked.

"I want you to start," Britt said. "You said you'd start."

"You said you'd bring it up." Gloria sat back in her seat and folded her arms.

"I did bring it up. I said we wanted to talk to him." Britt folded her arms too, her gaze locked on Gloria's.

Matt found the whole thing comical, and he burst out laughing. "I don't think you're going to win this one, sweetheart. I've seen that look on Britt's face before." He grinned at his daughter, because she did have a spirit with plenty of fire and spunk, and he adored that about her.

Keith grinned at her too, and Gloria finally released her arms. "Fine," she said. "I'll start."

CHAPTER 16

*G*loria loved Britt with her whole heart. "Britt would like to go blading with me."

"We found a stroller and everything," the little girl blurted out, and Gloria knew she wouldn't be able to hold her tongue.

"Are you going to tell it?" she asked, cocking her eyebrows.

Britt settled back onto her haunches and forked up another bite of cake. "No, go ahead."

"I'm getting Earl Grey out this week to try blading," Gloria said. "The weather's been great, and it's supposed to hold through the end of the month."

"If you believe forecasters," Keith said.

Gloria gave him a friendly smile too. He was definitely a tougher nut to crack than his sister, but their moment in the kitchen had helped. She also knew about Kassidy, the girl he wanted to ask to the prom, and she hoped to be able to help him with that too. She'd been praying for an opportunity to talk to him about it, but nothing had come up yet.

"Right," she said. "I figured I'd take Earl out alone for a few times. When he's doing well, I want to take Britt." She looked at Matt. "We talked about it a while ago."

"Yes," he said quietly, though she knew that wasn't him giving his permission for her to take his daughter.

"I'm wondering if your opinion on it has changed," she said, glancing at Britt. He'd already told her yes, but that was months ago, before all the other changes with Britt. *Good changes*, she told herself.

"How much is the stroller?"

"Pony Power will buy it."

His eyes widened, and he immediately shook his head. "No. No, I can afford it." His ice cream melted in front of him, testifying to Gloria that she'd forgotten about his fiercely prideful streak.

"But the equine therapy unit *needs* to fund things like this," Gloria said. "That way, it doesn't belong to me. I can take other children out blading with the horses. It could become part of our program."

Matt folded his arms this time, and what he didn't realize was that such movement only made him more attractive to her, not more foreboding.

"Daddy," Britt said. "Can I show you the stroller?"

He flicked his gaze toward her and back to Gloria in the blink of an eye. She reached over and put her hand on his leg, wondering if that was too forward or too much for his kids to see. No matter what, it softened him, and he used one hand to push his phone across the table to his daughter.

"It's so nice," Britt said. "Gloria said she could have Travis put nails in the barn to hang it on, and wait until you see the wheels."

Matt lowered his other hand to cover hers on his knee, his fingers curling around hers and squeezing.

"It's not charity," Gloria said quietly. "Except for me, maybe. To see if running the horses like I do is as good for kids as it is for me, even if they're not the ones blading."

Matt ducked his head, but without his cowboy hat to hide his face, she could still see the concern in his expression. "You like your solo blading."

"I'll still have plenty of time to do that," she said.

He picked up his fork and put together a bite of cake and ice cream.

"Look," Britt said, turning the phone toward him. She lurched forward, which had everyone else at the table tensing and flinching toward her too, Keith especially. "Isn't it so nice, Daddy?"

Matt took the phone and looked at the stroller Gloria had found. It seated one, up to one hundred and ten pounds, with huge wheels that were practically begging to be pushed along the farm roads out here, and a canopy that would keep the kids safe from the sun.

She could see Britt in it easily, singing as Gloria bladed. She thought the activity would be good for Claudia too, another little girl with dwarfism that left her physically incapable of doing a lot of things. She could saddle a horse now, and that had taken her two months to accomplish.

"It's very nice," Matt said, setting the phone down. Keith started to chuckle, and Matt threw him a look. "What?"

"Nothing," Keith said. "That's just your code for yes."

"Hmm."

Gloria beamed at Matt and then Britt. "Great. So I'll get it ordered through Cosette. Remember, Britt, I have to go out with him alone for a while. I have to make sure he knows the rules and can run with us safely."

"I remember."

"Great." Gloria turned her attention to Keith, who still grinned like he'd figured out how to get free hamburgers for life. "So, Keith, I hear you're looking for ideas for how to ask a girl to prom. You know, I was on my prom committee in Montana."

His smile fell from his face like a shooting star falling toward Earth. There, blink, gone. "Uh, yeah." He shot a look in his father's direction, but Gloria didn't look away from the teenager. "But I think I got it figured out already. Thanks, though."

"Oh," Gloria said, recognizing the lie as it came out of his mouth. Maybe the moment she'd thought had presented itself really hadn't. "Okay. But if you want to run something by me, let me know. I know what girls like."

"Do you?" Matt asked, clearly teasing. "What do girls like?"

Gloria felt him laying down a challenge, and the competitive spirit inside her reared up. "Well, let's see. Girls like it when you know what they like and bring it to them. Or do it for them." She watched Keith's face, and the wheels inside his head had definitely started turning.

"They like feeling special. That's why having a song written about them is *so* romantic. Some girls—not all, so you really have to be careful here—like others to know just how perfectly charming and romantic their boy is. So they like flowers in class, for example. Or a ton of those candy-grams that go out at Valentine's Day."

"It's way past Valentine's Day," Keith said, frowning.

"Right," Gloria said. "But any day can be like that, because there's social media. You make a big splash? She'll like it—if she's that kind of girl."

"Is she?" Matt asked.

Keith's face turned red. "I don't know."

Gloria leaned forward, wishing she could tell him not to be embarrassed about liking a girl. She didn't think she'd achieved that status yet, so she simply said, "I'm sure you do. Think about her social media. What does she post? How often? Does she write long captions or short? What does she say?"

Keith lifted his eyes to Gloria's and held her gaze. The boy was smart, and she knew the moment he realized he knew Kassidy better than he thought. "I think she'd like a big splash."

Gloria grinned and nodded. "Okay, you're halfway

there. Up next: Providing that splash with all of her favorites."

"I know she plays the piano."

Matt made a noise halfway between a laugh and a scoff. Gloria met his gaze and realized he'd started to laugh before knowing he shouldn't. "Buddy," he said quickly. "Most people don't like practicing the piano."

"No," Gloria said slowly. "But she'll like it if *Keith* plays the piano."

"I can't play though."

"But I can," Gloria said. "Let's make her a song."

The hope in Keith's eyes shot off the charts. "Would you...?" He cleared his throat. "Would you help me with that?"

"Sure," Gloria said easily. "I'm available in the evenings, usually about this time."

"I just wish I could go," Britt whined from where she leaned against the fence post.

"But then who would I have to open the gate for Earl?" Gloria grinned at her and adjusted the straps on her helmet. "I just need one more time with him," she said. "Plus, this is only the third time I've practiced with the stroller, and I need to be able to make the gait right. I don't want to fall or topple the stroller with you in it."

She rolled over to the little girl and held onto the fence as she sank into a crouch. "Soon, baby, okay?"

Britt looked at her with those soulful, light green eyes, begging her to take her blading that evening.

"Britt," Matt said at the same time Keith yelled, "Gloria!"

She rose and twisted in the same movement, catching the two of them coming toward her. Keith broke into a run, his face full of delight.

Gloria's pulse pounced through her body. He'd asked Kassidy to the prom today. He had to have, though he'd been saying every day this week that he was going to and hadn't for one reason or another. "Did you ask her? How'd it go?"

Keith laughed as he rushed at her and grabbed onto her. They twirled around as she already had her rollerblades on, and he had plenty of forward motion. "I asked her today." His breath rushed out of him as he stepped back, and he looked like he couldn't believe he'd asked a girl to the prom.

"I have a friend who works as a TA in the office, and he finally got me on the morning announcements."

"My goodness," Gloria said, covering her mouth with her hand. "You played it over the morning announcements? And I'm just hearing about it?" She swatted at him. "That's something you text the moment it happens."

"That's what I said," Matt said, leaning toward her with a smile. He seemed to realize at the last moment that he couldn't just kiss her right in front of his kids, and he jerked backward. "Britt was tryin' to persuade you to take her, I see."

"I wasn't," Britt said defensively. Tears filled her eyes, and she spun away from them. "Leave me be." She stomped away from them, as much as a tiny girl with a limp could do, at least.

"Britt," Matt called after her. "I didn't even say anything." He met Gloria's eyes, worry in his.

"She hasn't seen Doctor Pratchet today," Gloria said quietly. "I'm going to take her really soon." She couldn't explain how different it was to have a stroller in front of her as she stroked her blades back and forth. It was almost like she needed longer arms or the handlebars on the stroller to come out farther.

"I'll go take her over there," Matt said. "That's where she should probably be about now, right?"

"Yes," Gloria said, and Matt went after his daughter. Gloria took a big breath and looked at Keith. "Start talking, buddy. I want to know everything."

"You do?"

"From beginning to end. None of this one-word stuff either. *Details*, Keith. I want details." She grinned at him, and he seemed to grow ten inches under her attention.

"Well, there's not much to tell. They did the whole thing about the activities for the weekend, and what was for lunch. And then our student rep said, 'For our last thing today, we have a student-written song we'd like to play.'"

"Exciting," Gloria said.

"The song played, and it was during math, right?"

"Oh, you have math with her." Gloria could just see

how perfect this had gone. "That makes the story so much better."

She didn't think Keith could remove the smile from his face with a chisel. "Yeah, so after only about three words, everyone knew it was for her. There was this big uproar in the class, and the teacher shushed us all." Keith got a faraway look on his face, and it was oh-so-dreamy. Gloria's heart expanded for him over and over, because he was such a good kid. "I sit in the front in that class, and Kassidy sits a row over and one behind me. When I finally got up the nerve to turn and look at her, she had the biggest smile...."

He sounded so happy, and Gloria couldn't believe how unbelievably happy that made her.

"At the end, she stood up and threw herself into my arms, and said, 'Yes, I'd love to go to prom with you.' Then the whole class cheered." Keith reached up and pressed on the top of his cowboy hat. "It was pretty great."

"That sounds *amazing*, Keith." Gloria nudged him over. "I've got to get Grey out." Their eyes met, and Gloria paused. "It's hard to ask a girl out, but you did it. Do you feel good about it?"

"I feel great about it."

"Were you nervous she'd say no?"

"A little."

Gloria nodded and reached out tentatively to hug him. He stepped right into her arms and she held him tight, her eyes closing as she fell in love with this tender boy.

"You're so brave, doing it in a class where she could see you."

"She held my hand in the hall after class," he whispered. "Don't tell my dad, okay? We're going to Scooter's tomorrow for lunch too."

Gloria pulled back, her throat suddenly narrow. "Oh, honey, I have to tell your dad stuff if I think I need to."

"Not about the hand-holding," Keith said, darting a glance in the direction Matt had gone. "I already asked if I could leave campus and go to lunch."

"And he said yes?"

"Yeah, he said yes."

"Does he know Kassidy will be there?"

"You two must rehearse your questions," Keith said with a smile. "He asked it almost just like that. 'Will Kassidy be there?'" He lowered his voice to imitate his father, and Gloria tipped her head back and laughed.

Keith joined her, and she gave them a few seconds to just be together.

"Anything else, bud?"

"No," he said. "Just…thank you, Gloria." He looked nervous, like he'd been caught stealing cookies from the jar after his father had said he couldn't have any. "I know you're ready to go blading. I'll let you go."

"I have time," she said. "If there's something else you want to talk about." She wanted to tell him she'd always have time for him, but she bit the words back.

Keith looked torn for a moment, and then he shook his

head. "No, not right now. I'll talk to you later, okay? I have chores in the south stable."

"All right." She watched him walk away, her heart full. She'd had no idea Colorado would hold the things and people it did, and she pressed her eyes closed and added, "Thank you, Lord," to the silence around her before opening the gate.

"All right, Earl," she said. "It's you and me and this stroller today. Let's see what you can do." She'd started the horse with a bridle and reins, but he'd graduated to free running after only two sessions.

The big, gray horse with black spots huffed at her, and she grinned back at him. "Yes, we're running again tonight. It's better than the circle. Or would you like me to harness you and put you in that thing to go round and round?" She cocked one hip, and in rollerblades, dang near lost her balance doing it.

Earl shook his head as if saying no, and Gloria backed out of the gate. "All right, then. Let's blade." She turned and faced the farm road that led to the highway. The stroller sat dormant and waiting for her, weighed down with two twenty-five-pound bags of flour—almost the weight of Britt. She pushed off with her right leg, then her left, finding her stroke and rhythm easily.

She moved right into the stroller, and all of them got moving after some initial resistance. "Come on," she called to Earl. "Up here with me. Right here with me."

He eased up on her right side, where she'd trained him to run. He trotted, as she wasn't moving very fast yet, and he needed a few minutes to get up to speed anyway. She did too, because she was no spring chicken and couldn't just go from zero to sixty on rollerblades.

"Stay in the grass," she yelled to him, and she edged over on the right side of the road to keep him off of it. She wanted him beside her, but not on the road, and when they reached the highway, she turned left instead of right to go deeper into the wilds of Colorado. The other direction led to town.

This way would take her down to the next farm—the Harris Farm—which Poppy Harris ran on her own. Gloria didn't know the whole story there, but she knew Gray sometimes lent out his cowboys to Poppy when she needed help with something big. She had an eight-year-old son named Steele that Gloria had seen at church several times, as well as riding his bicycle along the property lines, where someone had built a track for him.

"By the time we hit Harris," she said to Earl. "We'll be flying, okay? I want you up in a gallop. Come on now." She increased the stroke of her blades, leaning forward into the stroller. It didn't give her much resistance at all, and blading with something in front of her was definitely different than having to balance herself with the motion of her arms.

Her breathing increased, and her arm muscles worked to keep that stroller moving. The wheels on it turned and turned like butter, and Gloria tilted her face into the setting sun up ahead. Pure joy and contentment filled her—this was what heaven would be like for her. The wind in her face. A horse at her side. A sunset with silence.

The sign for Harris Farms appeared up ahead, and Gloria pushed her stroke again. "Come on," she called to Earl, and he picked up his trot and began to gallop. "Good boy!" She laughed into the sky, feeling more free than she ever had before.

She bladed until her ankles trembled, and then she finally made it back to Ivory Peaks and the farm she'd grown to love. She brushed down Earl Grey and put him back in his stall. She fed and watered him, all the movement keeping her muscles from cramping up after such a long ride.

She left the stroller with the flour in it right where it was, grinning at it as she went by. She'd only taken one step out of the stable when Matt said, "You are the sexiest woman I've ever met," and chuckled as he took her hand and towed her toward the corner of the stable.

"Matt." She giggled as she stumbled after him. "What are you doing?"

"Shh," he said, ducking around the corner. "I just saw you get back with that horse, and." He smacked his lips and shook his head, obviously at a loss for words. He looked down at her, and though almost all the light of the day was gone now, she could still see the emotions swimming in his eyes.

Desire, love, hunger, want, need, attraction, worry, fear. "Thank you for helping Keith. Thank you for doing this for Britt." His voice cracked, and he quickly hugged her, making it impossible to see his face. "Thank you for being my friend and for being on this farm."

"Matt," she said again, this time softer. "You're welcome for all of those things, except one."

"Which one?"

"We're way more than friends." She inched away from him and tilted her head back to receive his kiss. "Aren't we?"

"I want you to be my best friend," he whispered.

"You *are* my best friend," she said back. "And so much more."

"You are way more than a friend to me."

She kissed him, and while they'd shared other kisses since the one in the garden at Rhodes Mansion, this one felt more meaningful. This one seemed to be made of honesty and everything real worth having. And just like Gloria had realized she loved this man's son earlier that evening, with this kiss, she knew she was falling in love with Matt Whettstein all over again.

CHAPTER 17

*B*oone Whettstein turned onto the farm where his brother worked, a sigh moving through his body. He wished some of his feelings about Ivory Peaks and the Hammond Family Farm would rub off on Gerty, but she sat in the passenger seat of their rental car, her arms cinched across her chest.

"We'll get to see the cabin today," he said.

Gerty made a sound halfway toward a grunt, about what she did every time Boone talked about Ivory Peaks and moving to Colorado. She claimed it was the "absolute worst time" for a move, but Boone disagreed. She wasn't in high school yet, and if he didn't get her out of Montana in the next two years, he'd be stuck there for six more.

No, the move had to happen now. If he didn't cut the ties as completely as Matt had, Boone would simply let Saffron Lake, the Big Sky country, and...Karley pull him back in.

His muscles tightened, and he stared straight ahead as he moved past the tall pines that concealed the farm from the main road. The land opened up before him once past the trees, and more relief filled him. Everything strung tight inside him released, and Boone blew out his breath.

He didn't know how to talk to his twelve-year-old daughter about Karley White. Gerty knew something had happened, because she used to spend every afternoon at Karley's office once school got out. That had stopped a week ago, but she hadn't asked any questions.

Boone wished his feelings for the pretty blonde woman would stop as easily as Gerty going to that office, but they still streamed through him. He'd been in love with Karley. He'd mentioned marriage earlier this year. They'd been dating for over a year, and Karley had been his wife's best friend. He'd known her for close to fifteen years. He'd never felt so low and so foolish and so unworthy as he had a week ago, when Karley had told him she'd started seeing someone else.

Oh, she was so sorry. She cried buckets. She hadn't wanted to hurt Boone, and especially not Gerty. But she *had* hurt them both, and Boone had to make sure that didn't happen again—at least for Gerty. She deserved his full attention and only the very best people in her life. People who loved her and wanted her to thrive, not a woman who only wanted the girl around so she could be praised in the small-town Montana circles for how "amazing" she was.

As the tires crunched over the gravel road, Boone cleared his throat. "Gerty, I...Karley and I broke up."

"I figured."

He glanced at her. "It's not why we're moving here. We were going to do that anyway."

"I guess." She looked out the passenger window, and he could only see her left cheek.

Boone pressed his eyes closed for a moment, a prayer flying heavenward in that single beat of time. If Nikki were here, she'd know what to say to Gerty.

"When your mom died," Boone said, and that brought Gerty's attention right back to him. She loved stories of her mother. She'd been six when Nikki had passed away from a rare blood disease, and she did have some memories of her. For the first year or so, Boone had told her stories about Nikki every night before bed. He showed her pictures, and they both grieved in their own way. She got to learn about her mom; he got to remember her and how much he'd loved her.

"She told me to date and find someone else to marry." He cleared his throat. "I didn't know how to do that. I loved her so much." He turned and looked out the window at the passing stables. A couple of cowboys walked along the road, and they lifted their hands in a wave. Boone returned the gesture, feeling the peacefulness of the land here. Everything quieted inside him, and Boone waited for his energy to center.

"I didn't date anyone until Karley. She was your mom's best friend, and she seemed real safe. She knew you already. The very last thing I want is for you to get hurt. You're my priority now, you know?" He swung his gaze toward her, and Gerty just looked at him with the widest, most absorbent blue eyes on the planet.

She wore her hair down today, as they hadn't been working outside, and she looked so much older than the image of his daughter Boone held in his mind. *She can handle the truth.* The thought entered his mind, almost in the same tone and timbre of Nikki's voice, though he couldn't really remember what that sounded like anymore.

"She didn't want to marry me," Boone said, the words so raw and so sharp as they left his throat. "She cheated on me and started seeing someone else. That's why you don't go over there in the afternoons anymore. It's not the only reason we're leaving Saffron Lake—I'd decided to do that before I found out about this other guy—but I knew there was a reason I'd felt the pull to come here with Uncle Matt. Maybe it was so we could get away from her. I don't know."

Gerty nodded, her arms unclenching. "Okay, Daddy."

"Yeah?"

"Karley is a real jerk for doin' that to you." Tears filled her eyes, and she looked away quickly. "Why do people have to be so mean?"

"I don't know, baby," Boone said almost under his breath. "There's so much I don't know. I don't know what Colorado has to offer us, but the Lord is telling me it's something we both need."

Gerty sniffled and didn't say anything else. Boone

drove around the main farmhouse and toward the row of cabins, where his brother lived in the very last one—the biggest one—on the far end, closest to the forest.

A man and a teen boy sat on the bottom of the steps at one of the cabins, both of them with wood and knives in their hands. "Hey," Boone said, easing up on the accelerator even though they were barely moving. "That's Michael Hammond."

"It is?" Gerty stretched to see out Boone's window. "Can I go say hi?" She started unbuckling her seatbelt and reaching for the door handle before Boone even had the car at a complete stop.

"Sure," he said. "I'll be down at Uncle Matt's. Come on down when you're done."

"Thanks, Daddy." Gerty's mood had flipped from sullen to sunny, and Boone smiled as she ran around the front of the rental car and waved to Michael. He got to his feet too, his smile as genuine as they came.

Boone knew the two had exchanged phone numbers a couple of visits ago. He checked his daughter's phone religiously, and she never said anything out of character or inappropriate. Michael hadn't either, and he smiled at him as he waved to Boone before continuing down the road.

He'd just put the car in park in front of his brother's cabin when his phone chimed. Matt had said, *Still in our Pony Power meeting at Gloria's. Come on in.*

Boone sighed and said, *Okay,* though he didn't want to interrupt a meeting. He got out of the car, the temperature in the air precisely how he liked it. "Three more weeks," he murmured to himself as he went next door to Gloria's cabin. Once the meeting ended, Matt would have the rest of the day off. He was going to show Boone his cabin here on the farm, where he and Gerty would live, and then he wanted to get Boone's opinion on two houses in town, where he was going to move his family that summer.

With such crispness in the air, the hint of pine, and the possibility of a fresh start on his mind, Boone climbed the steps to the front door.

He'd just lifted his hand to knock when the door opened. A woman with reddish-brown hair came outside, but she was walking backward and talking. "...I'll get that done."

"Whoa," he said, the first thing that came to his mind. It got horses to stop, usually.

This woman didn't stop. More people came behind her —or in front of her—and Boone had to think fast. He put out his hands and they slid along the woman's waist. She wore the same thing everyone on a farm did—jeans, boots, a shirt in various shades of plaid. Her plaid was definitely feminine and done in tiny boxes of blue and purple.

She cut off mid-sentence and yelped, spinning toward him. Since she hadn't figured out how to stall her forward movement, she rammed into Boone, and he found himself holding her in his arms.

"Who are you?" she demanded, immediately swatting at him with the clipboard in her hand. "Let go of me, you rascal." Fire beamed from those dark green eyes, and

Boone did what she said. Anyone would do what this woman said.

"You ran into me," he said, stepping back. "I was just tryin' to make sure you didn't fall."

She stumbled forward as he moved, and he lunged to catch her again.

"Cosette," another woman said, pushing past the other cowboys filling the doorway. "Are you okay?" Gloria appeared, and she looked from Cosette to Boone. A smile brightened her face. "Boone. Matt, Boone's here."

She moved into his personal space, and he released Cosette to hug Gloria hello. "How was the drive? The airport was crazy, I bet. They had to close it this morning. You're lucky you made it in."

"We did have to circle a couple of times," Boone said, glancing back at the pretty redhead. Gloria stepped back and he adjusted his cowboy hat.

"Guys, this is Boone Whettstein, Matt's brother. He's going to be joining us at Pony Power in a few weeks." She beamed out at the group now gathered on the front porch. "Cosette Brian is our administrative assistant. She works real closely with Molly and the counselors, and then me to make sure everyone is paired with the right horse and the right therapist."

Boone nodded at her, but Cosette simply continued to glare at him like he'd committed the worst crime possible by catching her before she fell flat on her face.

Rascal echoed through his head in her voice. He could be a rascal, but he hadn't been in this situation.

"Travis Thatcher," she said, indicating a tall cowboy. "He does all the horse care with me. I train them; he makes sure I don't train them too hard."

Travis nodded at Boone, and he'd actually met the man before, so he did the same.

"Mission Redbay. He works a ton with Matt on the farm, actually. We only pull him over to Pony Power when we've got something major going on, like our big open house coming up next month."

"Nice to meet you," Boone said, reaching to shake the man's hand. He had a kind pair of blue eyes and a firm handshake.

"Cody Peterson," Gloria said. "He does all of our kid coordination classes. He also makes sure every child gets where they need to go when they arrive on the farm."

"Pleasure," Cody said, shaking Boone's hand with a big smile. "You really are a lighter version of Matt." He looked back and forth between Matt, who stood right next to him, and Boone.

"I told them that," Matt said, grinning. He stepped into Boone and hugged him, clapping him heartily on the back. "Glad you made it, brother. Are you ready to see your cabin?"

"Matt," Molly said as she came out onto the porch too. "I need you and Gloria for two minutes." Her eyes slid around the group and landed on Boone. "Boone, hello." She hugged him too, and said, "I'm going to steal him for just a minute."

"It's fine," Boone said. "There's plenty of time to see

the cabin." He stepped back and tucked his hands in his pockets, feeling out of place among all these new people.

"Cosette can show you," Molly said. "Would you, Cosette? I might have them longer than two minutes, and I know Matt has an appointment with his realtor."

Boone's eyes flew to Cosette, and while she nodded at Molly, she certainly didn't seem too keen on spending any more time with the *rascally* cowboy who'd literally prevented her from embarrassing herself in front of everyone.

The group started to break up, with cowboys going down the steps, and Matt and Gloria going back inside the cabin with Molly. In less than five seconds, only Cosette and Boone stood on the front porch.

"It's just down here," Cosette said, her voice full of professional clip. She led the way back to the sidewalk, and Boone followed her, glancing down the lane to find Gerty. She walked with Michael toward him, and he whistled to get her attention.

Gerty lifted her head, as she'd been trained to do, but Cosette did that yelping again, as if Boone had electrocuted her with his voice.

"My goodness," she said, plenty of snap in her tone. "Are you trying to deafen me?" She pressed one hand to her breastbone as if trying to keep her heart from flying from her chest.

Boone blinked at her. "No, ma'am," he said. "Just trying to get my daughter's attention." He waved at Gerty to come with him, and she turned to Michael, said something, and then jogged his way.

"You have a daughter." Cosette watched Gerty approach too.

"Gerty," Boone said, trying to infuse some of Cosette's professionalism and detachment into his voice. "This is Cosette Brian. She's going to show us the cabin, because Uncle Matt is busy for a few more minutes."

"Nice to meet you, ma'am," Gerty said, extending her hand and offering Cosette a smile.

That got the stoic woman to crack, and she returned Gerty's smile. "Thank you," she said. "It's nice to meet you too." She met Boone's eyes, and he smiled too. She was pretty, he'd give her that. But he didn't need someone so stuffy they couldn't at least thank him for catching them when they fell. Not only had she omitted the gratitude, she'd actually accused him of being rascally with her.

He didn't need anyone at all, and as he and Gerty followed Cosette down the road, he prayed he could find healing and contentment for both himself and his daughter, nothing more.

CHAPTER 18

Cosette Brian stayed in the living room while Boone and his daughter explored the cabin. They came back into the main area, which housed the kitchen, a small area for a table that seated four, and the living room, and looked at her.

"It's real nice," Gerty said, and she wondered if Boone had told his daughter she had to do all the talking. "I have a bedroom, at least. Keith sleeps in a loft."

"What are you guys doing with the foreman's cabin?" Boone asked, that deep voice sending shivers through Cosette's blood. He'd definitely startled her, and she wasn't used to being touched so intimately by a man. Maybe she'd over-reacted. Maybe she'd snapped at the handsome cowboy. She had been doing her best to keep every human being with a Y-chromosome out of her life for a while now, and her barriers against good-looking cowboys had flown into place on their own at his touch.

"I'm not sure," Cosette said. "I mostly deal with Pony Power, not the family farm."

Boone nodded, his eyes up in the rafters. "It's great." He looked at her, and she didn't detect an ounce of interest in that brown-eyed gaze. He was a shade or two lighter than his brother in every way, from his eyes to his skin to his hair. Even his shirt was a washed out blue instead of the bright colors Matt usually wore.

"Great," Cosette echoed. "Well, I have to get back to work." She turned to leave the cabin, sure the air outside would be easier to breathe without Boone's masculinity and the scent of that oceanic, piney cologne.

"Cosette," Gerty said, hurrying after her. "Do you guys hire kids to work at Pony Power?"

Cosette paused on the front porch and looked at the girl. She was tall for her age, so she stood only a couple of inches shorter than Cosette.

"I'm really good with horses," Gerty said. "I've been ridin' since I was three. My daddy taught me how to handle 'em, clean up after 'em, feed 'em. We're moving here in the summer, and I was thinkin' I could work with the kids or the horses."

Cosette smiled at the light and hope in the girl's eyes, which weren't anything like her father's. They'd definitely come from her mother then. Cosette's curiosity flew toward the stratosphere, but she kept her questions to herself. It wasn't any of her business what had happened to this girl's mother, how long ago, or if her father was interested in slightly-standoffish, almost-broken, redheads.

"Cody might have something for you to do," Cosette managed to say through her narrow throat. "He could probably use a helper to get all the kids to their horses this summer. I know Keith helps out. You should talk to Cody."

"Cody," Gerty said, twisting back to the cabin. "Daddy, did you meet Cody?"

Cosette looked over her shoulder too, finding Boone framed perfectly in that doorway, one shoulder leaning into it, his arms folded. "I did, baby. We can talk to him."

Gerty gave Cosette a grateful smile. "Thanks, Cosette." She turned back to her father and went that way, and it took every ounce of willpower Cosette had to go in the opposite direction. She felt the weight of too many eyes on her as she went, and she couldn't shake the feeling until she made it all the way to the stable office on the other side of the farm.

With the door closed, she leaned against it and *breathed*. Breathed in oxygen. Breathed out fear. Breathed in calmness. Breathed out the image of the last handsome cowboy she'd let into her life.

The way he raised his voice, then his hand....

She yelped for the third time that morning as someone knocked on the door behind her. The vibrations ran through her body, and then Michelle said, "Open the door, Cosette. I saw you running in here as if the devil were on your heels."

She reached for the doorknob and yanked open the door. She met Michelle's kind blue eyes, wide with concern. "What happened?" The counselor stepped into the office and closed the door while Cosette retreated to her desk.

"Nothing," she said, her voice shaking as hard as her hands.

Michelle sat down and folded her hands in her lap. Her waiting pose. Cosette busied herself with the clipboard and waking her computer. She had notes to put into her to-do list, and then she had a few phone calls to make to ensure they'd have the food they needed for the open house in June.

After only a few minutes, and with her to-do items stored safely in a list she could check off later, Cosette finally felt calmer. She looked at Michelle. "A man touched me today."

Michelle's eyebrows shot up.

"I mean...that sounded bad." Cosette exhaled and reached for a tissue. At least her hand wasn't shaking anymore. She was in control in this office. She could control the things on her list. She could make it through each day if she simply stayed in control.

"I was walking out of Gloria's, and I wasn't watching," Cosette said, imagining herself as a bird above the situation at the cabin. "A man was behind me, but I didn't see him, and he...slid his hands along my waist. I spun around, and then I was in his arms."

"And that upset you."

"Yes," Cosette said, wiping her nose and discarding the tissue in the trashcan. "It upset me."

"Why did it upset you?" Michelle always led her to examine her own feelings instead of rushing to tell her how wrong they were. It was why Cosette had begged the woman to come work with the kids here at Pony Power.

"No one's touched me since Joel," she said, surprised at how steady her voice remained. "I don't let anyone get close enough to me to do that."

"You don't hug anyone?"

"No."

"Not your parents? Your sister? No one?"

"No one."

"You and I are friends," Michelle said, tilting her head to the side. "Good friends, I would say. If it was your birthday, I'd hug you."

Cosette swallowed. "I don't know."

"What don't you know? Are we good friends?"

"Yes," Cosette said.

"So you don't know about the hugging, even from a close friend."

Cosette looked down at the clipboard, but she'd already transferred everything to the computer. "Joel abused me in so many ways, one of which was physical. He could make a hug into...hurt." She looked up at Michelle again, trying to be brave. She wasn't a victim anymore. She'd left Joel, and she'd made a new life for herself here in Ivory Peaks.

"How?" Michelle asked.

"He'd squeeze too tight," Cosette whispered. "He'd hold on too long, even when I said to let me go. He'd whisper cruel things as if they were soft love notes. He'd dig his nails into my back."

"Did this man let you go when you asked him to?"

"Yes."

"So he's not Joel."

Cosette shook her head, her emotions scattering all over the place. "I know he's not. I know I could hug you, and you wouldn't hurt me. Intellectually, I *know*." She put her hand over her heart. "In here, it still hurts."

Michelle wore an empathetic look, and that was what Cosette liked most about her. She didn't sympathize. She *empathized*, and there was a significant difference.

"Perhaps it's time you moved past the intellectual," Michelle suggested. "I know a great role-play therapist. He's really amazing."

"No," Cosette said instantly, mostly because of the pronoun Michelle had used. "I can't see a male counselor."

Michelle nodded and got to her feet. "I'm going to give you his name anyway. You can do all the research on him you'd like. I know that's important to you." She gave her a warm smile. "Then decide."

Cosette nodded, though she'd already decided. Michelle said good-bye and left the office, and Cosette got up and stood at the window. The sun shone so brightly today, probably the brightest it had been all year. The sky didn't hold a single cloud, and everything out there seemed made of perfection.

Cosette knew better than most that outward appearances could be deceiving. Storms and pain could be raging behind closed doors, or behind carefully placed smiles and perfectly curled hair. She reached up and touched her curls, then adjusted her shirt and sat back down at the computer.

She could control the outside of herself. She could put on the makeup and make the clothes match. She could smile and welcome, and she could make phone calls and checklists that got done with precision.

The real work needed to be done beneath the surface, and Cosette had no idea how to do any of it. A thought entered her mind, and she picked up her phone. Her fingers flew across the screen as she typed out a text, and before she could second-guess everything that had happened that day, that week, that month, that whole year, she sent it.

To Matt: *Tell your brother I'm sorry I snapped at him.*

She could control an apology, and she *was* sorry she'd acted badly toward the new cowboy coming to Ivory Peaks. A piece inside her that had been flapping lay down and stayed flat, and Cosette drew another breath, further calming herself.

Maybe she did know how to do some internal housecleaning, if the apology counted as that. She knew it would take a lot more to truly clean out the damaged parts of herself and replace them with what it took to have healthy relationships again.

She imagined Boone's handsome face, and Michelle's friendship, and Cosette determined right then and there that she wanted to *try*—and that was more than she'd ever wanted before.

CHAPTER 19

*M*att looked down the road again, but it remained empty. He couldn't shake the nerves from his fingers, no matter how hard he flapped them.

"Dad."

He turned toward Keith, who approached with Jane, Deacon, and Tucker. "Yep."

"They're not back yet?" He too looked down the road.

Matt wanted to say, *Obviously*, but he shrugged instead. "I'm sure they'll be back soon." Gloria and Britt had been gone for almost an hour. The sun wasn't all the way set yet, as the days kept getting longer and longer the closer to June they got.

"Elise said she'd do my corsage for prom," Keith said. He lifted his phone. "Do you want to see some of the ideas?"

"Sure," Matt said, but his attention felt scattered. He

looked at the pictures, his son's voice going in one ear and out the other.

"Which one do you like?" Keith asked, sliding through the pictures again.

"Uh, I like the second one."

"Really?" Keith flipped back to that one and studied it. "I guess it's okay. I like this one with the two roses a lot better."

"Great, get that one," Matt said, looking back down the road again.

"You're not even listening to me." Keith turned and walked away, but it took Matt a moment to realize he'd even done that.

"Wait," he said, but Keith just threw one hand up in the air and kept going. A sigh moved through his whole soul, because he *hadn't* been listening to his son. He was always so worried about Britt, and the past few weeks had found Matt going out with Gloria early in the week while Hunter and Molly took care of the kids. Matt could admit that he liked coming home to the quiet cabin, with only low lights on in the kitchen, both children in bed, and Hunter and Molly cuddling on the couch.

Hunter was almost always asleep, and he'd groan as he eased himself to his feet and told Matt what great kids he had. Molly always hugged him, and Matt felt especially lucky to be at this farm with them and to count them as his friends.

Had he stopped paying attention to Keith? And if so, when?

The sound of singing reached his ears, and he turned back to face the road. Gloria came blading toward him, the hulking, black stroller in front of her, with Britt strapped in it. They both wore a smile to rival the beauty and majesty of the sunset, and Britt's voice lifted into the air as she sang along with her music.

Joy radiated from her, as well as the woman pushing the stroller, and the horse trotting along beside them. Earl Grey looked mighty fine thundering along the side of the road, and Matt grinned as he stepped out of the way to led Earl back into his paddock.

"Slow," Gloria said to the horse, and they both slowed way down. "Walk, Earl." Her voice cut through the night as if his ears were attuned to its frequency. He watched her roll up in those rollerblades, wearing a pair of black leggings and a tank top in bright yellow, orange, and red tie dye. She panted, and Britt finished her song at the top of her lungs.

"Hey, Daddy," she said, her voice so happy.

"Hey, baby." He stepped over to her and started helping her unbuckle all the restraints in the stroller. "How was it?"

"So amazing," she said, gushing with how fast they'd gone, and how Gloria kept Earl Grey right at her side, and how the horse could trot or gallop, jump over a fence if he wanted to, and that he was simply the best horse ever.

As Matt helped her out of the stroller, Gloria led Earl into his paddock and promised him she'd be back to brush him down and give him a snack. Britt seemed a little unsteady on her feet, so Matt kept one hand under her arm until she solidified.

"Gloria," Britt said, hurrying toward her. "I want to help with Earl. You said I could help."

"Yep," Gloria said with a bright smile. "I'll take the stroller inside, and you come get the oats. He'll be your best friend then."

"Okay."

The two of them bustled off toward the barn, leaving Matt alone near the road. He looked down the way his son had gone with the Hammond kids, and he looked toward the barn, wondering if he was making the right decisions when it came to his kids.

He'd put in an offer on the gray brick house, because it hadn't sold in the past month, and that felt like the Lord reserving it for him and Keith. That was the right move, wasn't it?

He'd been dating Gloria, and both of his children liked her. The relationship felt real and meaningful to him, and Matt knew he'd started to fall in love with her again. Was that the right thing to be doing?

The school year was almost over, and Britt had improved so much this year. He'd taken a lot of steps to help her, and while some of them had been a little painful, he'd done it. She was improving in her speech, and while she wasn't always perfect, she was stronger physically and mentally in so many ways.

He'd signed her up for a summer art therapy class, and she'd already started a yoga class for the physically challenged. Her feet had strengthened, and she'd been skipping better too.

Matt turned in a full circle, trying to figure out where he belonged in all of this. In some moments, it was crystal clear. He and Gloria belonged together. They'd get married and everything would be fields of tulips and rollerblading with horses.

Other times, like this one, Matt wondered where he'd gone wrong and if it was too late to fix it.

"Matt!"

He spun toward Gloria's panicked voice. She waved at him from the doorway of the barn, and he sprinted that way.

"Britt fell," she said, turning as he approached. He burst into the barn behind her, scanning for his daughter.

She sat on the floor, currently pushing against an apple box as she tried to stand.

"Hey, hey," he said. "Stay there. What happened?" He arrived and knelt in front of her, trying to take in everything at the same time. Cuts, bruises, tears. Britt didn't have any of them.

"My ankle just twisted," she said. "I step-p-ped on the rope."

"Okay," he said. "Let's get you up." He started to help her, but Britt pushed against his attempt.

"I can do it, Daddy."

Matt leaned back on his haunches, surprised at this attitude in her.

"I'm supposed to do it myself." She gave him a glare

Matt had never seen on his daughter's face, and his eyebrows went up.

"Okay," he said, because he didn't know what else to say.

"He's just there if you need him," Gloria said, and Matt glanced at her. She wore her nerves plainly, and they seemed to choke the air in the barn.

Britt used her skinny arms to press against the apple box, and she got her feet switched around so she could get to her knees. Every move seemed to take great effort, and each squeezed the life from Matt's heart.

Pain crossed her face, probably from her knobby knees against the dirty cement in the barn. But she got to her feet, keeping both palms pressed against the apple box as she steadied herself.

"I did it." She smiled, but the gesture sure didn't hold the same light and joy as it had only five minutes ago.

"You sure did," Gloria said, beaming at her. "Come on, now. Grab that bag of oats. Earl's probably starting to make a fuss."

"She can't do the oats," Matt said, getting to his feet too. He dusted his jeans off and gave Gloria a look.

"Sure she can," Gloria said easily, and Britt picked up the oats from the floor. She followed Gloria outside, once again leaving Matt to wonder what in the world was happening. Gloria simply didn't know or understand Britt's limitations the way Matt did.

He followed them, his footsteps sharp and sure. "Britt,

let Gloria finish up with Earl," he said. "We have to get home."

"But she said—"

"Britt," he barked. "Keith's waiting to show us the flowers for his prom date, and I still have dinner to make. Come on."

Gloria blinked at him for a couple of seconds, her disbelief tangible. Then she flew into action, taking the bag of oats from Britt. "Go on, Britt," she said. "Do what your daddy says."

"But I don't want to go," she said. "You said I could help take care of Earl after we bladed."

"I know, but I didn't know about Keith's flowers." She crouched down in front of Britt, her smile warm and genuine and covering up everything she'd let Matt see. "There are going to be so many times to blade and give Earl his oats. It isn't today or never."

Britt said something Matt didn't catch, and he felt like a real jerk as she threw her arms around Gloria and hugged her. Gloria closed her eyes and smiled, hugged the little girl back, and then nodded toward Matt.

She rose to her feet as Britt came to his side, her nerves back. She also wore something else in her eyes, and it took Matt the whole walk back to his cabin to realize what it was.

Displeasure.

Keith wasn't in the cabin, and Matt texted him to come home and have dinner.

Elise fed me, Keith said. *I'm helping Jane with her algebra. I'll be there in a bit.*

Matt's frustration rose up like a tidal wave. When had his kids turned into people who didn't listen to him? Who just roamed the ranch and did whatever they wanted?

He felt wildly out of control and like he wanted to send an all-caps text for his son to *COME HOME RIGHT NOW*. Then he'd need to text Elise and apologize to her for always taking care of Keith, when Matt should be doing that.

"Can we have quesadillas?" Britt asked. "Where's Keith and his flowers?"

"He's helping Jane for a minute," Matt said, tapping out a quick message to his son. *I want to see the flowers again. I'm sorry I wasn't listening earlier.*

If he sent the all-caps text, he'd have to apologize for that too. Matt was so tired of feeling like everything he did was wrong, and he'd enjoyed getting to know Gloria all over again, because she made him feel strong and necessary. She made him feel like he did things right.

"Daddy."

"Yeah, sure, quesadillas." He shoved his phone in his pocket, plenty of other words gathering in the back of his throat. He got out the tortillas and shredded cheese and set a pan on the stove.

"Britt," he said. "When I ask you to do something, I just need you to do it."

"I was going to help with Earl."

"And *not* argue with me." He gave her a pointed look. "*I'm* your father."

Britt was such a sweet girl, and her face fell. "Okay, Daddy. I was just so excited about Earl. You should see 'im run, Daddy. It's *amazing*."

Matt couldn't stay mad at her for very long, and he smiled as he spread cheese over the tortilla. "I know you want to work with Earl." He didn't know how to explain the nervous pit in his stomach. "How's your ankle?"

"Just fine," she said, her voice pitching up a little. "I got up fine."

"Yes, you did." He turned back to her and met her eye. "You know I worry about you, right? There's been times when you've fallen, and you *can't* get up fine."

"I know, but Doctor Lindsey has been teaching me how to be stronger."

"I know that."

"You have to *let* me be stronger."

Matt stared at her, this fierce spirit God had blessed him with. He swallowed and ducked back to the stove. "Okay," he said. "I'll work on it."

He had so much to work on, and after he flipped the first quesadilla, he got his phone back out and typed up a text for Gloria.

I'm sorry about earlier.

He didn't know what else to add, but what he had wasn't enough. He deleted the words he'd typed and tried again. *Can I come over in a little bit? At least try to explain?*

He sent that, hating the conveniences of modern technology sometimes. He wanted to see her face-to-face and try to articulate the confusing things streaming through him. She didn't answer right away, which only added to the weight on his mind. He managed to eat with his daughter, and he told her to go get her math facts.

When Keith walked in, he gave Matt an icy look and headed for the ladder that led to the loft. Matt got to his feet and went to intercept him. "Hey," he said, making his voice as gentle as possible. "Look, I'm sorry."

"It's fine."

"It's obviously not." Matt stood in front of the ladder. "You don't have to eat with the Hammonds."

"Elise asked me to stay, and I didn't know what you were doing."

Matt wanted to tell him he should've texted. He could've asked. He shelved the comments and frowned at his son. "I want to see the flowers."

"No, you don't." Keith glared at him. "All you care about is Britt. And Gloria."

"That is not true."

"It's fine. I'm used to coming last."

"Keith," Matt said, his heart shredding right in half. "You are never last to me."

"I get it," Keith said, his voice breaking. "You're busy with the farm. You have a new girlfriend now, and they're kind of exhausting. And Britt has a lot of needs. It's okay, Dad."

Matt stepped into him and pulled his son to his chest. "It's not okay if you're not okay."

Keith stood unyielding in his arms for a few seconds, and then he melted into Matt's embrace. "I'm sorry," Matt murmured. "You're just as important to me as Britt. I want to see the flowers. Please, show them to me again."

Keith sniffled as he stepped out of Matt's arms, and he took out his phone. "Elise is making them, and I texted Kassidy to get the color of her dress. It's this really pretty blue color." He swiped a couple of times and a blue gown came up in a picture. "I think it'll look good with my brown suit, don't you?"

"Yeah, totally," Matt said, taking the phone. "You're going to have so much fun."

Keith took the phone back. "Elise is making a wrist corsage, and she came up with a few options." He swiped through them again, and this time, Matt paid attention.

"You're right," he said. "The one with the two roses is definitely the best." He looked at Keith. "I can't believe Elise can do that."

"She works with a lot of flowers," he said. "And she doesn't mind feeding me."

"I know she doesn't." Matt turned back to Britt as she said she finished her homework. "It makes me feel...like I can't take care of you guys." He walked toward the table.

"That's not true," Keith said behind him.

"True or not, it's how it makes me feel." Matt picked up the paper and scanned it. He couldn't check the accuracy of all the facts so quickly, but right now, he didn't care. "Good job, baby. Go get in the tub, okay?"

"Okay." Britt shot a look in Keith's direction that Matt

didn't miss, then skipped in her haphazard way down the short hall to the bathroom.

"Dad."

Matt sighed and put the homework paper down. Exhaustion pulled through him. "Yeah, bud?"

"You're a great dad."

Matt put a weary smile on his face. "I'm trying, and I guess that's all I can do." He drew in a deep breath. "Do you have homework?"

"No, I finished it all on the way home."

Matt nodded, unwilling to probe more to find out if that was true or not. Keith didn't normally lie about his homework, and Matt didn't worry about him nearly as much as he did Britt.

"I was unkind to Gloria," Matt said with a sigh. "I have to go talk to her."

"Okay," Keith said.

Matt looked up from the table. "You like Gloria, right?"

"Yes, Dad, I like Gloria a lot."

Matt didn't detect any falseness in his son's voice.

"In fact, if I send you these pictures, will you show them to her and see which one she likes best?"

"Yeah, sure." He grinned at Keith. "What did you mean about girlfriends being exhausting?"

Keith reached up and ran his hand through his hair. "I'm pretty sure I said 'kind of exhausting.'"

Matt grinned at him and took a step toward him. "Is Kassidy your girlfriend, then?"

Keith sort of rolled his shoulders, looking a bit uneasy. "I mean, yeah."

"You kissin' her?"

"Not yet, sir."

Matt grinned at him. "Prom?"

"I honestly don't know." Keith pressed his palms together. "I've never kissed a girl, Dad."

"Mm." Matt gestured for him to join him on the couch. "It's not too terribly hard. It's normal and natural to like girls. You've got to be kind to them, show them respect, even during the kissing."

"What does that mean?"

"It means mind where you put your hands, son." Matt smiled at him as they sank onto the couch together. Matt groaned, knowing he wasn't getting off this thing without a strong helping hand.

"My hands?"

"I recommend keeping them up near her face," Matt said, smiling. "Something like that. It's the hands that get you in trouble when you're kissing." Matt closed his eyes and felt himself sinking toward sleep.

Keith swallowed audibly. "Noted." He nudged Matt. "Don't fall asleep, Dad. You still have to go talk to Gloria."

Matt groaned, though he did want to do that. "All right. Help your old man off this couch."

CHAPTER 20

Gloria sat on her back steps, the country silence surrounding her so perfect, peaceful, and pure. She heard the opening and closing of Matt's door, as their cabins only sat about twenty feet apart. He wasn't the softest step in the west, and she heard him go down his front steps, across the grass, then the slim road between their cabins, and up her steps.

She hugged her knees and said, "Bless me, Lord, to listen to him and make whatever I did wrong, right."

The cabins didn't have doorbells, and she didn't hear him knock, but she got up and went inside. She padded through the cabin to the front door and opened it to find him standing there, looking at her.

"I hadn't even knocked yet."

"I was on the back steps," she said. "I heard you come over." She indicated the cabin behind her. "Do you want to go sit back there? It's nice."

"Okay." He stepped past her and into her cabin, which wasn't nearly as big as his. Still, the path to the back door wasn't hard to find, and he led the way. Her back porch could house a single chair, which she'd put there as soon as she could afford buying one.

A set of wooden steps went down to the yard, but Matt sat on the top one, leaving just enough room for Gloria to sit beside him. She did, and he immediately took her hand into his. "Sorry about tonight."

Gloria had been thinking for the past forty-five minutes, trying to figure out what had made him flip from his usual strong, sexy, quiet self to the barking father who wouldn't let Britt stay to help with Earl Grey.

"I think maybe we need to be on the same page before I tell Britt she can do things," Gloria said. "I didn't realize it would be a problem to have her stay to help with Earl's after-run care." She took a moment to center her thoughts again. "I actually thought it would be good for her, as part of her therapy. There's more to animals than just the fun stuff, you know?"

"I know," Matt said, back his quiet, calm self. "I...she's not given me attitude like she did in the barn, ever. I'm just learning how to take care of her, and Keith, and us, and it's a lot. I feel like things change constantly."

"I suppose they do."

"She said I have to *let* her be stronger," Matt said. "She's right. Her therapist told her to tell me that, and Britt thinks I treat her like a baby. Keith was mad at me only a few minutes before you guys got back, because I was distracted worrying about you and Britt and I didn't look at his corsage options." He sighed and looked up into the sky. "I love the stars."

"I remember that about you." Gloria leaned into bicep and squeezed his hand. "Did you talk to Britt and Keith?"

"Yeah, we had a little chat. He wants you to weigh in on the flowers, of course." He took out his phone. "Yep, he sent me the pictures." He showed her the different options for corsage, and Gloria studied them all carefully.

"I like the third one or the last one."

"This one?" Matt swiped back to the one with two roses.

"Yep."

"And this one." He tapped and couple of times and landed on the one with a large rose with lots of bows.

"Mm hm."

"I'll tell him." Matt started typing on his phone, and a few seconds later, he put it away. "I have to confess something," he said.

"Go on."

"I don't know how to do this."

"Do what?"

"Take care of them the way they need to be taken care of. They change constantly. I don't know how to make sure you're happy, and that I'm happy. I don't know how to talk to my brother about his ex-girlfriend and his deceased wife. There's just so much, and I don't know how to manage it all."

"Matt."

"Tonight, you got caught in the crossfire of that, and I'm sorry."

Gloria didn't have nearly the commitments he did. She had no children. No siblings. She just took care of herself, and for a while there, she couldn't even do that. "I understand," she said.

They sat in companionable silence for a few minutes, and Gloria enjoyed the cool air, the night sky, and the warmth of the man beside her. Then Matt said, "You'll come over on Saturday before Keith goes to the prom, right? He wants to model the whole look."

"I wouldn't miss it," Gloria promised, and Matt pressed a kiss to her temple, stood, and went down the back steps.

"See you tomorrow, sweetheart."

She watched him disappear into the night, and she stayed on the back steps and prayed she could figure out how to keep Matt in her life, even when he tried to pull away, as he had tonight.

"Oh, my goodness," Gloria said on Saturday afternoon. Keith finished coming down the ladder from the loft, and he tugged on the ends of his jacket to get it to lay right. He buttoned it next, and Gloria got thrown right into the past when she'd seen a younger version of Matt do the exact same move.

"How handsome are you?" She wiped her hands on a

dish towel, tossed it on the counter, and went to examine Keith more closely. He wore a suit of chocolate fabric, complete with a vest in a slightly darker color. His tie bore bright blue stripes on a white background, with finer brown stripes woven throughout.

He'd combed his hair to the side and sprayed something in it to make it stay there, and his feet looked far too big for his body in a shiny pair of loafers that sat halfway between chocolate and charcoal.

"She is so lucky." Gloria took the teenager right into her arms without thinking too hard about it. Keith took an extra moment, but he did hug her back.

"Thanks, Gloria."

She stepped back and kept her hands on his shoulders. "All right. Show me how you dance with her."

"Oh, I, uh, practiced with Britt."

"It's about your hands," Matt said from the kitchen, and Gloria twisted to look at him. "Let's see."

"Fine." Keith put one hand on Gloria's hip, but she could barely feel it. "And up here." He took her other hand out to the side. "And we move. I'm actually pretty graceful."

"Better than your dad," Gloria mock-whispered, and Matt said, "Hey, I'm a great dancer."

She swayed with Keith while they both laughed, and then she stepped away from him, the timer on the oven encouraging her to do so.

"You've got money?" Matt asked, taking over as the

responsible parent he was. "Your phone is fully charged? What's our safe word?"

"Dad, I've got it all. Jordy's gonna be here any second."

"Pictures," Gloria said, practically throwing the tray of muffins on the stovetop. "We have to have a picture before you go."

"Kassidy's mom will take pictures," Keith said with a groan.

"And we won't be there," Gloria said, wondering if anyone caught the "we" the way she did. "Come on now. It's not hard. Let's go outside where the light is better." She met Matt's eyes as she hurried past, and he grinned at her.

She snapped her pictures, and Jordy pulled up in his king-cab pick-up a couple of seconds later, saving Keith from sure embarrassment. Gloria could almost guarantee that Jordy's mother had taken pictures too, but she retreated back to the cabin as Matt went to talk to the other teenager about driving.

When he came back inside, he was Keith-less, and he sighed. "Well, he's off."

"He's going to have so much fun," Gloria said. "Come on, we're having breakfast for dinner, and these blueberry muffins are to die for."

Instead of coming to get a muffin, Matt picked up a roll of packing tape and started putting together a box. "I asked Elise to keep Britt tonight."

Gloria turned from the muffin she'd been buttering. "You did?"

"Yeah." He looked at her, abandoned the box, and came straight at her. "How about we go have a romantic evening together too? Hm?" He swept her into his arms, causing a giggle to come from her mouth.

"With all the teens out there on the roads? Clogging up the restaurants?" Gloria held onto his strong shoulders and moved with him. He was a good dancer, and she smiled up at him and said so.

Instead of responding, Matt leaned down and touched his lips to hers, and Gloria had the distinct feeling she'd go anywhere and do anything to be with this man. He kissed her sweetly, despite her attempts to speed things up a little.

"We can go over to Golden," he said. "There won't be any teens there."

"Giddy-up, cowboy," Gloria whispered, but she guided Matt's mouth back to hers and kissed him again.

Hours later, she lay on the couch with Matt's arms around her. The only light came from a couple of bulbs above the stove and the flickering TV in front of them. Matt had fallen asleep at least twenty minutes ago, but Gloria remained awake.

She'd heard the slam of a truck door too, and she sat up and looked toward the front door. "Matt," she said at the same time Keith entered the cabin. His head hung down, and Gloria jumped up.

"Hey," she said softly, reaching for the remote control to switch off the TV. "Are you okay?"

On the couch, Matt had woken, and he yawned,

complete with a terribly loud almost-yell that made Gloria frown and shake her head.

But the smile on Keith's face erased all of her consternation. "Yeah," he said. "I'm great."

Matt got up too, and he went around the couch the other way. "How was it?"

"Good."

Gloria folded her arms, but she waited for Matt to tell his son he had to give more than one-word answers about a prom with his girlfriend. Matt reached his son and hugged him. "You had a good time?"

"Yes."

"Did she?"

"I think so."

Neither of them seemed bothered about the complete lack of details, but her frustration grew by leaps and bounds with every second that passed.

Matt released his son, who reached to loosen the tie around his neck. "I'm wiped out, though. Talking all day and all night is hard work."

Gloria giggled and even Matt smiled. "Did you kiss her?" Matt asked.

"Dad." Keith threw a look at Gloria, but she wasn't going to save him from this conversation. She wanted to know too. Matt had told her that Keith hadn't kissed Kassidy yet, and they'd talked about how to kiss a girl.

"It's a valid question."

"It's private."

"That means yes," Matt said, grinning even wider.

Gloria wanted to tell him not to tease the boy and he'd probably talk more, but she said nothing. "So, how was it? Was it a peck or you know, a kiss?"

Keith glared at Matt, and they were cut from so many of the same pieces. The dark, devilish, handsome cowboy cloth. The tall, quiet, strong, cloth. The kind, good, wants-to-do-what's-right cloth.

"It's a simple question," Matt said. "Peck or kiss?"

Keith folded his arms and settled his weight on one foot. "If I tell, can I go to bed?"

"I can't make any promises," Matt said. "I might have follow-up questions." He seemed pretty serious about that too, and Gloria almost wanted to fade into the background so Keith would open up to his dad. Maybe it would be easier for him to do that if she wasn't around.

"It's easy," Matt said. "Two four-letter words. Peck? Or kiss?"

"Fine," Keith growled out. "I kissed her."

"Where?"

"On the mouth?"

Matt chuckled and shook his head. "No, I meant, where did this kiss happen?"

"Her front porch."

"So when you dropped her off."

"Yes."

"Wasn't Jordy in the truck?"

"No, he dropped us off and took his date home. She only lives around the corner. Then he came back and got me."

"The hands?"

"I kept them up by her face," Keith said. "I might have wrapped this one around the back of her neck...." He brought up his right hand and looked at it like it had betrayed him. Gloria found the whole thing funny, but she held back her laughter.

She could remember her first kiss, and it had sort of stupefied her a little bit.

"Good boy," Matt said, slinging one arm around his son. "All right, you can go to bed."

"Thanks, Dad." Keith leaned into his father's chest for a couple of moments before he headed up the ladder. "Night, Gloria," he called down.

"Good night," she said.

Matt met Gloria's eyes, and she could see the laughter in his gaze too. "I'll walk you home," he said.

She met him at the front door, very happy to be the one under the weight of his arm now. "This time next week, you won't be able to walk me home," she said once they'd left the cabin.

"No, but I can drive you home. Then maybe we can kiss on your front porch." He chuckled, and they went down his steps, across the sidewalk, and past the narrow strip of grass before meeting the road that separated their cabins.

On her front porch, Matt did take her into his arms. "I'm ten minutes away in Ivory Peaks. It's not far at all."

"I know," Gloria murmured. "I'm still going to miss having you right there."

"Mm." Matt leaned down but didn't quite kiss her. She waited, her eyes closed, the anticipation ratcheting higher and higher with every breath. "Kiss or peck, sweetheart?"

"Oh, you better kiss me," she whispered, and Matt obliged. She sincerely hoped Keith had not kissed Kassidy with the level of intensity and outpouring of love she felt in every one of Matt's strokes, because if he had, the poor girl would be ruined for life.

Just like Gloria was.

CHAPTER 21

"Britt, grab that crate on the table, okay?"

"Okay." Matt's daughter walked past him as he went out of the cabin with a couple of boxes from the kitchen. The back of his truck was almost full, but the cabin was almost empty of their personal belongings too.

Hunter turned from the tailgate and took the top box from the stack in Matt's arms. "Dad's almost here with the horse trailer."

"Great." Matt slid the box of spices and boxed goods on top of another one further in the truck bed. "Thanks for helping."

"Of course," Hunter said with a smile. "We'd have brought the whole crew if you needed it. Travis said he'd rather schlep boxes than deal with nervous moms today." He looked past the truck and toward Pony Power, though the facility couldn't be seen from the row of cabins behind all the main farm buildings.

Matt knew exactly how those moms felt as they dropped off their children for a therapeutic riding lesson. For some of them, they'd tried so many other treatments, and nothing had worked. They had doubts that equine therapy would do anything for their mentally or physically handicapped child. They didn't know how their child would act or react. Anything could happen, and that unpredictability was very hard on people.

"Oh, and you never answered about that therapy dog program I emailed you about."

Matt tore his gaze from the road where Gray Hammond had just turned his monster-huge truck with a horse trailer behind it and looked at Hunter. "What are you talking about?"

"I emailed you earlier this week about a therapy dog for Britt. They need to know today."

Matt immediately pulled out his phone. "I didn't see that email."

"Shoot," Hunter said. "I thought you had. I should've said something sooner. This week has been a bear."

He didn't have to tell Matt, who'd packed up everything he owned in the past seven days while working, trying to get his kids through the last couple of weeks of school, and buying a metric-ton of furniture for their new house in town. Unlike this cowboy cabin, the house did not come furnished, a fact Matt had overlooked until Britt had asked if she could have bunkbeds in her room so Gerty could sleep over sometimes.

Matt had then ordered that bunkbed, as well as a

whole host of other items for the house. Some of it was delivered yesterday, some would be today, and a few items wouldn't be available until next week.

Matt wasn't one to check his email that often, but he found the one from Hunter easily enough. He tapped and read the short note, then tapped on the website Hunter had provided.

"I guess they're not really therapy dogs," Hunter said. "More like companion animals. But they can be trained to help if someone falls or to retrieve items if she can't get them herself."

"Yeah," Matt said slowly, trying to absorb what he'd said and everything he could see on the website. "How much are they? Are they puppies?"

"They're not puppies," Hunter said. "They come fully trained. They're like service animals. And Pony Power would buy the dog. Molly and I want to try them in conjunction with the equine therapy, and we thought Britt would be the perfect one to start with. We have easy access to her, and she's here all the time anyway."

Matt looked up at Hunter, having just tapped on the pricing page. "They're so expensive, they don't even put the prices on the website."

Hunter grinned at him. "It wouldn't be Britt's dog, though she can take it home and everything. But if another child needs it, we'd send the dog with them. Pony Power would pay for it."

Matt didn't want to think of it as charity. Molly and Hunter wanted Pony Power to be the best children's animal therapy unit in the west, and if that meant they brought in dogs too, that was what they would do. The Hammonds had a ton of money, and Matt actually admired Hunter, Gray, and Wes for how much they gave back to their communities.

"Sounds amazing," he said. "She would love a dog as a friend. She even told me the other day she wishes one of the farm dogs would go blading with her, Gloria, and Earl."

"That would be epic," Hunter said. "I'll call Tim right now." He stepped away from the truck as Gray got out of his.

"I've got your three horses loaded up," he said, coming forward to shake Matt's hand. "We're going to miss you."

"I still work here," Matt said, grinning at the man. "I hope. Right?"

Gray grinned back. "Of course you do. I know why you're moving." He gazed at the cabin. "I get it. It'll be a little different, that's all."

Britt and Gloria arrived at the back of the truck with the crate he'd asked his daughter to get and Gloria carrying the vacuum. "I got all the bedrooms," she said, hefting the appliance up and into the back of the truck.

"Thank you," Matt said, appreciating her so much. Another change was happening between them, and he sure hoped the physical distance wouldn't create any relationship distance that he couldn't overcome. "I'll just go do one last walk-through. Has anyone seen Keith?"

"He went up into the loft to make sure the bed up

there was made and ready." Gloria watched Matt as he passed, a couple of questions in her eyes. He didn't know how to answer them, so he just kept going.

Inside the cabin, Matt paused. This place had no air conditioning, and it was about to get hot in Colorado. The gray brick house would keep them cool. He looked around at the couch and loveseat, the television, the small dining room table where he'd fed his kids breakfasts, lunches, and dinners for almost two years now.

"The loft is clean and ready," Keith said, jumping down the last few steps of the ladder. "Dad?"

"Yeah, great, bud." He put his arm around Keith, and they looked at the cabin together.

"Thanks for getting us a house, Dad," Keith said, the words almost inaudible he spoke so quietly. "It means a lot to me."

Love swelled in Matt's chest. "I know it does, and I'm happy to do it. It was never my intent for us to be boarders permanently."

"Now, if we could start talkin' about a car...."

Matt flinched, surprise flowing through him, and looked at his son. "You have got to be kidding."

"I'm going to be sixteen this summer." He turned for the front door. "I have a ton of money. I'd love you to take me car shopping, but I can ask Gloria to do it." He walked out of the cabin, leaving Matt standing there slack-jawed.

He found his wits and jumped to follow his son. "No," he practically barked as he flew down the steps. "Don't ask her. I'll take you."

Keith grinned over his shoulder, scooped Britt into his arms, which caused her to squeal, and they got in the truck.

"Hurry up, Britt," Matt said a few weeks later. "Boone will beat us there if we don't get goin'."

"Gerty texted to say they're fifteen minutes out," Keith said from the front steps of the house. He stood and took Britt's hand as she came dashing outside.

"Yep, let's go." Matt led the way toward the truck in the driveway. He hadn't thought living in town would be that big of a difference than living on the farm, but it was. He got home later than usual, and everything seemed just a bit harder.

Keith loved it, as his friends picked him up for school and brought him home. Britt only had to ride the bus for fifteen minutes before it dropped her and the younger Hammonds off at her front door. Matt had adjusted his schedule to come to the house to pick up the kids in the afternoons instead of getting them at school.

He didn't get to see Gloria as casually, as she worked at Pony Power, and he ran the farm. Moving into summer was a crazy-busy time for everyone and everything at the farm, and he praised the Good Lord above that both Boone and Wes were arriving that day.

Once they got Boone moved in, they'd be ready for

anything to happen at the Hammond Family Farm. At least Matt hoped so, and he'd been praying for good weather and good fortune for Boone's first summer in Colorado.

"What time are we leaving tomorrow?" Keith asked.

"For what?" Matt asked.

"The camping trip?" Keith looked at him like he'd lost his mind.

Matt startled, because maybe he had. "Oh, right. Eight, I think."

Keith nodded. "Hunt said he'd teach me to drive while we're up in the mountains."

"I don't think so," Matt said.

"I've already taken driver's ed, Dad. I just need the hours."

Matt started the truck but didn't put it in gear. "Do you want to drive us out to the farm?"

Keith looked absolutely hopeful. "Can I?"

"Sure." Matt got out of the truck and switched places with his son. *Dear Lord, bless us to survive this ride,* he prayed as he buckled into the passenger seat. "Go slow. Ask questions if you need to."

"Okay." Keith kneaded the wheel, and he took a few seconds to adjust the rearview mirror, his seat, and the air conditioning. He finally flipped the gearshift into reverse, looked both ways backward, and eased his foot off the brake. The truck wasn't like one the Hammonds owned—brand new, with all the bells and whistles.

"You've got to give it a little gas," Matt said, and the

next thing he knew, the vehicle jerked backward. "A little. Just a *little* gas."

"Sorry, sorry." Keith made it out onto the street, and it seemed to take ten years to get the truck into drive and started forward.

Matt told himself to be patient, and driving forward was definitely easier for Keith than backing up. He didn't drive fast, and he checked both ways after coming to a complete stop every single time. He made turns flawlessly, and he got the truck up to forty on the way out to the farm.

"Nice job, son," Matt said as he turned onto the dirt road that led back behind the pines to the farm. "You can pull right up to the farmhouse." Once they made it past the guardian pines, he saw Boone's truck and trailer parked in front of the main farmhouse too. "Boone's here."

"Sorry," Keith said. "We're probably late because of me."

"There's no late," Matt said with a smile. "We're just helping him move today."

"I heard Michael is staying the summer too," Keith said. "Is he?"

"Yep," Matt said. "He's staying with Chris, because Gray and Elise will take their kids to Coral Canyon after the open house for Pony Power." Matt wasn't sure how he felt about that, and he'd offered to take Michael in for the summer. Chris was eighty-five years old, and he didn't work the farm anymore.

"Gray said if it gets to be too much for his dad, he'll have Mike come stay with us."

"I have that bunkbed," Britt said.

Matt grinned at her, bumping along between him and Keith. "Baby, he's almost fourteen. He needs his own bedroom."

"Plus, he's a boy," Keith said. "Girls and boys don't share bedrooms, Britt." He glanced at Matt and grinned.

"That's true," Matt said. "Rule number one, kids. Girls and boys don't share bedrooms until they're married."

"Are you gonna marry Gloria, Daddy?" Britt asked.

Matt choked and coughed, though he and Gloria had actually had a couple of brief conversations about marriage. "I...don't know, baby. Keith, you're too close on this side. Ease over to the left."

Keith did as he said and brought the truck to a stop in front of the farmhouse. "Looks like Wes and Mike are here too."

"It'll be a regular party," Matt said, already dreading going inside the farmhouse. He wasn't sure why; he hadn't seen Gloria outside of work for a couple of days, and he itched to be alone with her. He could admit to himself that he would like to marry Gloria, and he should probably bring up some of the more serious topics to see if they were still on the same page with regards to family and work.

She came out onto the porch, and he hastened to reach for the door handle then. "Let's go, guys. I see Gloria has a cupcake in her hand already." He grinned up at her, then turned back to make sure Britt could get down by herself.

She did, and she even skipped in her limping way toward the steps. "Are there vanilla ones, Gloria? Molly said she'd make vanilla ones with silver fairy dust."

"That's what this is, bug." Gloria met her at the top of the steps, crouched down, and hugged the girl. "I brought it out for you. There's a lot of boys in there, and they have grabby hands."

"Thanks." Britt peeled the paper off and bit into the treat while Matt climbed the steps.

Gloria rose to her feet, a hint of nerves in her expression Matt wished wasn't there. "Hey, beautiful." He leaned down and kissed her—by Keith's standards, it would've been labeled a peck—and asked, "A lot of boys?"

"Wes brought all of his kids this time," she said, giving him a tight smile. "Hey, Keith."

"Morning, Gloria." He went past, and Michael Hammond burst out of the door a moment later.

"Keith, come see this new game my dad bought. It's *insane*."

Matt watched them go back inside, Britt following. "Insane," he echoed, smiling down at Gloria. "We need a night out."

She cocked her eyebrows in a sexy challenge. "When do you propose we do that?"

"I don't know." He ran his nose down the side of her face. "When I get back from the mountains?"

"We have the open house," she said, holding onto his

shoulders in a way that made him feel like he could carry the weight of the world for her.

"Matthew." His brother's booming voice filled the porch, and Matt stepped away from Gloria to greet Boone. They laughed and pounded one another on the back. Boone put his arm around Matt's shoulders and guided him toward the house. "Come settle a little debate I'm having with the other cowboys, would you?"

Matt looked over his shoulder to where Gloria still stood on the porch, a smile on her face. It fell before he looked away, and she spun away from him as well. His heart beat at him to go make sure she was okay, but his brother had started outlining how he may or may not have told the Colorado cowboys that they didn't know what winter ranching was.

"Booney," he said with a warning note in his tone. "You didn't." They stepped out of the entrance hallway and the rest of the house opened up before them. Travis, Mission, and Cody all milled about the kitchen, and all six eyes landed on Boone the moment he returned.

He had. He totally had.

"You're not the brightest bulb in the box," Matt said with a sigh.

Boone just laughed, and Matt joined the fray of people, first lifting Gerty right up off her feet as he hugged her. "I'm so glad you live here now," he said, grinning at her. "Are you going to survive?"

"Honestly?" Gerty had always been such a sober child. "I don't know." She eyed her father. "I know it's what's best for Daddy, but I already miss Saffron Lake and Sugar Pond."

"I know, darlin'." Matt straightened and looked around for Keith. He crowded around a handheld device with Michael, Tucker, Deacon, and Hunter, who was playing the game, and a moment later, they lot of them erupted into shouts and then laughter.

Matt put his hand on Gerty's shoulder. "You can talk to Keith about leaving Montana anytime. He knows what it's like. And you can come sleep at our house any time your dad is bugging you."

"Can I stay tonight?" Gerty asked in a dark voice, her eyes trained on the group of boys taking up one of the couches.

"Matt," Boone called. "I need you over here."

Matt saw Elise and Molly working in the kitchen, Gray sitting with Wes and Chris at the kitchen table. Wes's other two children hovered on the edge of the other kids, and Hunter reached out and picked up the littlest girl. She was even younger than Britt, and Matt thought her name was Opal.

"You should go see what Hunt's playing." He looked at Gerty. "All the kids are over there." Even Britt went in that direction, and all the boys made room for her among them.

"All right." Gerty went, but she didn't seem too happy about it. She approached Keith and Michael, who both hung over the back of the couch, and they both looked at her as she arrived. Keith gave her a quick hug, and Michael sure looked like he wanted to do the same thing.

Matt sucked in a breath when he saw Michael's hand brush Gerty's, and the secret look they shared. Oh, that was trouble with a capital T, and Matt swung his gaze back to his brother. His very oblivious brother, who tipped his head back and laughed at something Travis had just said.

Matt looked over his shoulder to find Gloria, but she hadn't come in yet. He retreated back to the front porch, but she wasn't there either. In the distance, he saw her walking toward the barn, and he frowned.

She'd left the party? Why had she left?

He pulled out his phone to text her, but noise came at him like a tidal wave. "All right, boys," Gray said, the loudest voice among them. "Let's get these guys moved in. The sooner we finish that, the sooner we can eat lunch."

CHAPTER 22

*G*loria parked her truck in front of the simple front for Pony Power and got out. People checked in at a desk inside the front barn, but today, it had been moved outside. Two six-foot tables flanked it, and Gloria took one of the bags of plastic cups to the end one. She set it beside the twenty-five-gallon cooler that Hunter had filled with water before she'd left to get the paper goods.

"All right," Molly said, joining her with a stack of paper plates. She started unwrapping the plates and setting them on the table. Gloria did the same with the cups, removing them from their outer plastic layer. "We've got the cookies. The punch. The plates, cups, and napkins."

Molly twisted and looked down the road toward the farmhouse. "Now we just need the men to come get the horses out."

"I can start on that once we're done here," Gloria said

with a smile. Molly and Hunter had been advertising the open house at Pony Power for a solid month, and they both felt confident that a lot of people would show up. Some of their current clients were coming, and all of their counselors and staff should be here already.

For some reason, Gloria was as nervous about the open house as Molly seemed to be, and they both took an identical breath at the same time. She met Molly's eyes, and they laughed together.

"It's going to be great," Gloria said, though she wasn't sure if she was trying to reassure herself or Molly. "We have everything in place, and everyone knows all the answers to any questions someone could ask."

Molly tucked her arm through Gloria's. "You're right, of course. Not only all of that, but we have the best horse trainer in the world."

Gloria grinned into the morning sunshine. "I'm sure that's not true," she said. If it were, surely she wouldn't be working at a small farm in Colorado, but training the best racehorses in the world. At the same time, Gloria didn't want to train racehorses. She didn't want to be doing anything but what she currently did.

"The horses are ready," she said. "Because of Hunt's overbuying tendencies, and your ability to find quality counselors, we can take on about fifteen more clients."

"And what do you think? Do you think we can get them?" Molly wore her worry right on her eyebrows.

"I don't know," Gloria said, unlacing her arm and moving to put another stack of cups on the table on the opposite side of the desk. This cooler down here had been marked "cherry fruit punch," in messy cowboy handwriting, and Gloria smiled at it.

"Here's the real question, Molly," she said, turning back to her friend. "Why do you want it to operate at full capacity?"

"Because I...." She sighed and reached up to tighten her ponytail. Gloria loved Molly like a sister, though she had three of her own. Gloria didn't have any, and Molly had been nothing but kind to her from the moment they'd met. Last summer, they'd spent so much time eating lunch with Matt and Chris, and Gloria had been there, stuffed in the pantry with Matt, when Hunter had proposed to her.

"I quit my teaching job," Molly said. "I want it to be for something. I want to be busy here."

"You are busy here," Gloria said. "You come every day, and you manage to find things to do, don't you?"

"Yes," Molly said, sighing. "I don't know. Hunt and I aren't going to have kids for a while, and I just found out my sister's pregnant, and I just want my life to...mean something too."

Gloria approached Molly, trying to tame her surprise. "Molly, your life means a lot. It means a lot to me. Without you and this facility, I wouldn't have a job." She swallowed, so many words teeming beneath her tongue. "Who says that the only way to have your life mean something is if you're a mother?"

"Do you not want kids?" Molly asked.

Gloria looked off toward the big pines that hid the view of the main road. "I mean, I've thought about having kids."

"You and Matt must be getting pretty serious," Molly said.

"I guess," Gloria said. He'd been gone for a few days with Keith, and he'd left Britt with his brother. Now that Boone had arrived on the farm, Gloria had seen Matt less and less. Their time together had already been diminished after he'd moved with his children to town.

"What does that mean?" Molly asked, facing the same way as Gloria. "I've seen you two together. You're cute. You get along great."

Gloria smiled, her mind slowing enough to seize onto the thoughts that had previously raced around. "Do you ever wonder if there's an element of timing to a relationship?"

"I know there is," Molly said. "Hunter and I met as kids, you know? Things almost didn't work out even last year, what with him becoming the CEO and everything."

Gloria nodded and managed to smile, though Molly hadn't given her the answer she wanted to hear. "Matt and I dated a long time ago," she said. "Back in Montana." She glanced at Molly, because she knew Matt well too, and perhaps he'd told her this story already. Sure enough, Molly nodded.

"And now we're together, and he's wonderful." Gloria's breath burst out of her body, and she felt so helpless. "And I don't know. He just seems to have so much on his plate right now, and I don't know how to crowd myself into the corner." She reached up and brushed at her eyes, feeling absolutely ridiculous that she'd been brought to tears over Matt's absence in her life.

"That sounds so stupid," she said, spinning away from the empty road in front of her. "And selfish. The summertime is always busy. We'll be fine." She headed for the side-entrance to the barn, where she'd find the reins and bridles for the horses. "I'll go get the horses."

Before she could take more than two steps in that direction, Travis came around the side of the barn, leading two horses with reins in one hand. "Morning, Gloria."

"Hey," she said brightly, hoping Molly knew well enough not to say anything more. "Morning, Draco. How are you this morning, huh? You ready to meet the kids?" She ran her hand down the side of the black horse's face. "Morning, Oatmeal."

Of course, neither horse greeted her, but right behind Travis came Mission with two more horses. "How many more?" she asked.

"Oh, everyone's back there," Travis said. "We might need another body or two."

She nodded and continued on, smiling and greeting the cowboys and the horses as they paraded past her. Foolishness and apprehension filled her when she saw Boone, especially when he was bright and sunny toward her.

"Heya, Gloria," he said. "Matthew's right behind me."

"Thanks, Boone." She gave him the best smile she could muster, feeling even worse for being jealous that he'd come to Ivory Peaks and "stolen" some of Matt's time with her. He was the only one she'd ever heard call Matt "Matthew," and she did like the brotherly bond they shared.

So get over it, Gloria, she told herself. She heard Matt's voice before she saw him, and she wasn't surprised to see him leading Cinnamon Sugar while Britt led Sterling Silver. A real, genuine smile burst onto her face.

"Wow," she said at the same time Britt called over her shoulder, "Come on, Earl. Let's go show Gloria how clean you are."

"She's right there, baby." Matt grinned at Gloria, and all the familiar heat that had always sparked between them roared back to life. Perhaps she'd simply gotten too far inside her own head. He held the reins in one hand and slipped the other around her waist. "Mm, are you a sight for sore eyes, or what?"

He kissed her and Gloria lost herself for a moment. She knew then that she was in love with Matt Whettstein, and she hoped this summer of busyness didn't kill them. They hadn't survived something hard last time, and all Gloria could do this time was pray that they were more mature and better equipped to do so this time.

"You ready for this?" Matt asked.

"I hope so," Gloria said, turning toward Britt, who bounced on the balls of her feet. "Look at you, Britt. Leading a horse and controlling Earl too?"

"I told Daddy I could do it, and I'm doing it."

She exchanged a glance with Matt. "You sure are. Go

on, then. Take 'em out front. The people should be arriving soon." She ran her fingers through Britt's soft, blonde hair, and the girl continued on. "She's almost a different person."

"Right?" Matt tugged on his reins and got Cinnamon moving again. "We best be out there on time too. Hunter said in no uncertain terms not to be late."

"Yeah, he looked real stern going by just now too," Gloria quipped. "He was joking with his dad and Wes."

Matt smiled at her and kept moving. "You don't need those. We got all the horses."

"Okay." Gloria tucked the reins under her arm and followed him back to the front of the barn. They'd tied the horses along the fence that ran down the lane toward the farmhouse, and the cowboys milled about on the top of the fence, jawing with one another.

Gloria went to help Britt about the time the first car arrived, and Molly called her name a moment later. "You okay, baby?" she asked, realizing she spoke to Britt the same way Matt did.

"Just fine," Britt drawled.

"I'll help her tie up Earl," Cody said, and Gloria nodded at him to get that done.

She hurried back down the lane to help Molly, realizing she'd be doing a lot of talking that day. She didn't mind. If there was one thing Gloria could talk about, it was horses.

She stayed busy, only pausing to drink when Hunter or Molly or Matt put a cup of water in her hand.

"It's once a week for eighty-five dollars, yes," she said,

looking up at the parents of a boy who'd been born with cerebral palsy. "That includes a thirty-minute equine lesson and thirty minutes with a trained psychologist."

She noted that Mission and Wes had started to take back a couple of the horses, and she forced herself to focus on the people in front of her. Her stomach grumbled at her, but she was pretty sure all the cookies were gone.

"I think we should do it, Rachel," the father said. "Look at him."

The three of them turned to look at the eight-year-old boy, who stood in front of Draco. The horse held perfectly still, his eyes half-way closed, as the child patted him.

"We're taking names for interest," Gloria said, hopefully with just as much enthusiasm now as she had a couple of hours ago. But the sun had waxed higher in the sky, and she needed to get out of the heat. "You don't have to commit now. Someone on our staff will follow up with you. Probably Molly, the owner." She nodded to where Molly stood laughing at something her husband had said.

Time froze in that moment, and Gloria saw that even people who appeared to have it all on the outside could still hurt on the inside. They could paint over their doubts and their cares with smiles and laughter, but that didn't make them go away.

The world spun forward again, and Gloria blinked her way back to the clipboard so she could take down the couple's name, email address, and phone number. They called to their son, and together, they headed for their car.

Gloria glanced around, didn't see anyone else to talk

to, and made a beeline toward the barn. Inside, she breathed in the cooler air and wished she had someone to make sure she drank. Her head spun for a moment, because she needed to eat, and she pulled out her phone to text Matt.

Lunch? Me and you?

He didn't answer right away, and Gloria heard voices going past the barn, causing a real ruckus. Cowboys had never been known for being quiet when they got together, and Gloria didn't usually mind.

Today, however, after the busyness of the open house, she wanted an escape. Somewhere with air conditioning. Somewhere with good food. Somewhere with someone to take care of her for just an hour, before they both had to get back to work.

"Gloria," Molly said, and she turned toward the other woman. She giggled and shrieked and danced over to her. "That was so great. Thank you so much. I know you didn't anticipate being the voice of Pony Power, but you did *so* amazing."

Gloria hugged her, smiling and letting herself giggle too.

"You're coming back to the house for lunch, right?" she asked, linking her arm through Gloria's. She saw her quiet escape into cool darkness, with delicious food and a handsome cowboy, go right up in smoke.

"I don't know," she said with a moan. "I might just want some peace and quiet after that."

"It was intense, wasn't it?" Molly didn't seem affected

by it at all. "Reminded me of parent-teacher conferences. Such a rush." She headed for the door. "Come if you can, Gloria. You're a superstar, and all the cowboys will fall over themselves to take care of you."

Gloria just shook her head and smiled. Molly walked out, and Gloria walked toward the back of the barn. She sighed, trying to decide what to do. She'd left the farmhouse a few days ago once everyone had arrived, because the pulsating energy of it had been too much for her.

She was an only child, used to being by herself and doing things alone. The Hammonds didn't understand the meaning of the word "alone," or "solitary," though Hunter did like a quiet evening with his crossword puzzles sometimes.

With Wes here, and Boone...Gloria wasn't sure she fit as easily as she did in a smaller group.

Her phone chimed, and she tugged it from her pocket. *Lunch is at the farmhouse, remember?* Matt had added an emoji with crazy eyes. *You were so busy during the open house. Come and I'll get you whatever you want. Elise has that almond punch you love so much.*

The thought of Matt—and almond punch—had Gloria turning and leaving the barn, her destination down the road at the farmhouse. She didn't respond to Matt, and about halfway there, he came out onto the front porch, obviously looking for her.

"Yeah," she muttered to herself. "You just need to get out of your own head, Gloria."

CHAPTER 23

Matt laughed as the golden retriever ran after his giggling daughter. She stumbled, and he knew she was going down before she fell. He didn't immediately run to her aid, as he would've in the past. Tonight, he sat on the steps and watched Pearl, her new therapy dog, lick her face, nudge her with her doggy head, and give Britt something solid to hold onto while she got back to her feet.

Her face shone with radiance, and she said, "Did you see that, Daddy? She is so much fun." She came back toward Matt, who nodded.

"I saw it, baby."

Britt sighed as she sat on the steps beside him. "When is the pizza gonna be here?"

Matt looked down the street. "When Boone gets it and shows up."

"I'm so hungry." Pearl circled and collapsed at her feet,

and Britt smiled down at her. "Look how she sits right on my feet. She's so sweet."

"Tell me what you need to remember," Matt said.

"She's not my dog," Britt said dutifully. "She belongs to Pony Power, and she might go home with other kids who need her."

Matt lifted his arm and put it around his daughter. "Good girl." A tan truck turned the corner and came their way cautiously, and Matt got to his feet. "Dear Lord, he let Keith drive."

His son was actually a decent driver, and Matt had been letting him get behind the wheel every afternoon and evening to first go back to the ranch and then drive them home again. He needed time and experience behind the wheel, and when he turned sixteen at the end of the summer, he'd be ready to drive himself places.

A sliver of excitement stole through Matt at the idea of Keith waiting for Britt to get out of school and then being able to drive them both out to the farm. Matt's day wouldn't be interrupted at all.

He'll need a car to do that, he thought as Keith turned into the driveway and brought the truck to a stop. Matt grinned at his son, who had his window down. "Nice turning, bud."

"Thanks," Keith said, flashing a smile at his father before he killed the ignition. "Uncle Boone's in a bad way."

"What?" Matt's gaze slid past his son to his brother, who did have violent waves rolling from him. "Boone?"

"Hurry up, Gerty," he barked at his daughter, though she'd already unbuckled and started to open the back door.

She dropped to the ground and though Matt stood on the other side of the truck, he could see her glare. He himself withered from the hot disdain in it, and she stomped past her dad without speaking.

Boone jumped from the truck too, calling, "Keep up that attitude, and you'll never get this phone back!"

Matt tried to see her reaction, but she marched past him without giving him much of a glimpse. He backed up as Keith got out of the truck, and the two of them gathered the pizza boxes from the back seat.

"I'll take 'em," Keith said when Matt didn't move to go into the house. He passed the food to his son and stood at the front of the truck as Keith herded the girls—humans and dogs alike—into the house.

"Boone?" Matt didn't need to say more.

Boone's laser-gaze switched from Gerty to him. He visibly relaxed, but when he held up a shiny, purple phone, his knuckles were white. "She's texting Michael day and night. They're more than friends."

Matt swallowed, not sure how to address this with his brother. "Oh. What does that mean, more than friends?"

"What do you think it means?" Boone growled. "You're more than friends with Gloria."

"They're like, kissing, or just hanging out? Kid stuff?"

He shoved her phone in his back pocket and hung his head. "I don't think they've kissed."

"Okay."

"She's *twelve*," Boone said, as if Matt didn't know.

"Well, I mean, she'll be thirteen in a couple of weeks."

"Not helping." Boone glared at him, smashed his hand down on his cowboy hat, and started toward the door. "It's fine. I just need to eat and wrap my head around this."

Boone was still trying to wrap his head around moving to Colorado, and he'd been here for two weeks. He was still trying to wrap his head around his ex-girlfriend cheating on him, and he'd known about that for six weeks.

Gerty having a semi-boyfriend? Boone would never get his head all the way around that, and Matt sighed as he followed his brother down the sidewalk. "Can we just take the glaring and shouting down a notch or two?" Matt asked. "I gave up the chance to take Gloria to dinner to spend time with my family."

"I didn't ask you to do that," Boone snapped, which was technically true. But Matt didn't need Boone to ask him to spend time with him. Matt simply knew his brother needed as much support as he could get right now. He'd invited Gloria to come have pizza with them, but she'd said she didn't want to intrude on his family night.

He'd argued that if they'd lived right next door to one another, she'd have come. She hadn't argued back the point. In fact, she'd gone silent after that, which had only told him how right he was.

He didn't need or even want to be right. He wanted to

enjoy his evening with his kids and his brother and niece, but as Boone dang near ripped off the front door to go inside, Matt didn't think that was going to happen.

His time with Gloria had dwindled and dwindled over the past month or so, and Matt looked up at the roof over the porch. He'd wanted to move here. His son had needed it. But the physical distance between him and Gloria had amplified into more than that. It had created some relationship distance he was still figuring out how to bridge.

"Look, Daddy," Britt called from further inside the house. "Pearl can sit up like a bear!"

He found her holding out a piece of pepperoni, and the golden retriever balanced on her hind legs, her front paws in front of her, bent down like a t-rex. He laughed at the sight and cheered as Britt gave the dog her treat.

He picked up a paper plate and cut a glance at Boone, who'd put a couple of slices of the ham and pineapple pie on his plate. "So, Gerty," Matt said, grabbing a pepperoni slice and then a combination one. "Tell me what Gloria's given you to do in the stables. She seemed impressed by you."

"Did she?" Gerty's eyes lit up. "She is so great, Uncle Matt. She lets me wash the horses all by myself and doesn't treat me like I'm five years old." She threw a sour look at her father, who only cocked his eyebrow and then took another bite of his pizza, silent.

Oh, this wasn't going to end well for either one of them. She was so much like Boone, just with his wife's physical features, and Matt could practically feel the simmer start between them. By the time they got home, it would be a full boil, and they'd argue before he finally sent her to bed.

"Can I sleep over here tonight?" Gerty asked, looking at Britt and then Matt. He immediately cut a look toward Boone.

"We have harvest at five in the morning," he said. "That's not going to work."

"Keith will bring me out," Gerty said, meeting his cousin's eye. "He's going, right, Keith?"

"I was gonna go, Uncle Boone," Keith said almost under his breath.

"You don't have pajamas," Boone said.

"Yes, I do," Gerty said. "Britt let me put some in her dresser so I could stay over any time."

Matt wanted to tell them to both stop it. Just let things go and get along. In a year, this wouldn't even matter. Heck, next week, this wouldn't matter. Gerty would get her phone back, and she'd have a little first crush thing with Michael Hammond, and come autumn, he'd return to Wyoming and she'd start eighth grade, meet someone else, and fall madly in love with them.

"I have to be there too," Matt said. "Not to sway you one way or the other." He met his brother's eye, silently adding, *Let her stay. It'll be good for both of you to have some separation.*

Boone seemed to get the message, because he nodded. "Fine. You do everything Uncle Matt says. You don't have a phone, so I'll have to rely on him for a report."

"Yes, sir," Gerty said, and she might as well have saluted him for how mocking her voice sounded. Matt looked at Keith, who wore a horrified look on his face, and then Britt, who finally seemed to realize that everything at the table wasn't hunky dory.

"Gerty," she said. "Are you mad at Uncle Boone?"

"Yes," Gerty said simply.

"You should go play with Pearl," Britt said. "Come on. Let's take our pizza outside. She can make you feel *so* much better." She collected her plate and started to get off her chair. She couldn't really do it and ended up crashing into the table. It was Keith who lunged forward to help her, and he held her plate while she got down, then handed it back to her.

"Come on, Pearl. Gerty needs some cheering up." She led the two of them outside, and all the tension in the house went with them.

"She's going to be the death of me," Boone complained.

"Especially if you let her talk to you like that now," Matt said. "Not that I have room to talk. I'm a total softie with my kids." He met Keith's eye, and when he didn't argue, Matt knew he'd spoken true.

"You're not soft, Dad," he said, his eyes showing wisdom. He clearly seemed to be thinking hard about something. "You're...trying to make sure we don't suffer more than we already have. Because of Mom. That's all." He looked at Boone and offered him a smile. "My guess is you're doing the same thing with Gerty."

"She's just not as good as you," Boone grumbled, eyeing the back door where his daughter had gone.

"Boone," Matt said gently. "Nikki's been gone for six years. Gerty doesn't need to be protected from that."

"Yeah, and then I brought another woman into her life," Boone said bitterly. "Someone else she fell in love with and wanted to be her mother. Someone who duped us both." He tossed down his crust and got to his feet. "I'm leaving. Sorry I ruined tonight."

"You didn't," Matt said, but his brother stuffed his trash in the can and headed for the front door. "You don't have to go."

"Let me know if she gives you the same attitude," Boone said, plucking his hat from the hook beside the front door. "She can talk to me like that, but I'll be darned if she does it to other people." He met Matt's eye, a fierce determination in his. Matt nodded, and Boone left.

Keith sighed and got up with his empty plate too. "Wow. I didn't know about Karley. What happened?"

Matt sighed and looked at his growing-cold pizza. "I think she cheated on him," Matt said. "He's...like you said. In a bad way."

"I'll say," Keith said. "Good thing he has you, Dad."

"You think so?"

"I mean, you know what it's like to leave Montana and move here alone with your kids." He shrugged, and Matt once again marveled at the maturity in his son. He'd grown up so much since they'd come to Colorado.

"Hey, since he didn't stay, and Gerty's with Britt, could

I go over to Jordy's? They're playing Monsters and Magic tonight." Keith wore a hopeful look in his dark eyes.

Matt frowned, but in the end, he couldn't deny his son. "Sure," he said. "Let me get the keys and tell the girls."

A COUPLE OF HOURS LATER, HE SAT ON THE BACK porch, pushing himself back and forth with his toe in a rocking chair. He felt geriatric, but he didn't care.

"You're kidding," Gloria said over the phone, and Matt chuckled.

"I wish I was kidding," he said. "I just got the girls to bed, and now I'm waiting up for Keith."

"Poor Boone," she said, and Matt detected something in her voice.

"You like Boone, right?" he asked.

"Sure," she said, and he identified what she carried in her tone. Falseness.

His heart thundered through his chest. "Talk to me," he said, his throat so dry. "I feel like you might not be telling me the truth."

Gloria hesitated, which spoke volumes, and then she sighed. A white noise rushed in Matt's ears, and he worked to quiet it so he could hear what she had to say.

"I just...of course I like Boone. He's your only brother, and he's a great guy," she said. "I think I just feel...left out. Like, you moved, and he showed up, and now I'm the last one on the list."

"That's not true," Matt said instantly. "I invited you to come tonight."

"I know."

"If I still lived next door, you would've come." He wasn't asking, but he gave her plenty of space to deny it or to say that she really was too busy or too tired.

When she didn't, he said, "It's a ten-minute drive, Gloria. And you could've ridden with Boone."

"I just need...I don't know. The farm feels very loud right now, and I'm not good with loud."

She never had been, and Matt nodded into the night. "How can I make it quieter for you?"

"I don't know," she whispered. After several seconds of silence, she added, "I'm scared, Matt."

"Of what?"

"Of this not being the right time for us."

"Why wouldn't it be the right time for us?" he asked.

"When's the last time we went out?" she challenged.

Matt clamped his mouth shut.

"When's the last time you snuck me around the back of the barn just to steal a kiss?"

Still, he said nothing. He couldn't name a day, because it *had* been a while. *How long?* he wondered, and in the back of his mind, the answer emerged. *Weeks, at least.*

"When's the last time we talked about something that wasn't farm-related, therapy-related, or kid-related?"

"I thought you liked my kids."

"I do," she said, her voice powerful now, no whisper in

sight. "I love your kids, Matt. I know they're your priority, and I guess I thought I was too."

Until Boone showed up rang in his ears, unspoken but oh-so-loud.

"Boone's just going through a really hard time right now," Matt said. "I know exactly what that feels like. You do too, Gloria. We both came to Ivory Peaks under the same conditions as he did. I can help him."

His son's words from earlier that night rang in his ears. *Good thing he has you, Dad.*

He'd wished and prayed for someone to help him when he'd come to Ivory Peaks, and that person had been Gray Hammond, and then his son Hunter, and then his father, Chris. All three of them had showed Matt that life was good and worth living, and that he could overcome the depression and fight back the black clouds that had followed him around for the first few months after moving.

If he could be that person for Boone, he wanted to be.

"You can help him, but you can't save him," she said.

"I'm not trying to save him," Matt said. "I *don't* have a Savior complex." She'd accused him of that in the past, and he didn't appreciate it cropping up again. "I thought we weren't going to make assumptions that were two decades old."

"Some things about a person don't change," she said.

Frustration and irritation fired through him. "What do you want me to say, Gloria?"

"Nothing."

"Let's go out tomorrow night. Me and you."

"After getting up at four-thirty for harvest?"

"It's the first one," he said. "It'll be small and done by eight."

"And then I have twelve kids coming for therapy tomorrow, and I'm pretty sure you're rebuilding a fence in the back lot."

"Are you saying no?"

She hesitated, and then she said, "Yes, I'm saying no. I don't think either of us will be fit for dinner tomorrow night."

Matt rolled his eyes. "Okay, but then don't blame me for not getting together for dinner."

"I wasn't blaming you."

"Sounded like it."

"I'm going to go," she said abruptly. "I'm getting angry, and I should've been in bed an hour ago, and I don't want to say something I'll regret later."

"Great, sure," he said.

"See you tomorrow." The call ended before Matt could respond, and he let his hand drop to his lap, his phone almost bouncing down to the deck. He rocked as he replayed the conversation once, then twice.

"What just happened?" he asked, more stupefied than ever. When he realized it was ten o'clock and Keith wasn't home yet, he dialed his son, a yawn pulling through the back of his throat.

"I'm on my way, I swear," Keith said, sounding breathless.

"We have to be leaving the house again in six and a half hours," Matt said, his fatherly tone employed. "I should've been in bed an hour ago."

"I know," Keith said. "I'm coming. Ten minutes."

"If it's eleven, you won't be going to Jordy's again for a week."

"Ten minutes," Keith repeated. "Go to bed. I'll check in when I get home."

"Mm." Matt hung up, set a timer for ten minutes, and went to brush his teeth. When the front door opened, Matt glanced at his phone. "Thirteen seconds," he called, and the timer went off as Keith filled the doorway to the master suite.

"But I made it." His son grinned at him, and the lamp-light caught on something shiny on his lips.

Matt saw his rest that night evaporate. He patted the empty side of the bed. "Come talk to me for a few minutes."

Keith pushed away from the doorway and entered the bedroom. "About what?"

"About that pink shiny stuff on your upper lip."

His son quickly wiped his mouth and looked at his fingers. Matt watched the emotion run through Keith's eyes as he saw that yes, he was wearing his girlfriend's lip gloss. Keith lifted his eyes to Matt's. "It was just a kiss," he said.

"Did you even go to Jordy's?"

"Yes," Keith said, settling on the bed. "Of course I did, Dad. I wouldn't lie to you about that."

Matt reached for his phone and swiped to get to his map app. He saw Keith's smiling, more youthful face on a house several blocks over. Jordy's. He handed it to Matt. "I have your pin activated. I'll know if you go somewhere you haven't told me about."

"Kassidy just came over," he said, looking at the phone. "The game was over, but no one was leaving yet, so we went out to the trampoline. That's all."

"Just you and her?"

"Yes, sir." Keith handed the phone back to Matt, his eyes wide and pleading. "Kissing her is fun, Dad. You said it would be easy and fun, and it is."

Matt regretted saying that, and he connected to Boone on a new level. What would he be feeling and thinking if Keith was only twelve?

"A moment ago, you said 'a kiss.' Now we're talking about kiss*ing*. Plural."

"I mean, it was more than one," Keith said.

Matt's mind could conjure up all kinds of things that two teenagers could do on a trampoline, in the dark, without anyone watching. "And the hands?" He swallowed and closed his eyes, praying for an answer that would allow him to fall asleep that night.

"I swear, all I think about when I'm kissing her is where my hands are," Keith said dryly. "You've ruined me, Dad."

Matt opened his eyes and looked at his son. "For real?"

"For real." Keith held up both of his hands. "They stayed in a safe zone, I promise."

Matt reached over and put his arm around his son. He curled into Matt's side, and he thoroughly enjoyed this tender moment between them. "I hope I'm always the voice in your head, reminding you of who you are and what you should be doing. I don't regret that."

"I know, Dad." Keith sighed. "I'm sorry."

"You have to be careful with girls, Keith," Matt said, thinking of Gloria. "Things can change so quickly, and then you'll be wondering how they did."

"Okay." Keith scooted to the edge of the bed and got up. "We have to get up early. I can go to bed now?"

"Yes, go." Matt smiled his son out of the room, then switched off his lamp. He settled down to sleep, but his mind switched back and forth between concern for his son and worry that he'd messed up with Gloria.

Help me to fix it in the morning, he prayed.

CHAPTER 24

*D*irt covered Boone from head to toe. All he wanted was a big basin of cold water. Ice cold water. First, he'd drink as much as his belly could handle, and then he'd dunk his whole body into the water.

He reached for the door handle of the stable, pausing when he heard a salty voice come from inside. Matt's voice.

And Matt was never salty. Okay, hardly ever.

"...I don't know what you want from me," he said, and Boone left the door open a few inches and pressed his back against the brown-painted wood. He didn't want to overhear this, but he couldn't walk away either.

Matt had been the only lifeline Boone had since arriving in Colorado, and if he needed help, Boone would do his best to offer it.

"I don't know what I want from you either," Gloria said, her voice equally as frustrated. "I feel like there's all this space between us, and I don't know how to fix it. I feel like I've tried, but you're fine with how things are."

"Relationships ebb and flow," Matt said, and Boone pressed his eyes closed. *Wrong answer*, he thought.

"I'm not fine with it," Matt continued. "You make me sound like I don't care about you. I do. I think about you all day. I want you to come to dinner at the house. You won't. I asked you to dinner tonight. You said no."

"I'm just trying to figure out where we are."

"We're standing in the stable, arguing about me spending time with my family."

Gloria said nothing, and Boone's guilt punched him like a fist to the nose. He couldn't be the reason Matt couldn't be with Gloria. He'd fallen in love with her twenty years ago, and they seemed so perfect for each other now.

"Maybe we need a break," she said, her voice the thing that was breaking.

"I don't want a break," Matt said. "I want to kiss you in the stables. I want to call you at night when conversations go awry. I want to tell you about Keith and his girlfriend and how he was only thirteen seconds away from losing all of his freedoms."

"You want me to be available when it suits you," she said, nothing breaking in her voice now. "What about what *I* need, Matt?"

His brother didn't answer, which told Boone that he hadn't given much thought to what Gloria actually needed. Matt spent so much time thinking about others and giving to others that he wasn't surprised that he was more of a taker in his romantic relationship with the woman.

"What do you need, Gloria?" Matt asked, his voice tender and soft.

"I need a break," she said. "I need things to quiet down. I need to know that if we get married, I'm not going to be fourth or fifth after your kids, then your niece, then your brother. Oh, and behind all the Hammonds too. What does that make me? The past month or so I've been tenth or eleventh on your list. It doesn't make me feel good, Matt."

Boone didn't stay to hear what Matt said after that. He pushed away from the stable and strode toward the paddock, several feet away. "Help him," he prayed right out loud. "Help them both."

In Boone's eyes, Matt and Gloria were perfect for each other. He'd seen the way his brother looked at that woman, and the way she watched him. He'd seen her with Britt and Keith, and both kids loved her. She clearly loved them.

Boone would not wish the heartache currently storming through his life, ripping apart his ribs and infecting every breath, on anyone, least of all his brother.

"Please, please don't let me be the reason they can't be together. I can't handle that. Not with everything else." He looked up into the cloudless sky, wishing God would send a ray of light to his mind so he'd be healed. He had no idea how to talk to Gerty. Every time he tried, she shot him down and burned him with her eyes, which were so much like her mother's.

Nikki had been fiery like that too, though she'd calmed with every passing year they'd been married. She'd fought hard against her illness, but in the end, her spunk and sass had not saved her.

Boone's breath shuddered out of him, and he let it. He didn't even try to strengthen his resolve or his determination not to break down. If he let himself keep going, he'd spiral right into a sobbing mess. He felt it coming on.

Thankfully, behind him, a door slammed, and Boone spun that way. The problem was, he saw Matt striding away from the stable in the same manner Boone just had —angry, defeated, desperate.

He had the very real feeling his brother and Gloria had just broken up, and as she exploded out of the front of the stable, Boone got confirmation of that.

"Dear Lord," he whispered. "Lead me, guide me, help me help them both." He didn't know what to do, or what to say. The Lord didn't lead him or guide him, and Boone ended up simply standing beside the paddock until Travis happened by, and then they went into the stable to wash up together.

BOONE'S SKIN ITCHED, AND HE RUBBED HIS hands together while he waited for Gloria to unclip the papers from her board. "Here you go," she said, smiling at him. She'd been as professional as ever the past couple of weeks, like nothing had changed in her life at all.

Boone knew better.

He'd been with his brother often, and Matt was definitely not okay. Boone didn't know what to say to him. He and Matt had always sort of suffered in their own way, only coming to each other once they saw a light at the end of the tunnel. Boone wondered if, this time, he should switch on a floodlight and start waving to Matt.

"And it just goes to Cosette," Boone said, looking at the invoice.

"Yes," Gloria said, her attention getting diverted to another child who'd just arrived. "She knows what it's for. Thanks, Boone." She walked away, greeting the child with enthusiasm and smiles. Boone wondered what her life looked like behind closed doors, and how tired pretending made her.

He opened his mouth to say something, thought better of it, and spun away from Gloria. *Not your business,* he told himself.

Cosette worked out of an office in the big, red barn with the neatly painted white trim. Once Boone dropped off this paperwork, he'd go collect Gerty from the stables, where she worked with the horses in the mornings, and together, they'd go find Matt.

Matt usually went to Chris Hammond's for lunch, where he made the meal for the older gentleman. Boone and Gerty had been tagging along with Matt and his kids so far this summer. In fact, Boone felt like he'd been tagging along after his older brother his whole life. Moving to Ivory Peaks was just another example.

So far, in Boone's opinion, life here was better than it would've been in Montana. Even with Gerty's attitude. Even with her insane statements about how much she liked Michael, and it was perfectly normal for a twelve-year-old girl to like a thirteen-year-old boy.

Boone supposed it was normal, but he'd bucked against the idea so hard, it had taken Matt to calm him down and remind him of the first girl he'd ever had a crush on. Boone had been eleven.

He scratched his hand again, wondering if he'd gotten into something that morning while checking the pastures where the therapy horses who weren't working today got to graze and roam. It sure felt like he had, and he couldn't wait to wash his hands and switch roles from Pony Power over to the main farm.

Gerty and Britt would go back to his cabin for the afternoon, and he'd probably find the two of them at the main farmhouse with Molly Hammond that evening. Gray and Elise had taken their younger kids to Coral Canyon immediately following the open house, and Hunter and Molly now lived on-site.

Boone found their movements in life fascinating. He'd lived at Saffron Lake for so long, never wanting to go anywhere else. He still didn't really want to leave that patch of land behind, and he hadn't listed it for sale yet.

"Howdy, Boone," Travis said, and Boone looked up from the ground.

"Howdy, Trav." He nodded at him, his gaze sliding to the teenager next to him. "Mike."

"Sir." Michael Hammond didn't look nervous or afraid of Boone, but ever since Boone had laid down the law about where he and Gerty could go, and when, and if they should really be alone together or not, Michael hadn't called him anything but *sir*.

Boone supposed he didn't mind the formality. It showed respect, and he'd give Michael credit for that.

"You comin' to the hot dog roast tonight?" Travis asked, turning to walk backward as they passed.

"Wouldn't miss it," Boone said over his shoulder, though the idea of going and socializing made him sigh in exhaustion. The work on the farm in the summer started early and went all day. About the only thing a cowboy could rely on was a slow, hot evening on the back porch, a guitar in his hand and the promise of cooler mountain air that night.

Boone loved summertime, that was for sure, and he did like a good weenie roast. Gerty would love it, and Boone wanted her to spend time with Matt's kids—and Michael, under his supervision—and he couldn't keep her cooped up at home because he didn't want to talk to anyone.

He pulled open the main door of the barn, where all the parents and children came when they first checked in for their therapy sessions. He went past the desk there, where a woman named Dani sat.

"Heya, Boone," she said without looking up from her

novel.

"Howdy, Dani. Is Cosette in her office?"

"Should be."

He kept going into the barn and made the first right. The door to the executive administrator's office sat open, with lilting, flowery music filling the air. "Cosette?" he asked, knocking on the door frame.

She looked up from her work, her eyes the color of a grassy meadow on the side of a hill in Montana. Boone found her extremely pretty. If pressed into a corner, he might even admit he was attracted to her.

At the same time, he wasn't ready to be in a relationship right now, and he had serious doubts that he ever would be again. Likewise, Cosette always seemed as jumpy as a drop of water on a hot skillet when Boone was around, and she got to her feet today, her nerves plain.

"Gloria sent this over for you," he said, stepping into the office and then extending his arm as far as possible while he leaned forward. Doing that, he could drop the paper onto her desk and stay as far from Cosette as he could.

That seemed to be what she wanted—him as far from her as possible. He had apologized for grabbing onto her, and she'd apologized for not watching where she was going. They could work together without it being too terribly difficult. Still, so much awkwardness stemmed between them, and Boone didn't know where it came from or how to eliminate it.

He liked most people, and he got along well with them.

He wasn't sure what he'd done that had been so wrong with Cosette. He just hadn't wanted her to fall or for him to be plowed over.

Rascal.

He wasn't a rascal, he knew that.

"What is it?" Cosette reached for the paper as it fluttered to the desktop.

"Gloria said you'd know what it was," Boone said. "I didn't look at it."

"Oh, it's the invoice for the Myers twins." She glanced up, something softening in those eyes. Some of the tension bled away. "Thanks, Boone."

He reached up and touched the brim of his cowboy hat. "Ma'am." He turned to leave the office, glad this interaction had gone well. He'd strung several of them together over the past couple of weeks, and he hoped that first experience with her would soon fade in her memory.

Why? he asked himself as he left the barn. *Why do you care what Cosette Brian thinks of you? It's not like you're going to date her.*

"Dad," Gerty called, her voice full of excitement.

He couldn't answer the questions in his head once he laid eyes on his daughter. She was fair and beautiful, just like her mother, and Boone loved her with every fiber of his soul. "What's up, baby?"

"Come see the new horses Hunter just bought." She gestured for him to hurry up and follow her, and Boone did just that. His daughter loved horses, and Boone did too. As he joined her, he suddenly knew the answer to his questions.

He wanted to have a good reputation around Ivory Peaks. He was a hard worker, a kind man, full of faith and devotion to his family. He wasn't a rascal, and it bothered him that Cosette had called him that without even knowing him at all.

As he watched Gerty's excitement over the new mare and her foal, he also knew that no, he wasn't going to be dating Cosette—or anyone—any time soon. His focus needed to be on his daughter and fulfilling her needs. Not his.

He thought of Matt, and the last two years he'd taken to really focus on his kids. Once again, his brother had shown him the right path to take, and as Boone settled his foot on the bottom rung of the fence separating him from the new horses, a sense of peace and happiness came over him.

"They're amazing," he said to Gerty, who looked at him with that childlike wonder in her eyes. Love for her filled him, and Boone prayed that he could be the best father for her that he could be.

That would be enough.

CHAPTER 25

*G*loria pulled her tank top over her head and collapsed onto the bed. "I do not want to go to this bonfire tonight."

She did, and she didn't.

She wanted to, because Chris had suggested it, and he was excited for everyone to come. Since Gloria had asked Matt for a break, they'd perfected a delicate dance around lunchtime. They usually ate with Chris, and Matt made delicious sandwiches, wraps, and even salads. With Boone here, however, it had been easier for Gloria not to go.

She didn't know if Chris had asked about her or not. Matt did text her in the morning if he wasn't going to Chris's for lunch, and then Gloria would go. On those occasions, Chris fed her from his fridge.

Hunter and Molly and Michael were staying with him, and the generational house where he lived vibrated with good energy every time Gloria went there.

Tonight, however, she wouldn't be able to avoid Matt. "It's not like you can anyway," she muttered as she reached for her cowgirl boots. She had to coordinate with him for Britt's therapy, and she took Britt out in the stroller at least twice a week, even now. He didn't want anything to change for his kids, and Gloria loved the little girl too.

Someone knocked on her front door, and Gloria called, "Just a sec," as she pulled on her second boot. "Come on in," she said as she hurried down the hall.

The door opened just as she reached the kitchen, and she found Keith entering the cabin. "Hey, Gloria."

"Keith." The name gushed out of her. Since she'd paused things with his father, she hadn't seen the boy all that much. She rushed him now, her maternal instincts taking over. She took him right into a hug. "Hey, baby. How are you?"

He gripped her tightly, and he'd grown up so much in the past couple of years. "I'm good," he said, his voice throaty. He stepped back, his eyes flitting all over the cabin. "Listen, I just wanted to talk to you for a minute before we go to the hot dog roast."

Gloria stepped back, surprised by the surge in her own emotions. She tucked her hands into her back pockets. "Okay."

"First, Kassidy is comin' tonight, and I want you to meet her."

Gloria's eyebrows shot up. "She's coming to the farm? Tonight?"

A smile decorated his face. "Yeah. It's crazy, I know. I shouldn't bring her to something with everyone. It's going to be so loud."

"It'll be fun," Gloria said, suddenly more excited to go to the bonfire. "I can't wait to meet her." She grinned at Keith. "How's your dad handling that?"

"He's what I wanted to talk to you about." Keith cleared his throat, and he took a few more moments to get his gaze to meet hers. When it did, he looked fierce and calm at the same time. "He's so miserable, Gloria. He loves you so much. Britt and I do too, and I just know there has to be a way for you to work it out with him."

He took a giant breath and then another one, and when he reached up and brushed at his eyes, Gloria had to look away. Her own eyes felt so hot, and she blinked rapidly to keep the tears inside.

She didn't know what to say. Keith would be sixteen in a couple of months, but he was still a child. She firmly believed that children didn't need to take on adult problems or responsibilities. He wasn't even her child.

She finally raised her eyes to find he'd ducked his head too, and with his cowboy hat, he could conceal his face easier than she could. A shot of bravery moved through her like a flash of lightning, and she said, "I love you and Britt too."

Keith's head shot up. "You do?"

She nodded, sniffling and knowing she was going to lose the battle against her tears. She never cried, and she didn't want to now either. She drew in a breath and steadied herself. "I...don't know what to say."

"Just give him another chance."

"Does he know you're here?"

"No, ma'am."

"He's not going to like it."

"No, he won't." Keith didn't look ashamed of being there though.

"What has he told you?"

"Nothing," Keith said, sighing in frustration. He took off his hat and ran his hand through his hair in such a classic-Matt-move that Gloria smiled. "He won't say anything, and that's the most maddening part."

Gloria waited, because she sensed there was more to the story.

"I overheard him talking to Uncle Boone this afternoon though. He said he wasn't going to feel guilty for putting his family first, whatever that means."

Guilt gutted Gloria, and she couldn't articulate how she felt. She had not asked him to put her before his family, but in a way, she had. She just wanted to be as important to him as Boone or Hunter, and she hadn't felt like she was.

"Me and Britt are okay," Keith said. "I don't know what he means."

"I do," Gloria said, finding her voice once more. "I told him I felt like he was choosing anyone and everyone over me." By the time she finished speaking, her voice had declined to a whisper. "Essentially, I told him I wanted him to pick me sometimes."

Keith simply looked at her. The silence between them lengthened, until the slamming of a car door tore his attention from her. "That's probably Kassidy. I told her to come to our old cabin." He ducked outside and added, "It is."

He turned back to Gloria, his dark eyes blazing with bright fire. "He's just overprotective."

"I know," Gloria said, her throat closing around the words.

"Let me grab Kassidy." Keith ducked out of the cabin, calling his girlfriend's name. Gloria turned back to the kitchen and tried to gather herself together. She wasn't sure where all the pieces were, so it was harder and took longer than she'd like.

"This is Gloria," Keith said from behind her, and Gloria put a smile on her face before she turned to meet the girl.

Kassidy wore a bright smile too, along with the cutest sundress in blue, yellow, and white. It fell to her knees, where a pair of cowgirl boots rose to meet the hem, and went over her shoulders in wide straps.

She held Keith's hand with a strong grip, but she released him to step forward and greet Gloria.

"It's so great to meet you," Gloria said. "You're such a pretty girl." Her long, auburn hair hung in waves over her shoulders and down her back, and she'd pinned back the sides.

"Thank you," Kassidy said, moving right into Gloria for a hug. She wasn't normally the huggy type of person, but she didn't mind. "Keith's told me so much about you."

"I'm sure none of it's true," Gloria said, squeezing the girl and letting her go.

Kassidy glanced to where he stood smiling at the two of them, and then back to Gloria. "He said you're the best horse trainer he's ever met."

"That's because he's only met one." Gloria smiled at Keith, her heart expanding for the boy in ways she'd never anticipated.

"That's not true," Keith said quietly as Kassidy returned to his side. When he looked at her, the soft feelings he had showed spectacularly on his face. He faced Gloria again. "I better go. Dad's waiting to meet Kassidy too."

Horror flowed through Gloria. "Don't tell him I met her first."

Keith grinned at her. "I value my life more than that." He took Kassidy's hand. "Come on, let's go find him. He's probably pacing down at the fire pit." He flashed Gloria a smile and a wave, and then he led Kassidy out of the cabin.

Gloria followed them to the doorway and then the top of the steps. She remembered what it was like to be young and "in love," and as she stood there, she realized that the one person she thought of when she reflected on that time of her life, twenty years ago...was Matt.

A sob caught somewhere between her stomach and her

heart, making her torso tight and breathing difficult.

Fifteen days had passed since she'd told Matt she needed a break to figure out what she wanted. A break to decide if she'd rather be in his life in tenth or eleventh place than not at all.

As Keith's and Kassidy's footsteps faded and the silence returned, Gloria had her answer. She hated her nights alone, with only a microwave to keep her fed and a television to keep the silence from infecting her mind.

"How do I get him back?" she asked herself. She repeated the question for the Lord, and ideas began to flash through her head. She dismissed all of them, because she wasn't the type of person who liked the spotlight on her. She didn't make a big deal of things.

Most importantly, Matt didn't either.

He wasn't a simple man, but he liked simplicity, Gloria knew that. Good food, and good friends, and a good horse.

"Does he really have room for me?" Gloria wondered as she turned back to her cabin. "Can I really just sit beside him tonight and see what he does?"

She wasn't the best cook in the world, but he'd said he liked her cinnamon rolls. Perhaps she could get up early and make those for him tomorrow. She could leave them in the hay barn here at the farm, where Matt went every morning when he got to work. Maybe a card, telling him how sorry she was and that she'd like their second chance to become forever.

"That's stupid," she muttered. She wasn't going to

apologize to him through *a card*. No, it had to be done face-to-face. With plenty of frosting.

Tomorrow was the Sabbath, and she knew exactly where Matt would be, at what times. He didn't bring the kids out to the farm until afternoon on Sundays, as Hunter took care of the morning feedings.

Knowing Matt as she did, he wouldn't be sleeping in either. Cinnamon rolls tomorrow morning could work....

"Tell me if I shouldn't do this," Gloria whispered as she reached for her cowgirl hat and placed it on her head. The Lord didn't do any such thing, and she took a steeling breath before she left her cabin.

"Please bless him to be forgiving," she prayed as she went down the steps. "I do love him, and I do love those kids. What Keith said is true. There has to be a way for us to make it work."

She wasn't sure, but Gloria had never shied away from a challenge. She told herself this as she walked down the lane lined with cabins and around the end one to the wide backyard of the farmhouse. The fire pit already had blazing flames spouting from it, and several people had gathered around.

Matt was definitely one of them, as he stood with Keith and Kassidy, a smile stuck to his face Gloria could see from two hundred yards away.

"You took your ex-fiancé to court," she told herself. "You lived out of your truck for two weeks. You worked on that almost-broken ankle for nearly a month before Daddy made you go to the hospital. You can make some cinnamon rolls and go apologize to the man you love."

Determined in her plan, and marveling that Gloria had admitted that she was in love with Matthew Whettstein, she walked straight over to the bonfire.

att saw Gloria coming toward the roasting area, and his first instinct was to find her a place to sit. Preferably next to him. Then he could hold her hand and listen to her soothing voice for the whole evening.

Then he remembered that they barely spoke in person these days. Texts didn't seem to be off-limits, and he was glad for that. He might have gone completely crazy had he not been able to text her and talk to her about Britt, or let her know that Chris would be alone for lunch that day.

On this fine June evening, Gloria wore a pair of jeans that hugged her legs to her calf and then flared over a pair of cowgirl boots. Her bright teal tank top showed off her muscular arms and slim shoulders and made everything male inside him flare to life.

He was aware of his son speaking, but Matt couldn't focus on the words. Not with Gloria so near, at such a casual event. If they'd been at work, he'd have something else to occupy his mind.

You have to get her back, he thought, but he had no idea how to do that.

"Matt'll know," Boone said, and he turned toward his brother.

"Hey," Matt said, his mind still on Gloria. He glanced at Boone and the man next to him. "Evening, Chris. How are you?" He stepped forward and embraced the older gentleman. "I know Hunter brought out a chair just for you." He looked around for the other man, but he couldn't see Hunter.

"I can stand for a minute," Chris said, and Matt watched Gloria ease into a conversation with Cosette and Travis, a few people away from him. He didn't want to stare at her, but he couldn't help himself. He swallowed just thinking about spending a couple of hours with, but absolutely without, her tonight. He wasn't sure he could do it.

He started making contingency plans for his kids should he need to leave. Kassidy had driven out to the farm, and she could bring Keith home. Britt could sleep over with Gerty. Easy. Done. Matt could leave any time he wanted, and his muscles twitched to do that right now.

"Chris was wondering how many beef cattle Hunter got this year."

"Let's see," Matt said, blowing out his breath. "He asked everyone if they wanted one." Matt and Boone had signed up together to split the cow. "I think we've got fifteen on the farm this year."

"That boy has more ideas than anyone I know." Chris shook his head, but pride so clearly emanated from him. "Where does he come up with raising beef cows for the cowboys here?"

"I think it's a great idea," Matt said. "You've got the land."

"It's a good idea," Chris said. "I just don't know where he comes up with them."

"Probably while he's doing his crossword puzzles," Matt said, smiling. "I find my best ideas come when I allow my mind to quiet down."

"Grampa," Hunter said, arriving on the scene. "Come sit down. Molly's got those blondie bars you like." He put his arm around the older gentleman, his love for his grandfather etched in every line on his youthful face. "Then I need to ask you something about one of the charities at work."

Chris allowed himself to be led away by Hunter, who nodded at Boone and Matt before they left. Matt wanted a blondie bar too, because every baked good Molly had a hand in creating melted in his mouth. He moved over to the two long tables they'd used for the open house a few weeks ago and found fruit salad, water bottles, lemonade, hot dog buns, hot dogs, potato salad, and rocky road brownies. Molly arrived with a tray of blondies and set it in the only remaining spot.

She wiped her brow and surveyed the food. "I think

there's enough."

Matt grinned at her, so glad he knew these good people. "Mols, there's more than enough."

She looked at him and then the still-gathering crowd. "Have you seen how much you cowboys eat?" She shook her head, her eyes catching on Hunter and his grandfather. "It's unbelievable."

"It takes a lot of muscles to work a farm," Matt said, reaching for a plate and then a couple of hot dogs.

"You sound just like my husband." She grinned in a way that said she didn't mind at all, loaded a plate with blondie bars, and said, "Excuse me, Matt. Eat as much as you want."

He nodded at her and put more hot dogs on his plate. He went to get Britt, Keith, and Kassidy, and the four of them found sticks and places around the fire to cook their dinner. His kids talked and laughed with each other, other cowboys, and Matt, but every time he saw a flash of teal, he was reminded of how very alone he was.

After about forty minutes, after almost everyone had eaten and dusk had fallen, Matt leaned closer to his son. "If I left, could you get a ride home with Kassidy?"

Keith looked at him with alarm. "Why would you leave?"

Matt told himself not to, but he looked over to Gloria, who sat next to Travis, chatting. "I'm just not feeling like staying."

"Dad," Keith said. "Just go sit by her. She's got an empty seat over there."

Gloria did have an empty seat on her right, and her whole body was turned left, toward the people she was conversing with. If he sat down, would she even notice him? He'd been watching her since the moment she arrived, and as far as he could tell, she hadn't looked his way once.

He shook his head. "It's been a long week. I just want to go home."

"I can drive him home, sir," Kassidy said. "Britt too."

"I'll talk to her," Matt said with a nod. "Thanks, Kassidy." He turned away even as Keith tried to protest again. He cut his son a look that said *Drop it,* and Keith fell silent.

Britt sat on a blanket with Gerty, Michael, and Steele Harris, the boy from the farm next door. He was close to Britt's age, and he seemed like a nice kid. Matt had met his mom a time or two, but he didn't know where she was at the moment.

"Britt," he said, crowding in close and talking low. "I'm going to head home. Uncle Boone is in charge of you, okay? Kassidy is going to give you and Keith a ride home. You be real polite and listen now, okay?"

Britt turned toward him, her eyes wide and innocent. "Why are you leaving?"

"I don't feel too good," he said, flashing her a smile. "I just need some peace and quiet."

She squished her hands against both of his cheeks. "Okay. Love you, Daddy."

"Love you too, baby." He got up and went to find his

brother, who thankfully stood near the back of the group of chairs all crowded around the bonfire. "I'm headed home."

Boone said nothing as he lifted his lemonade bottle to his lips. "You don't have to leave."

"I do," Matt said. "I can't breathe here." He took a breath, trying to get the air to fill his lungs. It refused. "Kassidy has a car, and she's going to bring the kids home for me. Will you just keep an eye on Britt for me?" He glanced over to where Keith and Kassidy had smashed themselves into a single chair. "And my hormonal son?" Maybe he shouldn't leave after all.

"Of course," Boone said, and he met Matt's eye. "I think you should walk over to Gloria and ask her if she'd like to go with you. She doesn't look like she's having all that much fun either."

Matt looked at her, and her conversation with Travis had died. She looked around at the others nearby, and she did seem a bit lost. "I don't know what to say."

"You say, 'I'm in love with you, and I'll put you first from now on.'" Boone drained the last of his lemonade while Matt's heart flopped around inside his chest. He'd never told Boone anything about what Gloria had said.

"You're miserable, brother," Boone said. "A blind man can see it. Go get her. Go now."

"She wanted a break," Matt murmured.

"No," Boone said, and he sounded like he knew. How he did, Matt wasn't sure. "What she wants is for you to choose her. Pick her."

"I have to pick my kids sometimes."

"Not tonight," Boone said, and he took a few steps away to put his empty bottle in a recycling can. When he returned, he looked right into Matt's eyes. "Tonight, you're choosing yourself. You're leaving your kids here with me, and you're slinking away in the night, because you're afraid to talk to her."

Challenge and defiance rose within him. But he couldn't deny what his brother had said. "I am afraid to talk to her," he said. "Last time, it went so badly."

"Here's what you say, one more time." Boone offered him a smile that barely touched his lips. "You walk over there, and you lean down, and you whisper in her ear: Gloria, I miss you so much. I love you, and I will put you first from now on. Will you please come talk to me?"

Matt looked over to her again. She put a spoonful of vanilla ice cream in her mouth, and Matt wanted to taste it so badly. He swallowed. "You make it sound so easy."

"Take one step," Boone said. "Say one word. It'll be easy after that."

Matt nodded, but it still took him a good minute or two to take that first step. The second wasn't any easier, and his back actually complained at him as he leaned down.

His voice betrayed him by breaking over her name. He cleared his throat, her tension filling the entire sky around them. Boone's words scrambled and left his mind, and Matt could only come up with, "I'm in love with you. Can we talk?"

CHAPTER 27

*G*loria's muscles seized the moment Matt touched her back. She'd known it was him, because the gentle pressure could only come from him. Her heartbeat had gone from strolling to galloping when his voice broke on her name.

He'd said he loved her, and a melty, oozy feeling moved through Gloria.

She turned toward him, getting the scent of clean clothes, something woodsy, and chocolate, most likely from the brownies on the tables behind her. If she angled her face just a little more, and he moved forward a couple of inches, she could kiss him.

Her brain screamed at her about all the spectators, and she managed to say, "Now?"

"Now would be great," he said, pulling back, taking the delicious heat of his hand with him and retreating from her. She wanted to grab onto his face and pull him in for a kiss.

Instead, she got to her feet as she said, "Okay."

He faded into the background, moving toward the house and the farm at the same time. She looked around for his kids, and she spotted Britt sitting on a blanket with the other kids near her age. She had no idea where Keith was. Her eyes found Boone, and he nodded at her, his face stoic as his gaze switched to his brother's retreating back.

Gloria hurried to keep up with Matt, who reached back for her as she drew closer. She easily slipped her hand into his, and it felt like all of her cells finally aligned. They knew how to hold Matt Whettstein's hand, and they'd been completely scattered for the past fifteen days.

"Where are we going?" she asked.

"I don't know," he murmured. They went around the side of the farmhouse, and all the cars and trucks came into view from those who'd driven over for the hot dog roast. He slowed, his hand in hers tightening. "We could just sit in my truck. It's kind of windy out here."

"You want to sit in your truck?" She wasn't sure why that surprised her, only that it did. "I think we're too old to sneak away from a party and go parking."

He looked at her, his smile slow, somewhat sober, and oh-so-sexy.

"I was going to bring you cinnamon rolls in the morning," she blurted out. "And apologize, and beg you to forgive me, and then hopefully we could just forget that the past two weeks have happened, and you'd kiss me and tell me we're going to be okay."

Matt absorbed what she said while Gloria gulped at the thickening night air. "Is that what you want, Gloria? For us to be okay?"

She looked out over the farm in front of them, the barns and stables where she dedicated so much of her time and energy. "More than anything," she whispered. "I love you, Matthew Whettstein, though you have one ridiculously long name and I have no right to love you when I told you I wanted a break."

He reached over with his free hand, turning his body into hers to do so. He curled his fingers along the side of her face, and she leaned into the touch, closing her eyes to truly experience it. He guided her to face him, and his eyes searched hers once she opened hers.

"You think my name is ridiculously long?"

She shrugged, trying a smile on. It didn't fit too harshly, and one danced along the corners of Matt's mouth too.

"You love me?"

"Yes," she said.

"I love you too." He leaned down as if he'd kiss her, but Gloria tensed. "What?"

"That's it? Just like that? We're okay?"

"I was hoping so," he said. "But I can see not." He put a touch more distance between them. "I ate way too many desserts. Can we at least go sit on the tailgate or something?"

Gloria gestured for him to lead the way, which he did. He lowered the tailgate on his truck, and they both hopped up. He immediately put his arm around her, and Gloria thought she'd always had the best view of the sunset while she rollerbladed with her horses.

She'd been wrong.

Sitting in the back of Matt's truck, cuddled into his side, was the only way to watch the sun set.

"I'll still take the cinnamon rolls in the morning," he said.

"Even after all of your desserts tonight?" she teased.

"If I can see you, yes," he said seriously. "I will put you first, Gloria. Well, I guess I can't promise that. I do have Keith to worry about, and Britt takes up a lot of my time now that she's ten going on twenty." He sounded half-tired and half-sarcastic, and Gloria wrapped her arms around him.

"I can help you with them," she said. "If you'd let me, I could help you with them."

"Yeah," he said. "We need to talk about that."

"You don't want me to?"

"I do want you to," he said. "But I think we should talk to the kids about it and make sure we all know going in what your role is, what my role is, and how they'll treat us both."

She nodded. "Okay." She wanted to tell him Keith had stopped by earlier, but she didn't. If he wanted his dad to know, he could tell Matt. "I love those kids as if they were my own."

"Mm, I know you do." He pressed a kiss to her temple. "Thank you for that. I'm a lot to handle, and you have to take on three of us."

"You're not a lot to handle," she said. "I didn't mean to make you feel like that."

"It's true, whether you made me feel like that or not," he said. "Which you didn't." He sighed into the sky. "I want to be there for Boone, because he's really struggling right now. But Gloria, I can't live without you. I'm miserable, and I can't think straight, and I will do everything I can to make sure you know you're number one in my life, even if I have to choose Keith sometimes, or Britt sometimes, or Boone sometimes."

"I don't want to take you from your family."

"I want you to *be* my family."

"I want that too."

He ran his hand up and down her arm. "So can I kiss you now?"

Gloria's smile filled her whole face now, and she turned her face toward his. "Oh, all right." She kissed him, and she poured everything she felt into every stroke, every touch, and every breath, hoping he would know how very miserable she'd been without him too.

He finally pulled away and tucked her back into his side. "I'm an old man, Gloria."

"You are not," she said. "You're forty-one. That's hardly old."

"It is to be having babies."

She pulled away and looked at him, her eyes widening. "You want more kids?"

"I do if you want one of your own," he said. "You did, once."

Gloria faced the sunset again, searching her feelings. In her younger years, she'd fantasized about what a baby who came from her and Matt would look like. She hadn't thought about that in a very long time.

"I'm thirty-eight," she said. "I'll be thirty-nine in the fall."

"It's only the very beginning of the summer," he said.

She didn't think it was possible, but her eyes widened even further. "You want to get married *this* summer?"

He grinned at her. "I do if you do." He nuzzled her neck and kissed his way up to her ear. "Who do you need to invite, sweetheart? I just need to let my folks know, but they won't come anyway."

"Your mom might," she said, her voice caught somewhere behind the desire raging through her throat. Could she really become this man's wife before the end of the summer? Her mind rebelled against the idea, but in a small corner hidden in the back of it, a voice whispered, *Why not?*

"She might," he conceded. "But two months or eight isn't going to make a difference. Boone's here. The farm is available, I'm sure. You'll go get a dress, and I'll get a tux, and we'll get it done. I even know a pastor."

"Are you proposing tonight then?"

"No," he said quickly, pulling away. "Absolutely not. Just...feeling out the situation."

"And how does it feel?"

Matt pulled her close and wrapped her up in both arms. "To me, it feels like the right thing to do. It feels like joy. It feels like a bright future, with a family I want to come home to every single night."

Gloria knew he hadn't always had that, and as she gazed at the last of the sunlight before it disappeared, she could see that future too. She and Matt were blissfully happy in that gray brick house. Keith and Britt were there, with horses in the back pasture. Dogs. And another, smaller child with eyes as deep as midnight, like his father, and hair that reminded her of the sand on the beach, like his mother.

"All right," she said with a sigh. "I suppose if this handsome, kind, strong cowboy I'm in love with asked me to marry him this summer, I'd say yes."

Matt chuckled, and Gloria joined her giggle to his. "Good to know," he said just before kissing her again.

THE NEXT MORNING, GLORIA PARKED IN FRONT of Matt's house, collected the long aluminum tray of cinnamon rolls, and headed for the front door. The clock had barely touched eight-thirty, but Gloria had been up at dawn to get the dough made, give it time to rise, and then shaped. Then more rising, and then finally the baking.

No one came out before she reached the porch, which surprised her a little. She and Matt hadn't gone back to the party last night, but they'd stayed on his tail gate, talking, until others had started leaving. His kids had never come, and he told her he'd made other arrangements for them so he could spend all of his attention on her.

He'd walked her back to her cabin, and he'd kissed her so completely on her front porch that Gloria had regretted the past two weeks without him even more. When she'd apologized again, he'd covered her lips with his finger and said, *Enough. Your feelings are and were valid. You don't need to keep apologizing for them.*

She knocked on his front door and adjusted the tray so it wouldn't fall. She'd used one of those disposable ones, and they bent so easily if they weren't supported properly.

"I'll get it!" Britt yelled from the other side of the door. A male said something in response, but whether that was Keith or Matt, Gloria couldn't tell. Some scuffling came on the other side of the door, and Gloria backed up a step, expecting Pearl to come barreling out of the house once the door opened.

Britt finally pulled the door open, and her face lit up. "Gloria." Her therapy dog, Pearl, did accompany her, but she stayed right at Britt's side. "What is that?"

"Cinnamon rolls," she said, crouching down so the girl could see. Pearl's nose started working, but she didn't move a muscle. She really was well-trained, and Gloria reached out and patted her too. "I brought breakfast to share with y'all. You haven't eaten, have you?"

"Nope," Britt said. "Come in. Daddy's not even dressed yet."

"Yes, I am," Matt said, but he was pulling a shirt over his head as he entered the living room. "I could smell that frosting all the way down the hall." He beamed at her as he came closer, and he took the cinnamon rolls in one large hand and swept the other along her waist. "Hey, sweetheart." He kissed her right there in front of his daughter, only breaking their connection long enough to say, "Britt, go get your brother up. Tell him Gloria brought breakfast for him, and he better be in a good mood about it."

"Okay, Daddy." Britt skipped away, calling for Pearl to go with her.

Matt set the cinnamon rolls on the back of the couch and stepped Gloria backward to get her out onto the porch. He pulled the door closed and kissed her again. Happiness beamed through Gloria's whole soul, and she smiled against his mouth.

"I love you," he whispered. "I love seeing you in the morning. I love seeing you at night. I want to be with you all the time."

Gloria was never as good as him at articulating her feelings, but she did say, "I love you too, Matt," before kissing him again. When she broke the kiss, she said, "You better ask me to marry you soon, and then we'll both get what we want."

"I'm working on a plan," he said.

The door behind him opened, and Keith said, "Oh,

they are out here." He looked past his father to Gloria, a knowing smile touching his lips. "Yeah, I think Gloria dropped her keys." He stepped back into the house. "Dad's helping her find them. Let's take the cinnamon rolls into the kitchen, sissy." His voice faded as he closed the door again, and Gloria giggled as she buried her face in Matt's chest.

He laughed too and said, "He's helping me with the proposal."

"I'm glad." She looked up at him, and everything in the world stilled into pure perfection. She couldn't believe how different this morning was from the one previous, and she closed her eyes and thanked God above that Matt had such a forgiving heart.

CHAPTER 28

"Can you turn the phone around, Britt?" Matt closed his eyes as his daughter clearly did not know where the camera was on her phone.

"My word," Keith muttered beside him. "You should've let me go in."

"It's right here, Daddy," Britt said over the video. "Can you see it?"

"No, baby, because the camera is at the top of the phone. Remember Keith showed you where it was?" Matt spoke in his most patient voice, the one he used with his most difficult goats—and apparently his daughter.

"Oh, just a sec." She started flinging the phone around again, and Matt looked away from the violent images on the screen. He grinned at Keith, who just shook his head.

"I couldn't have you go in," he said. "Then it really would be like breaking and entering."

"Having Britt pretend to be sick so she can root through a jewelry box is hardly different," he said dryly.

"But Gloria let her in," Matt argued back. He wanted to ask Gloria to be his wife, but he also knew she wanted to wear her mother's diamond ring as her own. He wanted to know if she had it in her house, and if so, if he could somehow "borrow" it and use it during the proposal.

As he'd talked about it with his kids, Britt had actually come up with a pretty great idea.

"There," she said. "I got it to work."

Matt looked at the screen again, and sure enough, the image now showed the inside of a jewelry box.

"I think it's that black box, Daddy," Britt said. "Should I open it?"

"Yeah, go ahead and open it," he said. Matt wasn't exactly sure what the setting looked like, but he figured he'd know.

Britt sprung the top on the box and sure enough, an older, aged ring sat there.

"It needs to be cleaned," Matt said. Maybe he should do that before the proposal. He immediately rejected the idea, because that would take time. He didn't want Gloria to realize the ring was missing before he asked her, and he didn't want to wait another day.

"This is it, right, Daddy?" Britt swung the phone around to face her, and he got a screen-full of her light green eye.

"Yes, baby." He smiled and lowered his phone. "Can

you put it in your pocket and sneak it to the back door? I'm sending Keith over right now."

He and his son turned as the door opened. They'd sequestered themselves in the storage shed on the farm, because no one ever came in here.

"Shoot," Keith muttered, ducking down.

Matt did the same, though he wasn't sure why. He could mute the call, shove his phone in his back pocket, and see who'd come inside. He was allowed to be inside the storage shed, for crying out loud.

He straightened and did all of that, moving toward the door. "Oh, hey, Mike. What's up?"

Michael looked relieved to see him. "My granddad said there's some old war boxes out here? He wanted me to get them for him."

Matt turned down the first aisle in the shed. "Yeah, I think I saw them over here."

"What is all this stuff?" Michael asked. "Personal stuff? Or farm stuff?"

"Oh, this place has a little bit of all of it," Matt said with a smile. "I think those are the boxes from your granddad's time in the war." A pair of rough-hewn, navy blue boxes sat on the shelf at Matt's eye level. "He got a couple of medals, I thought."

"Yeah, he wanted to show them to me," Michael said. "I told him I'm thinking about joining the military when I get older."

Matt's surprise sent his eyebrows up. "Really? Good for you."

"Don't tell my dad," Michael said, reaching for the first box. "All he ever talks about is HMC and how I'll take over there once Hunter is ready to retire from being the CEO."

"You don't want to do that?"

Michael shrugged and stacked the second box on top of the first. "I'm not...Hunter."

"What does that mean?" Keith asked, coming down the aisle behind them. "You're a Hammond."

"Not one of the smart ones," Michael said. He bumped Keith's fist. "What are you guys doing out here?" He looked from Keith to Matt.

"My dad's stealing his girlfriend's ring so he can ask her to marry him with it."

"Keith," Matt said, chastising him. "We're not stealing it," he assured Michael. "Besides, I'm not doing anything. You're supposed to go get the ring from Britt right now."

"Yes, sir." Keith grinned as he saluted, and he and Michael left the storage shed together. Matt quickly pulled out his phone, but the call with Britt had ended.

He's coming, he texted to her, and he hoped that Gloria wouldn't see her phone or any of the messages.

Five minutes later, Matt got another text, this one from Keith. *The shipment is secure. I repeat, the shipment is secure.*

He grinned as he sagged against the door of the shed. It was starting to get hot in there, and Matt had work to do.

"Tonight," he told himself as he opened the door and let the fresh air hit him in the face. "You'll ask her tonight."

"WE DON'T HAVE TO GO," GLORIA TOLD HIM later that afternoon. She glanced at him as she looped the reins of a horse over the top rung of the fence.

Matt stroked the cream-colored horse's face. "Why wouldn't we go?" The ring Keith had passed him half an hour ago felt like a fifty-pound brick in his front pocket. He worked hard not to move his hand there. She couldn't see it. He told himself over and over that she couldn't see it.

"Britt's not well." Gloria faced him, obviously confused and concerned. "You got my text, right? I took her back to my house to take a nap. When I stopped by an hour ago, she was conked out on the couch."

Matt swallowed, not sure what to say. He didn't want to lie to Gloria. "It's Stephen Mustave. You love him, and he doesn't come to Colorado very often."

"It's a concert," she said. "There will be other concerts. I get it if you'd rather stay home with your *sick daughter*." She stared at him, a level of disbelief in her eyes.

Matt reached into his pocket. "Okay, so I was going to do this tonight, but I really don't want to lie to you."

Gloria folded her arms. "Lie to me?" The fire raging in her gaze made Matt swallow and reassess everything he'd just said.

"Britt's not sick," he said. "We created a little...ruse, so she could get inside your house legally."

"You're using a lot of words I don't like," Gloria said, her eyes narrowing. "Ruse? Legally?"

Matt dropped to both knees, right there between two stables, with a cream-colored horse named Underbelly watching. "I'm in love with you. I want to marry you. I want to be your husband, and there's nothing I want more than for you to be my wife, my partner, my best friend, and the mother of my children."

He withdrew his hand and held up the ring. "I know how much your mama meant to you. So yes, Britt and Keith and I came up with a plan to get this ring from your jewelry box. Technically, there was no stealing or breaking or entering involved, as you let Britt into the cabin." He grinned at her. "She's just tired, because she stayed up too late last night drawing plans for how we could get the ring out through a window."

Gloria's eyes widened as she stared at the ring. Joy filled her expression when she looked at Matt.

"Will you marry me?" he asked.

Gloria didn't hesitate at all before she said, "Yes. Yes, I'll marry you." She laughed and swiped at her eyes with her right hand while she held out her left. Matt slipped her mother's wedding ring onto the appropriate finger and rose to his feet.

He took her into his arms, cradled her face, and kissed her. The air vibrated around them with the emotions streaming between the two of them, and Matt honestly couldn't wait the two months before he could kiss this woman and then call her his wife.

"I love you," he murmured against her lips. "I know I'm not perfect, and I'm going to mess up again. But I love you, and that's not going to change."

"I love you too," she said. "I'm not perfect either." She looked up at him. "We just have to *try*, Matt. We have to forgive each other."

"No breaks," he said.

"No breaks," she promised, and when she kissed him this time, Matt lost himself to the taste, the scent, and the touch of his fiancée.

Keep reading for the first two chapters of **HIS THIRD TRY**, which features Matt's brother, Boone, and the administrative assistant at Pony Power, Cosette!

SNEAK PEEK! HIS THIRD TRY
CHAPTER ONE

*B*oone Whettstein pulled up to his brother's house, and all the balloons in the cab of his truck flew forward, booping him in the back of the head. He swatted at them while his daughter, Gerty, giggled and did the same.

Boone could listen to her laughter all day, every day, and he grinned at her. "You get the cake, and I'll get the balloons?" he suggested.

"No way," Gerty said. "I want to take in the balloons. I'll just drop the cake."

"Why would you drop the cake?" Boone put the truck in park and looked up at Matt's front windows. He was getting married in the morning, but tonight was his son's sixteenth birthday. Boone loved living near his brother again, and he'd missed Matt and his kids when they'd left Montana a couple of years ago.

He'd never in his wildest dreams thought he'd follow

Matt to Ivory Peaks, Colorado, but he wasn't unhappy that he had. In fact, Boone was happier now than he'd been in a long, long time—even when he'd been with Karley, before he'd known about her infidelity.

"Because I'm tripping over everything lately," Gerty said. "You get the cake, Daddy, please?"

"Yeah, sure," he said easily. He could carry a cake as easily as he could a bunch of balloons, and he opened the door to get out of the truck. Gerty did the same on her side, and she gathered all the blue, white, purple, and green ribbons together to get the bunch of balloons back together.

With all those floating orbs gone, he collected the big, pink pastry box. He'd been more than willing to stop in town and get all the things Matt needed for the party, because he had about fifteen hundred things on his plate right now.

Boone turned as a car engine filled the country silence on his brother's street. A pick-up truck full of cowboys pulled up to the curb, with another one not far behind. The second one only held a single person—Matt's fiancée —and Boone grinned at Gloria Munson.

"Need any help, Boone?" she asked as she got out of her truck. She stood back, and a golden retriever jumped down from the cab too.

"Yeah, my gift is still in there." He nodded toward the back seat as Gloria approached. Gerty had gone ahead to the front door, which now stood open, and Matt came down the front steps to welcome everyone.

"Did you get it?" Matt asked, arriving at Boone's truck too.

"Right there," Boone said, nodding to the wrapped package on the back seat. "Gloria was going to grab it for me."

"And we're a go for everything?" He looked at Gloria, slid his arm around her and kissed her. "Hey, sweetheart. You look fantastic."

"Hey, baby." She beamed up at him, and Boone's jealousy soared toward the sky.

He turned away from the truck, the weight of the enormous cake shifting in his hands. He steadied it and said, "Someone just needs to grab it, please."

"I'll get it," Gloria said. "We're a go for later, yes."

"Perfect," Matt said. "Thank you both." He turned toward the cowboys crossing his lawn and started greeting them. Boone knew them all too, because they all worked at the Hammond Family Farm, about fifteen minutes from downtown Ivory Peaks—if such a small town could have a downtown.

Ivory Peaks did, and it housed a Cowboy Church, a general store, a small grocery store, two gas stations, a barber and salon that shared the space—men on one side and women on the other—and a pet supply store. A couple of restaurants, a dollar store, and the elementary school rounded out Main Street, and Boone sure did like the town.

He liked the huge mountains to the west, even if he was used to seeing them in the east. Well, all around, if he was being honest. Montana seemed covered with hills and mountains and snow—and sky.

He looked up into the Colorado sky and drew a deep breath before going up the steps to Matt's house. Since it was the height of summer, he had all the windows closed and the air conditioning pumping hard.

Thank you, Lord, Boone thought, because he spent far too many hours outside without the cooled air. He went past the men and women milling about in the living room, waiting for the party to start, and into the kitchen, where he slid the cake box onto the counter.

Keith stood there with his friends, and Boone grinned at him. "There you are. I haven't seen you yet today." He stole a hug from his nephew, clapping him heartily on the back. "Happy birthday, bud."

"Thanks, Uncle Boone." Keith laughed, and it sure did Boone's heart good to see how happy Keith was. He hoped Gerty would achieve something similar after acclimating to her new school, a new house, and hopefully new friends.

They'd moved here at the beginning of the summer, and she'd spent the past few months with her cousins, a boy who lived at the farm next door to where they lived, adults, and horses. His daughter loved horses more than people, which actually worried Boone. He wanted her to fit in here; he'd been praying for eighty-two solid days and nights that Gerty would find just one friend in the junior high on the outskirts of Denver, another ten minutes past Ivory Peaks.

Just one, he thought as he released Keith.

"These are my friends," Keith said. "Jordy, Luis, Dalton, and Bennie."

"Nice to meet you fellas," Boone said. "Where's Kassidy?"

"She and Izzy are coming in a minute," Keith said, looking toward the front door. "My Uncle Boone. My dad's brother."

"Nice to meet you, sir," chorused around, and Boone looked at the kids.

"Any of you have siblings that will be in eighth grade?"

"I got a brother who'll be in eighth grade," Luis said, and Boone didn't correct him on the grammar. "His name's Alberto."

Boone nodded.

"My sister is going into seventh," Jordy said. "Is Gerty going into eighth?"

"Yep." Boone looked around for the mass of balloons, and they stood over by the garage entrance. "There she is, behind that mass of balloons."

Keith's face lit up, and he went to help Gerty. He took some of them from her, and they started tying the balloons to the backs of chairs, rails on the lamps, and even the handle of the fridge.

"This is her," Boone said when Gerty came into the kitchen with Keith. He introduced her around to his friends, though they were all a few years older than her. Boone just watched, because Gerty was a pretty girl, and she'd liked a boy named Michael Hammond all summer.

He'd be fourteen in November, and Gerty had turned thirteen several weeks ago.

Boone had spent more time on his knees this summer than any other, because he could see the changes in his daughter. She'd been wearing a bra before she needed one, but when she needed new undergarments now, she went with another woman.

Before they'd moved to Colorado, that had been Boone's steady girlfriend, Karley. This past summer, he'd let her go with Molly Hammond and Gloria, who both worked at the farm where Boone and Gerty lived.

Matt and Gloria finally came inside the house and closed the front door, leaving Boone to wonder what had taken them so long. He knew, because they were set to be married tomorrow. It wasn't hard to figure out that they'd snuck away to kiss for a few minutes.

"All right," his brother called into the chaos. "I think we're ready to start." He waited a couple of seconds while conversations finished, and people turned their attention toward him. "We've got tables and chairs outside on the deck and in the yard. There's pizza and cheesy bread. Some of those garlic knots and the cinnamon twists. Keith set up the volleyball net, and Britt got out all the roller skates and long boards we own or could find. There's a big cement pad back there for that, and we can put the sprinkler on it."

He looked around at the group, and Boone could read the expression on his brother's face. He was overwhelmed with love and gratitude for all the people who'd come to celebrate this birthday with his son.

"Thank you all for coming," he said, his voice thick. "We'll eat first and do presents after that. Right, Keith?"

"Sounds good, Dad."

"Okay, let's pray first, and then you can lead us out."

Cowboy hats started getting removed, as most people had left theirs on as they'd all end up outside again anyway.

"Gray, would you pray?" Matt asked, and Boone's eyes flew to the tall cowboy who acted as patriarch at the family farm where he worked. Technically, Gray Hammond signed Boone's paychecks, but he'd been gone all summer. He and his family went to Wyoming for the summer months, and they'd only just returned yesterday. Apparently, he and his wife usually stayed until later in August, but they'd wanted to be here for Keith's birthday party and Matt's wedding.

That made sense, because Matt had been working for Gray as the caretaker and foreman of his farm for seventeen years now. For fifteen of those, he'd just come down in the summer and run the farm while Gray and Elise left town. Now, he lived here permanently and worked there full-time.

Gray didn't do much around the farm anymore, as he was close to sixty years old. His son, Hunter, had been living there all summer, and he and his wife had opened and currently operated Pony Power, a children's equine therapy unit.

"Of course," Gray said, and he bowed his head. "Dear Lord, we thank Thee for the opportunity to gather as friends and family. It's such a blessing to be able to get together, and please bless each of us to look for ways to serve those around us, some of whom might even be right here at this party. Bless this year for Keith Whettstein, that it'll be one of his best, and bless his family, especially Matt and Gloria, who are getting married tomorrow. Bless those who haven't arrived yet, that they'll do so safely, and bless us all with Thy spirit of guidance and the bravery to go where Thou leads us. Amen."

"Amen," echoed through the house, and the front door opened. Kassidy and her girlfriend entered the house, and instead of leading everyone out the back door to the deck, Keith went toward the front.

"This way," Boone said, his voice plenty loud enough to get people to follow him. He led the way out to the back deck, where the noise of conversation and laughter didn't get quite so trapped and reverberate around inside his head quite so much.

Outside, he started opening the pizza boxes as the line queued up behind him. He didn't actually take any food— until the end of the line and those delicious, buttery cinnamon twists. He did nab one of those and take a crunchy, sweet bite as he got out of the way.

A cheer went up inside the house, and he looked through the glass doors where people were still coming out. Wes Hammond had walked in, and he'd brought his wife and children with him. Boone immediately looked for

Michael, and he found the boy right beside Gerty.

Of course.

He frowned, and then got over it. Michael would go home in three days, and Gerty would have to figure out her own friendships here in Colorado.

"Mike," he called, and the boy looked his way. "Your family is here."

"They are?" He swung his attention back toward the house, immediately starting that way. He pushed back through the crowd, and Boone watched through the glass as he ran toward his mom and dad, throwing himself into his father's arms first. Wes grinned as wide as the lake that used to sit outside Boone's front door, and Boone could admit that their relationship touched his heart.

Michael Hammond was a good boy. He'd worked tirelessly around the farm this summer, separated from his own family, and living with his cousin and his grandfather as his only support. He probably hadn't been any happier to be in Ivory Peaks than Gerty had been, and they'd probably been good for each other.

Boone switched his gaze back to his daughter, who now stood in line alone. She reached for a plate, definitely an island among the cowboys behind her and the smaller girls—Britt's friends—in front of her.

Boone's heart expanded once again, because Gerty was a good girl too. In that moment, he had the overwhelming impression that she'd be okay. The words actually flowed through his mind and everything.

She'll be okay, Boone. Stop worrying and start trusting.

337

Boone swallowed, because he didn't know how to do that. He needed a guide for how to trust in the Lord more completely. He heard pastors from here to Sugar Pond talk about it. It sounded good in a sermon.

Put your faith in God.

Trust in the Lord with your whole soul.

Learn to rely on the arm of Jehovah.

What he didn't know or understand was *how* to do that. The Lord was surely tired of Boone's constant pleadings and just wanted him to stop, but he found himself asking exactly that: *How, Lord? How can I trust You more?*

The Lord had moved on to someone else, and Boone didn't get an answer while standing there at his nephew's birthday party. He did feel loved and cared for, and he appreciated that so very much.

Gloria poked her head out of the house. "Boone, it's here. Could you...?"

"On my way," he said, turning to go down the steps and away from the party. He could sneak away without Keith noticing, and he did, easily slipping into the garage a moment later. The lack of light in there took a moment for his eyes to adjust to, and he blinked for a few seconds before continuing. He went up a couple of steps to hit the garage door opener, and then the evening light started to flood the garage from the front driveway.

As he walked toward the still-rising door, he heard a woman said, "...has to move. Who's the moron who parked here?"

The door made it all the way up, and Boone saw

Cosette Brian standing there. She took his breath away in her denim pencil skirt and nearly sheer blouse with bright green stick bugs on it. She wore a camisole underneath that, the fine lines of the thin straps going over her shoulders clearly seen through the blouse.

Though she was beautiful, she had that forked tongue that always seemed to whip at him personally. "I am," he said, raising his hand. "Sorry, I had cake and balloons. I can move the truck."

Cosette spun toward him, her eyes widening. "Boone." She'd once looked terrified of him. She'd called him a rascal a few months ago, on the day he'd arrived on the farm to stay for good. Then she'd run away, and he'd had to ask Gloria for her number so he could apologize for whatever he'd done wrong. They'd worked it out, and they'd been dancing around one another since.

An easy hello there. A hand-off for a receipt there. Nothing major. Nothing to paint him in a bad light in her mind.

Until now.

"Sorry," he said, digging in his front pocket for his keys. "I'll be out of the way in two shakes."

Cosette reached up and tucked her hair behind her ear as Mission, the cowboy she'd been talking to, walked away. She watched him go, and Boone didn't dare move now that they stood on the front driveway alone. She switched her gaze back to his when Mission made it to the front porch, and Boone's mouth turned dry.

He wasn't ready to date again. He wasn't. He absolutely was not, and he absolutely would not.

Cosette, to his knowledge, did not have a boyfriend and had not gone on a date with a man all summer long. But he didn't know her that well, and she didn't live on-site at the farm, so anything was possible.

Except the lightning currently arcing between them. *That* wasn't possible, and Boone threw up every defense he had against the sizzling attraction, because he did not have time for it. He did not want it.

He did not—fine, he did, but he couldn't risk his heart again, and he one-hundred-percent would not subject Gerty to yet another disastrous relationship that would result in a woman walking out on her. Been there, done that. Twice, even if the death of her mother had not been anything any of them had wanted.

He swallowed, sure he was reading the situation all wrong anyway. Cosette had never liked him all that much.

"After you move your truck, would you stay and help me put the bow on Keith's present?" she asked, letting her hand drop to her side.

Boone said the first thing that came to his mind, the thing he said as easily as he breathed, the thing he said whenever anyone asked him for help. She wasn't special; he was just a nice guy.

"Sure."

SNEAK PEEK! HIS THIRD TRY
CHAPTER TWO:

Cosette Brian reached into the back of the truck she'd just parked in the driveway, her fingers brushing the huge, red ribbon before it got pulled away from her. Boone had picked it up ahead of her, and he stared at the enormous bow.

"This is amazing," he said, finally looking across the bed of the truck to her. "Where did you get this?"

"I made it," Cosette said, feeling her defenses rise up. She told herself to relax, that Boone wasn't judging her. He'd already said the bow was amazing. She had to mentally remind herself to smile, and when she did, the gloriously handsome Boone Whettstein did the same.

My goodness, she thought. *He should not be allowed out in public with that smile.* It would blind drivers and send them right into the ditch on the side of the road. The brilliance of it would make women swoon from here to the state line. That had to be a crime, didn't it?

Cosette's heart started jack-hammering in her chest, despite her clear attempts at being kind to Boone. She thought of Louisa and what she would say, and she kept her smile hitched in place.

Cosette wasn't getting up at five a.m. because she liked it, though she had grown to love her early-morning walks with her neighbor. Louisa Knotts had quickly become Cosette's best friend, despite her living in the small town of Mountain Glen for the past fifteen years. Louisa had moved in at the beginning of June, and she'd claimed to be pre-diabetic. She'd asked Cosette if she'd like to go walking with her in the mornings, as she needed the exercise.

It had turned out that Louisa was a former psychiatrist for a university, specializing in young adults who'd been through trauma. She'd retired from that job and worked as a paralegal now, for a small law office on the outskirts of the city.

Cosette wasn't actually all that young, but she'd found Louisa really easy to talk to. She'd told her about Boone, and they'd been talking about him for months. They'd been talking about Cosette's trust issues for just as long, and Louisa had asked Cosette to think about what the worst thing that could happen if she spoke to Boone.

What would be the worst thing? The absolute worst? she'd asked.

The best Cosette had been able to come up with was: *He'll talk back.*

And that's bad? Louisa had asked.

To Cosette, speaking to a male—especially one as handsome, as tall, and as obviously cowboy as Boone—was bad, yes. She had no good relationships with males, and once she'd told Louisa that, the challenge had come.

What if he could be the first?

She brought herself back to the present when Boone cocked his right eyebrow. She'd missed something, if the confusion running through those dark eyes was any indication.

"What?" she asked.

He leveled his eyebrows. "I asked how you learned how to do this." He held up the multi-looped bow.

"I took a class one Christmas," she said. "They're usually about a hundred times smaller than that. I just went big for this. We're going to put it right on top of the truck."

Boone looked to the top of the truck, which stood about as tall as Cosette. Matthew Whettstein had bought a small truck for his son's sixteenth birthday from Cosette's sister, who owned a used car lot here in Ivory Peaks.

She'd picked up the truck that morning, as Raven had been holding it at the lot, and Cosette was getting a ride home with Gloria from this party. She glanced toward the open garage. This party. She normally wouldn't even attend a party like this, though she knew Matt, and she knew all the other cowboys, cowgirls, and staff from Pony Power had been invited and were likely in the backyard.

So she was doing a lot outside her comfort zone today.

She couldn't wait until Monday morning so she could tell Louisa.

Boone stepped to the side and reached up to put the bow on top. "How are you going to keep it there?"

"I've always wanted to be able to cock one eyebrow," she said, moving to open the back door of the truck. It had four doors and a shorter bed, and it was the perfect little vehicle for a high school student. It was about ten years old, but didn't have a lot of miles, as the previous owner had kept it out on his ranch and only used it to get from his house out to the far fields on his property.

Raven had only had it on the lot for six hours before Matt had showed up and bought it. Once the connection had been made between Raven, Matt, and Cosette, the plan for her to pick up the truck and bring it to the party had come together.

"You have?" Boone asked, staring openly at her now.

"Yeah," she said. "I can't do anything like that." She opened the back door and took out a big roll of duct tape. She pulled out a long piece, ripped it with her teeth, and stepped up into the truck, boosting her height. "Lift it up."

She looped the tape around itself, making a circle with sticky stuff all around, and plopped it right in the middle of the roof. "Stick it to that."

Boone did, and not a moment too soon. Cosette fell backward off the truck, managing to catch herself against the open door, but hitting her elbow in the process. A cry flew from her mouth, and Boone must've been a superhero, because he arrived at her side in less than two seconds flat.

"You okay?" he asked, his voice the tender, kind timbre she'd heard men use with their loved ones before.

She clutched her elbow as humiliation ran through her. "Yeah, I just hit my funny bone."

"Nothing funny about that bone," he said with a smile.

"No," was all she could come up with. He really couldn't smile like that. It erased the female mind, and how unfair was that?

Maybe just yours, she thought as her brain started working again. She tried to move, but the door had been pushed open as far as it would go, and she couldn't back up. Boone did, and they shuffled out of the doorway enough for her to close it.

"That's all?" he asked.

"I think so," Cosette said. "I'd just splay out the ends...." She started doing that, pulling the longer ends of the ribbon down over the rearview mirror on the front of the truck while Boone did the same over the back. He tucked them into the bed of the truck, and Cosette smiled to herself, because that was what she'd have done.

With the six ends billowing slightly in the breeze, she faced Boone again. "Thank you, Boone," she said, really trying out his name in her throat. It seemed to fit...okay.

"Yep," he said. "Are you gonna come back and eat?" He indicated she should go in front of him. "They'd just started when I came out."

"Oh, I don't know," she said.

"There's tons," he said, and he obviously had no qualms about joining the fray of people she could hear in the backyard. Of course he didn't. Boone Whettstein was a people person, and in Cosette's opinion, that was the worst type of person imaginable.

"It's pizza and salad," he said. "Have you eaten?"

"No," she said.

He paused, something marching across his face she couldn't identify. "If you don't want to stay here, we could just go grab something." He cocked that right eyebrow again, this time the smile coming with it.

Cosette dang near blacked out. Instead, with her pulse rioting and her cells buzzing at her, she laughed.

She *laughed*.

Cosette couldn't even remember the last time she'd laughed in mixed company. Sure, she did with Raven and her kids sometimes, but that was it. Never at work. Never if Raven's boyfriend was over to the house. Never if even a male neighbor was nearby.

Boone joined her, and the harmony and melody of their voices mingling in happiness as they did made Cosette long for something she'd vowed she did not want.

Companionship.

Not only that, but *male* companionship.

"You should stay," she said, because she had no idea how to flirt. Panic started to build beneath her breastbone. She'd gone too far already, and her vision swam slightly. "It's your nephew."

Boone lifted one hand toward her face, slowly. Oh-so-slowly, almost like someone had made the world start to spin backward. Cosette lifted her chin in defiance and to brace herself, all traces of laughter vanishing.

He paused, something curious in those eyes now. He dropped his hand without touching her and backed up. "I only want to stay if you're staying," he said. Just like that. Right out loud.

She'd known the cowboy was confident and bold, but she'd had no idea men talked like that. There wasn't any hidden meaning in those words, was there? Was he playing some game she didn't know about?

"I don't know," she said, glancing over her shoulder and into the garage again. Matt's truck sat parked there, with the other half of the two-car garage filled with broken-down boxes, a lawn mower, a weed-eater, and various other equipment and supplies.

Just the fact that she looked away from Boone when he stood so close to her told her how far she'd come. She hadn't realized it until that moment.

"I'm not really a party person," she said, facing him again.

"Then let's go grab something," he said. "No one's going to miss me, and I know they have these huge taco boxes on Friday nights at South of the Border." His eyes sparkled with mischief, and she wondered what a Friday night with Boone and a two-dozen pack of beef tacos would actually be like.

The fact that she wondered that baffled her.

"I've always wanted to get one," he said.

"You haven't yet?" She smiled at him again, reached up, and tucked her hair behind her ear. Shyness and awkwardness combined inside her, the same way they always had around good-looking men.

"Honestly?" he asked, but he didn't wait for her to answer. "I'm bushed by Friday night. If I make it back to the cabin and put a frozen pizza in the oven, I call it a win." He chuckled again, the sound like heavenly music to Cosette's ears.

"So no driving to town for a taco box."

"No, ma'am." He rocked back onto the heels of his cowboy boots.

"You're not bushed tonight? It's Friday." Her mind screamed at her that there was no way she was going with him to South of the Border. That would require riding in a vehicle with him—alone. Nope. She wouldn't do that.

"I got off early to come pick up things for the party."

"I really can't make you miss your nephew's sixteenth birthday party," she said. "It's a big deal." He looked like he was going to argue again, so she quickly added, "Did you know we're partnered up for tomorrow's wedding?"

Surprise darted across his face. "We are?"

"You're the best man, right?"

"Yes."

"I'm not the Maid of Honor, but Molly is walking with her husband. Gloria put me with you." Cosette had known for about a week, and maybe that was why she hadn't been able to stop thinking about Boone Whettstein over the past several days.

Truth be told, she'd been thinking about him since she'd run into him—literally—on the front porch of the farmhouse, months ago. But she wasn't ready to admit that yet.

Boone looked down to her hand. "Are we gonna...you know."

"What?" Cosette looked at her hands too, her skin suddenly tingling.

"Do you—?" He cleared his throat in a somewhat violent manner. "Link your arm through mine? Something like that?" A hint of redness crept into his neck and cheeks, and Cosette marveled at his embarrassment. "I don't want to make you uncomfortable."

A sigh filled her whole soul, but she only let it out in measured lengths. "You don't make me uncomfortable, Boone."

"You sure?" he challenged, all of that confidence on display. "It sure seemed like I did, when I touched you...before."

"I was just startled." Cosette had the distinct thought that she'd have to tell him everything if they honestly started a relationship. *Don't be ridiculous,* she told herself. *No one is starting a relationship.*

Certainly not her.

"Okay," Boone said, his higher-pitched tone indicating he didn't believe her.

"Okay," she said, as if the matter was now decided because she wanted it to be. "So...we'll walk down the aisle together tomorrow, and then, I don't know what your family responsibilities are after that, but I don't have anyone to sit by at dinner."

That smile spread across his face, and because he controlled it and it moved slowly, Cosette didn't swoon. Her knees only went weak for a moment, and she leaned her hip into the hood of the truck to mask it.

"I'm sure I can sit by you," Boone said.

"Great," she said. "Then I'll take a raincheck on the tacos."

Both eyebrows flew up now, and she grinned and shook her head. "You're an enigma, Cosette Brian," he said. "I'm not real good at mysteries or solving puzzles, but you...I want to figure you out."

"Do you just say whatever comes into your head?" she asked, straightening away from the truck. "If so, that's kind of unsettling."

"My daddy always said I didn't have a filter," Boone said with a laugh, as if that was a good thing. Cosette wasn't sure if it was or not, but she liked that he didn't play games.

"Dad, no way!"

Cosette turned at the excited yell of a teenager, and she got out of the way as Keith Whettstein came barreling toward her and Boone. She knew her place among a crowd, and it was definitely near the back of it. People came pouring through the front door and down the side-walk, as well as through the garage, all of them coming to see Keith's gift.

Keith looked around wildly, his gaze finally landing on

Matt and Gloria, who stood at the front of the crowd, their hands locked together. "This is insane," he said. "You said you weren't going to get me a car."

"I didn't get you a car," Matt said, his grin as bright as and powerful as the sun. "I got you a mini-truck, and don't forget. You paid for half of it."

Keith whooped and threw himself into his father's arms. They laughed together, and then Keith faced the truck again.

"I have the key," Boone said, and he put his hand out in front of Cosette. She certainly didn't want the spotlight, and she quickly extracted it from the front pocket of her skirt and placed it in his palm. He lifted it high above his head. "You want it?"

Keith looked at that key the way a hungry man would eye a doughnut. Boone laughed, and he stepped through the crowd to hug his nephew too, and as Keith got behind the wheel of the mini-truck, everyone who'd come to the party began to applaud.

Cosette looked around, her hands coming up to clap too, and she felt…something. Something she hadn't felt in a long, long time. It took her a moment to understand, and another to give it a name, but when she did, tears pricked her eyes.

Belonging.

Everyone here belonged here—including her.

She couldn't be seen crying in a crowd, so she kept her composure. She'd cry later, when her knees hit the floor in prayer. Right now, she thought, *Thank you, Lord. Thank you for giving me a new place to belong. Thank you, thank you, thank you.*

Boone returned to her side as the truck's engine roared to life and the applause started to die. As the crowd broke up and people began to return to the food in the backyard, he leaned down and said, "I'm looking forward to tomorrow, Cosette. And to the tacos," in a voice half the volume he normally used, which only made his tone that much sexier.

With that, he left Cosette to shiver in the summer evening as he joined his brother and Gloria. The trio moved to the front sidewalk to watch Keith drive down the road in his new truck, and Cosette realized she didn't have a way to leave the party.

So she did something completely insane. She walked over to Boone's side and looked down the road at the mini-truck trundling away too. When Boone looked at her, she simply said, "Gloria's my ride home. Guess I'll have to stay after all."

His First Love (Book 1): She broke up with him a decade ago. He's back in town after finishing a degree at MIT, ready to start his job at the family company. Can Hunter and Molly find their way through their pasts to build a future together?

His Second Chance (Book 2):
They broke up over twenty years ago. She's lost everything when she shows up at the farm in Ivory Peaks where he works. Can Matt and Gloria heal from their pasts to find a future happily-ever-after with each other?

His Third Try (Book 3): He moved to Ivory Peaks with his daughter to start over after a devastating break-up. She's never had a meaningful relationship with a man, especially a cowboy. Can Boone and Cosette help each other heal enough to build a happily-ever-after...and a family?

The Mechanics of Mistletoe (Book 1): Bear Glover can be a grizzly or a teddy, and he's always thought he'd be just fine working his generational family ranch and going back to the ancient homestead alone. But his crush on Samantha Benton won't go away. She's a genius with a wrench on Bear's tractors...and his heart. Can he tame his wild side and get the girl, or will he be left broken-hearted this Christmas season?

The Horsepower of the Holiday (Book 2): Ranger Glover has worked at Shiloh Ridge Ranch his entire life. The cowboys do everything from horseback there, but when he goes to town to trade in some trucks, somehow Oakley Hatch persuades him to take some ATVs back to the ranch. (Bear is NOT happy.)

She's a former race car driver who's got Ranger all revved up... Can he remember who he is and get Oakley to slow down enough to fall in love, or will there simply be too much horsepower in the holiday this year for a real relationship?

The **ONSTRUCTION** of *Cheer*

USA Today Bestselling Author
LIZ ISAACSON

The Construction of Cheer (Book 3): Bishop Glover is the youngest brother, and he usually keeps his head down and gets the job done. When Montana Martin shows up at Shiloh Ridge Ranch looking for work, he finds himself inventing construction projects that need doing just to keep her coming around. (Again, Bear is NOT happy.) She wants to build her own construction firm, but she ends up carving a place for herself inside Bishop's heart. Can he convince her *he's* all she needs this Christmas season, or will her cheer rest solely on the success of her business?

The Secret of Santa (Book 4): He's a fun-loving cowboy with a heart of gold. She's the woman who keeps putting him on hold. Can Ace and Holly Ann make a relationship work this Christmas?

The Harmony of Holly (Book 5): He's as prickly as his name, but the new woman in town has caught his eye. Can Cactus shelve his temper and shed his cowboy hermit skin fast enough to make a relationship with Willa work?

The Chemistry of Christmas

of Christmas

USA Today Bestselling Author
LIZ ISAACSON

The Chemistry of Christmas (Book 6): He's the black sheep of the family, and she's a chemist who understands formulas, not emotions. Can Preacher and Charlie take their quirks and turn them into a strong relationship this Christmas?

The Delivery of Decor (Book 7): When he falls, he falls hard and deep. She literally drives away from every relationship she's ever had. Can Ward somehow get Dot to stay this Christmas?

The Blessing of Babies (Book 8): Don't miss out on a single moment of the Glover family saga in this bridge story linking Ward and Judge's love stories!

The Glovers love God, country, dogs, horses, and family. Not necessarily in that order. ;)

Many of them are married now, with babies on the way, and there are lessons to be learned, forgiveness to be had and given, and new names coming to the family tree in southern Three Rivers!

The Networking of the Nativity (Book 9): He's had a crush on her for years. She doesn't want to date until her daughter is out of the house. Will June take a change on Judge when the success of his Christmas light display depends on her networking abilities?

The Wrangling of the Wreath (Book 10): He's been so busy trying to find Miss Right. She's been right in front of him the whole time. This Christmas, can Mister and Libby take their relationship out of the best friend zone?

USA Today Bestselling Author
LIZ ISAACSON

The Hope of Her Heart (Book 11): She's the only Glover without a significant other. He's been searching for someone who can love him *and* his daughter. Can Etta and August make a meaningful connection this Christmas?

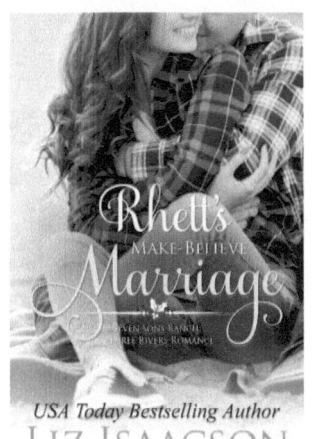

Rhett's Make-Believe Marriage (Book 1): She needs a husband to be credible as a matchmaker. He wants to help a neighbor. Will their fake marriage take them out of the friend zone?

Tripp's Trivial Tie (Book 2): She needs a husband to keep her son. He's wanted to take their relationship to the next level, but she's always pushing him away. Will their trivial tie take them all the way to happily-ever-after?

USA Today Bestselling Author
LIZ ISAACSON

Liam's Invented I-Do (Book 3): She's desperate to save her ranch. He wants to help her any way he can. Will their invented I-Do open doors that have previously been closed and lead to a happily-ever-after for both of them?

Jeremiah's Bogus Bride (Book 4): He wants to prove to his brothers that he's not broken. She just wants him. Will a fake marriage heal him or push her further away?

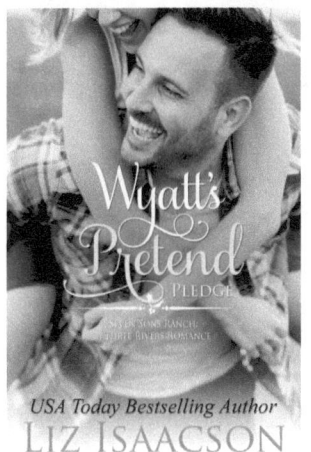

Wyatt's Pretend Pledge (Book 5): To get her inheritance, she needs a husband. He's wanted to fly with her for ages. Can their pretend pledge turn into something real?

Skyler's Wanna-Be Wife (Book 6): She needs a new last name to stay in school. He's willing to help a fellow student. Can this wanna-be wife show the playboy that some things should be taken seriously?

USA Today Bestselling Author
LIZ ISAACSON

Micah's Mock Matrimony (Book 7): They were just actors auditioning for a play. The marriage was just for the audition – until a clerical error results in a legal marriage. Can these two ex-lovers negotiate this new ground between them and achieve new roles in each other's lives?

Her Cowboy Billionaire Birthday Wish (Book 1): All the maid at Whiskey Mountain Lodge wants for her birthday is a handsome cowboy billionaire. And Colton can make that wish come true—if only he hadn't escaped to Coral Canyon after being left at the altar...

Her Cowboy Billionaire Butler (Book 2): She broke up with him to date another man...who broke her heart. He's a former CEO with nothing to do who can't get her out of his head. Can Wes and Bree find a way toward happily-ever-after at Whiskey Mountain Lodge?

Her Cowboy Billionaire Best Friend's Brother (Book 3): She's best friends with the single dad cowboy's brother and has watched two friends find love with the sexy new cowboys in town. When Gray Hammond comes to Whiskey Mountain Lodge with his son, will Elise finally get her own happily-ever-after with one of the Hammond brothers?

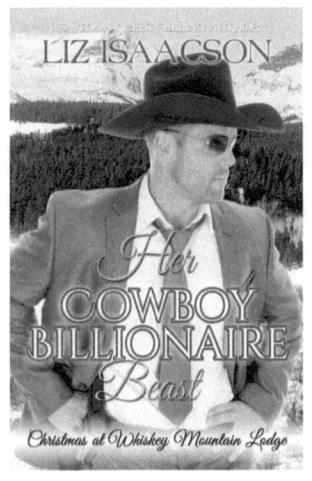

Her Cowboy Billionaire Beast (Book 4): A cowboy billionaire beast, his new manager, and the Christmas traditions that soften his heart and bring them together.

Her Cowboy Billionaire Bad Boy (Book 5): A cowboy billionaire cop who's a stickler for rules, the woman he pulls over when he's not even on duty, and the personal mandates he has to break to keep her in his life...

Her Cowboy Billionaire Best Friend (Book 1): Graham Whittaker returns to Coral Canyon a few days after Christmas—after the death of his father. He takes over the energy company his dad built from the ground up and buys a high-end lodge to live in—only a mile from the home of his once-best friend, Laney McAllister. They were best friends once, but Laney's always entertained feelings for him, and spending so much time with him while they make Christmas memories puts her heart in danger of getting broken again...

Her Cowboy Billionaire Boss (Book 2): Since the death of his wife a few years ago, Eli Whittaker has been running from one job to another, unable to find somewhere for him and his son to settle. Meg Palmer is Stockton's nanny, and she comes with her boss, Eli, to the lodge, her long-time crush on the man no different in Wyoming than it was on the beach. When she confesses her feelings for him and gets nothing in return, she's crushed, embarrassed, and unsure if she can stay in Coral Canyon for Christmas. Then Eli starts to show some feelings for her too...

Her Cowboy Billionaire Boyfriend (Book 3): Andrew Whittaker is the public face for the Whittaker Brothers' family energy company, and with his older brother's robot about to be announced, he needs a press secretary to help him get everything ready and tour the state to make the announcements. When he's hit by a protest sign being carried by the company's biggest opponent, Rebecca Collings, he learns with a few clicks that she has the background they need. He offers her the job of press secretary when she thought she was going to be arrested, and not only because the spark between them in so hot Andrew can't see straight.

Can Becca and Andrew work together and keep their relationship a secret? Or will hearts break in this classic romance retelling reminiscent of *Two Weeks Notice*?

Her Cowboy Billionaire Bodyguard (Book 4): Beau Whittaker has watched his brothers find love one by one, but every attempt he's made has ended in disaster. Lily Everett has been in the spotlight since childhood and has half a dozen platinum records with her two sisters. She's taking a break from the brutal music industry and hiding out in Wyoming while her ex-husband continues to cause trouble for her. When she hears of Beau Whittaker and what he offers his clients, she wants to meet him. Beau is instantly attracted to Lily, but he tried a relationship with his last client that left a scar that still hasn't healed...

Can Lily use the spirit of Christmas to discover what matters most? Will Beau open his heart to the possibility of love with someone so different from him?

Her Cowboy Billionaire Bull Rider (Book 5): Todd Christopherson has just retired from the professional rodeo circuit and returned to his hometown of Coral Canyon. Problem is, he's got no family there anymore, no land, and no job. Not that he needs a job--he's got plenty of money from his illustrious career riding bulls.

Then Todd gets thrown during a routine horseback ride up the canyon, and his only support as he recovers physically is the beautiful Violet Everett. She's no nurse, but she does the best she can for the handsome cowboy. **Will she lose her heart to the billionaire bull rider? Can Todd trust that God led him to Coral Canyon...and Vi?**

Her Cowboy Billionaire Bachelor (Book 6): Rose Everett isn't sure what to do with her life now that her country music career is on hold. After all, with both of her sisters in Coral Canyon, and one about to have a baby, they're not making albums anymore.

Liam Murphy has been working for Doctors Without Borders, but he's back in the US now, and looking to start a new clinic in Coral Canyon, where he spent his summers.

When Rose wins a date with Liam in a bachelor auction, their relationship blooms and grows quickly. **Can Liam and Rose find a solution to their problems that doesn't involve one of them leaving Coral Canyon with a broken heart?**

Her Cowboy Billionaire Blind Date (Book 7): Her sons want her to be happy, but she's too old to be set up on a blind date...isn't she?

Amanda Whittaker has been looking for a second chance at love since the death of her husband several years ago. Finley Barber is a cowboy in every sense of the word. Born and raised on a racehorse farm in Kentucky, he's since moved to Dog Valley and started his own breeding stable for champion horses. He hasn't dated in years, and everything about Amanda makes him nervous.

Will Amanda take the leap of faith required to be with Finn? Or will he become just another boyfriend who doesn't make the cut?

Her Cowboy Billionaire Best Man (Book 8): When Celia Abbott-Armstrong runs into a gorgeous cowboy at her best friend's wedding, she decides she's ready to start dating again.

But the cowboy is Zach Zuckerman, and the Zuckermans and Abbotts have been at war for generations.

Can Zach and Celia find a way to reconcile their family's differences so they can have a future together?

Second Chance Ranch: A Three Rivers Ranch Romance (Book 1): After his deployment, injured and discharged Major Squire Ackerman returns to Three Rivers Ranch, wanting to forgive Kelly for ignoring him a decade ago. He'd like to provide the stable life she needs, but with old wounds opening and a ranch on the brink of financial collapse, it will take patience and faith to make their second chance possible.

Third Time's the Charm: A Three Rivers Ranch Romance (Book 2): First Lieutenant Peter Marshall has a truckload of debt and no way to provide for a family, but Chelsea helps him see past all the obstacles, all the scars. With so many unknowns, can Pete and Chelsea develop the love, acceptance, and faith needed to find their happily ever after?

LIZ ISAACSON

A THREE RIVERS RANCH ROMANCE

Fourth and Long: A Three Rivers Ranch Romance (Book 3): Commander Brett Murphy goes to Three Rivers Ranch to find some rest and relaxation with his Army buddies. Having his ex-wife show up with a seven-year-old she claims is his son is anything but the R&R he craves. Kate needs to make amends, and Brett needs to find forgiveness, but are they too late to find their happily ever after?

Fifth Generation Cowboy: A Three Rivers Ranch Romance (Book 4): Tom Lovell has watched his friends find their true happiness on Three Rivers Ranch, but everywhere he looks, he only sees friends. Rose Reyes has been bringing her daughter out to the ranch for equine therapy for months, but it doesn't seem to be working. Her challenges with Mari are just as frustrating as ever. Could Tom be exactly what Rose needs? Can he remove his friendship blinders and find love with someone who's been right in front of him all this time?

Sixth Street Love Affair: A Three Rivers Ranch Romance (Book 5): After losing his wife a few years back, Garth Ahlstrom thinks he's ready for a second chance at love. But Juliette Thompson has a secret that could destroy their budding relationship. Can they find the strength, patience, and faith to make things work?

The Seventh Sergeant: A Three Rivers Ranch Romance (Book 6): Life has finally started to settle down for Sergeant Reese Sanders after his devastating injury overseas. Discharged from the Army and now with a good job at Courage Reins, he's finally found happiness—until a horrific fall puts him right back where he was years ago: Injured and depressed. Carly Watters, Reese's new veteran care coordinator, dislikes small towns almost as much as she loathes cowboys. But she finds herself faced with both when she gets assigned to Reese's case. Do they have the humility and faith to make their relationship more than professional?

Eight Second Ride: A Three Rivers Ranch Romance (Book 7): Ethan Greene loves his work at Three Rivers Ranch, but he can't seem to find the right woman to settle down with. When sassy yet vulnerable Brynn Bowman shows up at the ranch to recruit him back to the rodeo circuit, he takes a different approach with the barrel racing champion. His patience and newfound faith pay off when a friendship--and more-- starts with Brynn. But she wants out of the rodeo circuit right when Ethan wants to rejoin. Can they find the path God wants them to take and still stay together?

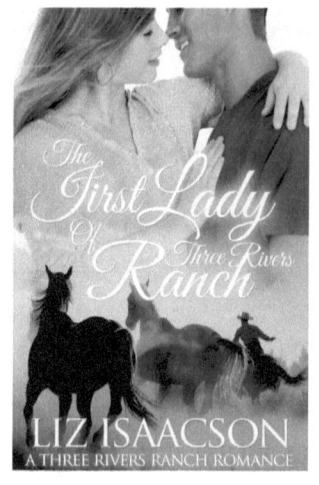

The First Lady of Three Rivers Ranch: A Three Rivers Ranch Romance (Book 8): Heidi Duffin has been dreaming about opening her own bakery since she was thirteen years old. She scrimped and saved for years to afford baking and pastry school in San Francisco. And now she only has one year left before she's a certified pastry chef. Frank Ackerman's father has recently retired, and he's taken over the largest cattle ranch in the Texas Panhandle. A horseman through and through, he's also nearing thirty-one and looking for someone to bring love and joy to a homestead that's been dominated by men for a decade. But when he convinces Heidi to come clean the cowboy cabins, she changes all that. But the siren's call of a bakery is still loud in Heidi's ears, even if she's also seeing a future with Frank. Can she rely on her faith in ways she's never had to before or will their relationship end when summer does?

Christmas in Three Rivers: A Three Rivers Ranch Romance (Book 9): Isn't Christmas the best time to fall in love? The cowboys of Three Rivers Ranch think so. Join four of them as they journey toward their path to happily ever after in four, all-new novellas in the Amazon #1 Bestselling Three Rivers Ranch Romance series.

THE NINTH INNING: The Christmas season has never felt like such a burden to boutique owner Andrea Larsen. But with Mama gone and the holidays upon her, Andy finds herself wishing she hadn't been so quick to judge her former boyfriend, cowboy Lawrence Collins. Well, Lawrence hasn't forgotten about Andy either, and he devises a plan to get her out to the ranch so they can reconnect. Do they have the faith and humility to patch things up and start a new relationship?

TEN DAYS IN TOWN: Sandy Keller is tired of the dating scene in Three Rivers. Though she owns the pancake house, she's looking for a fresh start, which means an escape from the town where she grew up. When her older brother's best friend, Tad Jorgensen, comes to town for the holidays, it is a balm to his weary soul. A helicopter tour guide who experienced a near-death experience, he's looking to start over too--but in Three Rivers. Can Sandy and Tad navigate their troubles to find the path God wants them to take--and discover true love--in only ten days?

ELEVEN YEAR REUNION: Pastry chef extraordinaire, Grace Lewis has moved to Three Rivers to help Heidi Ackerman open a bakery in Three Rivers. Grace relishes the idea of starting over in a town where no one knows about her failed cupcakery. She doesn't expect to run into her old high school boyfriend, Jonathan Carver. A carpenter working at Three Rivers Ranch, Jon's in town against his will. But with Grace now on the scene, Jon's thinking life in Three Rivers is suddenly looking up. But with her focus on baking and his disdain for small towns, can they make their eleven year reunion stick?

THE TWELFTH TOWN: Newscaster Taryn Tucker has had enough of life on-screen. She's bounced from town to town before arriving in Three Rivers, completely alone and completely anonymous--just the way she now likes it. She takes a job cleaning at Three Rivers Ranch, hoping for a chance to figure out who she is and where God wants her. When she meets happy-go-lucky cowhand Kenny Stockton, she doesn't expect sparks to fly. Kenny's always been "the best friend" for his female friends, but the pull between him and Taryn can't be denied. Will they have the courage and faith necessary to make their opposite worlds mesh?

Lucky Number Thirteen: A Three Rivers Ranch Romance (Book 10): Tanner Wolf, a rodeo champion ten times over, is excited to be riding in Three Rivers for the first time since he left his philandering ways and found religion. Seeing his old friends Ethan and Brynn is therapuetic--until a terrible accident lands him in the hospital. With his rodeo career over, Tanner thinks maybe he'll stay in town--and it's not just because his nurse, Summer Hamblin, is the prettiest woman he's ever met. But Summer's the queen of first dates, and as she looks for a way to make a relationship with the transient rodeo star work Summer's not sure she has the fortitude to go on a second date. Can they find love among the tragedy?

The Curse of February Fourteenth: A Three Rivers Ranch Romance (Book 11): Cal Hodgkins, cowboy veterinarian at Bowman's Breeds, isn't planning to meet anyone at the masked dance in small-town Three Rivers. He just wants to get his bachelor friends off his back and sit on the sidelines to drink his punch. But when he sees a woman dressed in gorgeous butterfly wings and cowgirl boots with blue stitching, he's smitten. Too bad she runs away from the dance before he can get her name, leaving only her boot behind...

Fifteen Minutes of Fame: A Three Rivers Ranch Romance (Book 12): Navy Richards is thirty-five years of tired—tired of dating the same men, working a demanding job, and getting her heart broken over and over again. Her aunt has always spoken highly of the matchmaker in Three Rivers, Texas, so she takes a six-month sabbatical from her high-stress job as a pediatric nurse, hops on a bus, and meets with the matchmaker. Then she meets Gavin Redd. He's handsome, he's hardworking, and he's a cowboy. But is he an Aquarius too? Navy's not making a move until she knows for sure...

Sixteen Steps to Fall in Love: A Three Rivers Ranch Romance (Book 13): A chance encounter at a dog park sheds new light on the tall, talented Boone that Nicole can't ignore. As they get to know each other better and start to dig into each other's past, Nicole is the one who wants to run. This time from her growing admiration and attachment to Boone. From her aging parents. From herself.

But Boone feels the attraction between them too, and he decides he's tired of running and ready to make Three Rivers his permanent home. **Can Boone and Nicole use their faith to overcome their differences and find a happily-ever-after together?**

The Sleigh on Seventeenth Street: A Three Rivers Ranch Romance (Book 14): A cowboy with skills as an electrician tries a relationship with a down-on-her luck plumber. Can Dylan and Camila make water and electricity play nicely together this Christmas season? Or will they get shocked as they try to make their relationship work?

Last Chance Ranch (Book 1):
A cowgirl down on her luck hires a man who's good with horses and under the hood of a car. Can Hudson fine tune Scarlett's heart as they work together? Or will things backfire and make everything worse at Last Chance Ranch?

Last Chance Cowboy (Book 2): A billionaire cowboy without a home meets a woman who secretly makes food videos to pay her debts...Can Carson and Adele do more than fight in the kitchens at Last Chance Ranch?

Last Chance Wedding (Book 3): A female carpenter needs a husband just for a few days... Can Jeri and Sawyer navigate the minefield of a pretend marriage before their feelings become real?

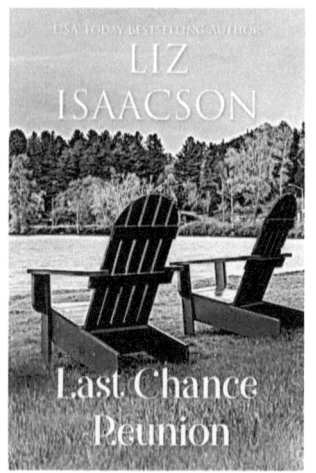

Last Chance Reunion (Book 4): An Army cowboy, the woman he dated years ago, and their last chance at Last Chance Ranch... Can Dave and Sissy put aside hurt feelings and make their second chance romance work?

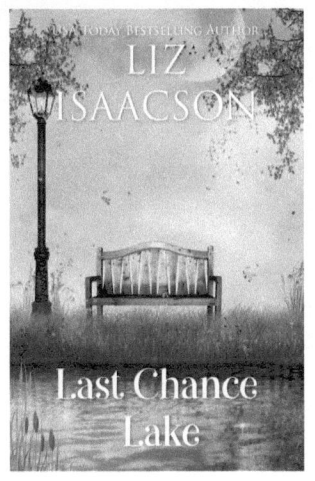

Last Chance Lake (Book 5):
A former dairy farmer and the marketing director on the ranch have to work together to make the cow cuddling program a success. But can Karla let Cache into her life? Or will she keep all her secrets from him - and keep *him* a secret too?

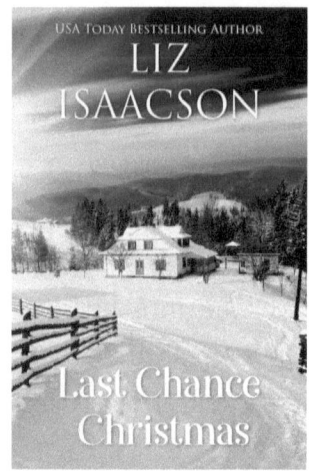

Last Chance Christmas (Book 6): She's tired of having her heart broken by cowboys. He waited too long to ask her out. Can Lance fix things quickly, or will Amber leave Last Chance Ranch before he can tell her how he feels?

Her Billionaire Cowboy (Book 1): Tucker Jenkins has had enough of tall buildings, traffic, and has traded in his technology firm in New York City for Steeple Ridge Horse Farm in rural Vermont. Missy Marino has worked at the farm since she was a teen, and she's always dreamed of owning it. But her ex-husband left her with a truckload of debt, making her fantasies of owning the farm unfulfilled. Tucker didn't come to the country to find a new wife, but he supposes a woman could help him start over in Steeple Ridge. Will Tucker and Missy be able to navigate the shaky ground between them to find a new beginning?

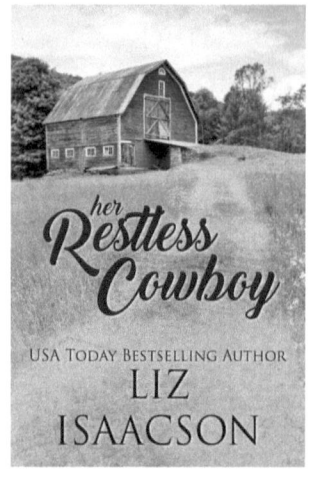

Her Restless Cowboy: A Butters Brothers Novel, Steeple Ridge Romance (Book 2): Ben Buttars is the youngest of the four Buttars brothers who come to Steeple Ridge Farm, and he finally feels like he's landed somewhere he can make a life for himself. Reagan Cantwell is a decade older than Ben and the recreational direction for the town of Island Park. Though Ben is young, he knows what he wants—and that's Rae. Can she figure out how to put what matters most in her life—family and faith—above her job before she loses Ben?

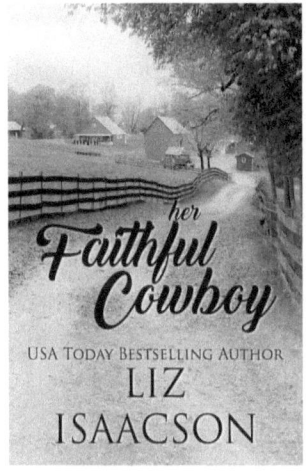

USA TODAY BESTSELLING AUTHOR

LIZ ISAACSON

Her Faithful Cowboy: A Butters Brothers Novel, Steeple Ridge Romance (Book 3): Sam Buttars has spent the last decade making sure he and his brothers stay together. They've been at Steeple Ridge for a while now, but with the youngest married and happy, the siren's call to return to his parents' farm in Wyoming is loud in Sam's ears. He'd just go if it weren't for beautiful Bonnie Sherman, who roped his heart the first time he saw her. Do Sam and Bonnie have the faith to find comfort in each other instead of in the people who've already passed?

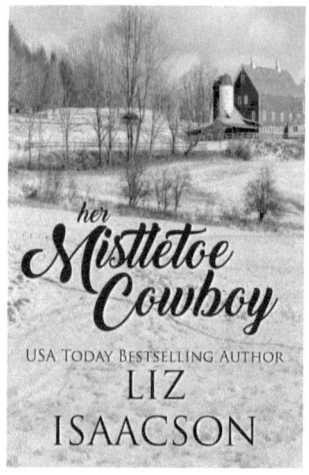

Her Mistletoe Cowboy: A Butters Brothers Novel, Steeple Ridge Romance (Book 4): Logan Buttars has always been good-natured and happy-go-lucky. After watching two of his brothers settle down, he recognizes a void in his life he didn't know about. Veterinarian Layla Guyman has appreciated Logan's friendship and easy way with animals when he comes into the clinic to get the service dogs. But with his future at Steeple Ridge in the balance, she's not sure a relationship with him is worth the risk. Can she rely on her faith and employ patience to tame Logan's wild heart?

Her Patient Cowboy: A Butters Brothers Novel, Steeple Ridge Romance (Book 5): Darren Buttars is cool, collected, and quiet—and utterly devastated when his girlfriend of nine months, Farrah Irvine, breaks up with him because he wanted her to ride her horse in a parade. But Farrah doesn't ride anymore, a fact she made very clear to Darren. She returned to her childhood home with so much baggage, she doesn't know where to start with the unpacking. Darren's the only Buttars brother who isn't married, and he wants to make Island Park his permanent home—with Farrah. Can they find their way through the heartache to achieve a happily-ever-after together?

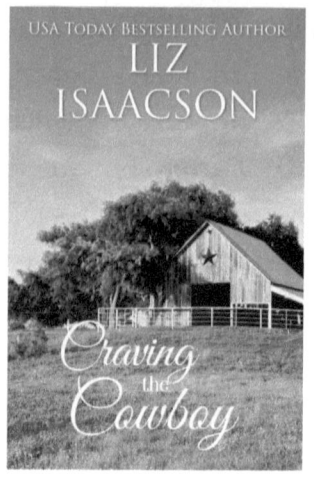

Craving the Cowboy (Book 1): Dwayne Carver is set to inherit his family's ranch in the heart of Texas Hill Country, and in order to keep up with his ranch duties and fulfill his dreams of owning a horse farm, he hires top trainer Felicity Lightburne. They get along great, and she can envision herself on this new farm—at least until her mother falls ill and she has to return to help her. Can Dwayne and Felicity work through their differences to find their happily-ever-after?

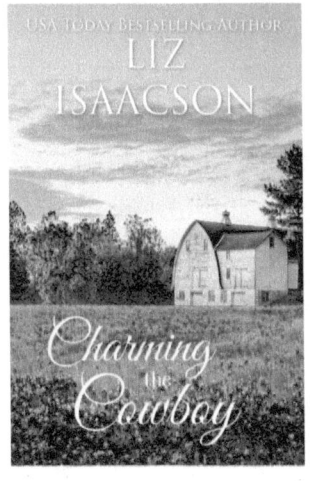

Charming the Cowboy (Book 2): Third grade teacher Heather Carver has had her eye on Levi Rhodes for a couple of years now, but he seems to be blind to her attempts to charm him. When she breaks her arm while on his horse ranch, Heather infiltrates Levi's life in ways he's never thought of, and his strict anti-female stance slips. Will Heather heal his emotional scars and he care for her physical ones so they can have a real relationship?

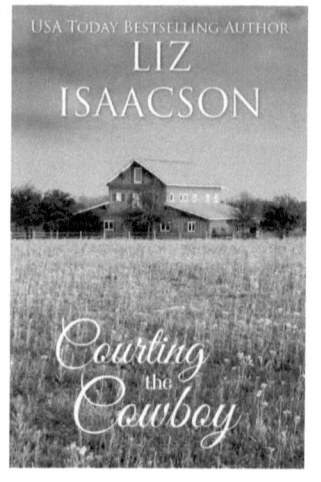

Courting the Cowboy (Book 3): Frustrated with the cowboy-only dating scene in Grape Seed Falls, May Sotheby joins TexasFaithful.com, hoping to find her soul mate without having to relocate--or deal with cowboy hats and boots. She has no idea that Kurt Pemberton, foreman at Grape Seed Ranch, is the man she starts communicating with... Will May be able to follow her heart and get Kurt to forgive her so they can be together?

Claiming the Cowboy, Royal Brothers Book 1 (Grape Seed Falls Romance Book 4): Unwilling to be tied down, farrier Robin Cook has managed to pack her entire life into a two-hundred-and-eighty square-foot house, and that includes her Yorkie. Cowboy and co-foreman, Shane Royal has had his heart set on Robin for three years, even though she flat-out turned him down the last time he asked her to dinner. But she's back at Grape Seed Ranch for five weeks as she works her horse-shoeing magic, and he's still interested, despite a bitter life lesson that left a bad taste for marriage in his mouth.

Robin's interested in him too. But can she find room for Shane in her tiny house--and can he take a chance on her with his tired heart?

Catching the Cowboy, Royal Brothers Book 2 (Grape Seed Falls Romance Book 5): Dylan Royal is good at two things: whistling and caring for cattle. When his cows are being attacked by an unknown wild animal, he calls Texas Parks & Wildlife for help. He wasn't expecting a beautiful mammologist to show up, all flirty and fun and everything Dylan didn't know he wanted in his life.

Hazel Brewster has gone on more first dates than anyone in Grape Seed Falls, and she thinks maybe Dylan deserves a second... Can they find their way through wild animals, huge life changes, and their emotional pasts to find their forever future?

Cheering the Cowboy, Royal Brothers Book 3 (Grape Seed Falls Romance Book 6): Austin Royal loves his life on his new ranch with his brothers. But he doesn't love that Shayleigh Hatch came with the property, nor that he has to take the blame for the fact that he now owns her childhood ranch. They rarely have a conversation that doesn't leave him furious and frustrated--and yet he's still attracted to Shay in a strange, new way.

Shay inexplicably likes him too, which utterly confuses and angers her. As they work to make this Christmas the best the Triple Towers Ranch has ever seen, can they also navigate through their rocky relationship to smoother waters?

Choosing the Cowboy (Book 7): With financial trouble and personal issues around every corner, can Maggie Duffin and Chase Carver rely on their faith to find their happily-ever-after?

A spinoff from the #1 bestselling Three Rivers Ranch Romance novels, also by USA Today bestselling author Liz Isaacson.

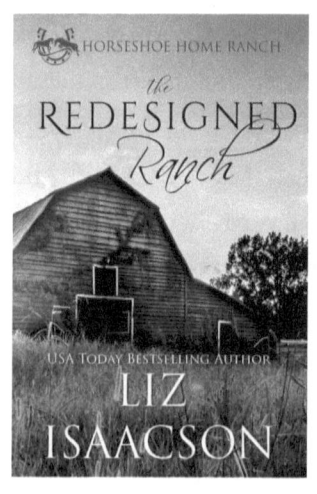

The Snowstorm in Gold Valley (Book 2): Professional snowboarder Sterling Maughan has sequestered himself in his family's cabin in the exclusive mountain community above Gold Valley, Montana after a devastating fall that ended his career. Norah Watson cleans Sterling's cabin and the more time they spend together, the more Sterling is interested in all things Norah. As his body heals, so does his faith. Will Norah be able to trust Sterling so they can have a chance at true love?

The Cabin on Bear Mountain (Book 3): Landon Edmunds has been a cowboy his whole life. An accident five years ago ended his successful rodeo career, and now he's looking to start a horse ranch--and he's looking outside of Montana. Which would be great if God hadn't brought Megan Palmer back to Gold Valley right when Landon is looking to leave. Megan and Landon work together well, and as sparks fly, she's sure God brought her back to Gold Valley so she could find her happily ever after. Through serious discussion and prayer, can Landon and Megan find their future together?

Be sure to check out the spinoff series, the Brush Creek Brides romances after you read FALLING FOR HIS BEST FRIEND. Start with A WEDDING FOR THE WIDOWER.

The Cowboy at the Creek (Book 4): Twelve years ago, Owen Carr left Gold Valley—and his long-time girlfriend—in favor of a country music career in Nashville. Married and divorced, Natalie teaches ballet at the dance studio in Gold Valley, but she never auditioned for the professional company the way she dreamed of doing. With Owen back, she realizes all the opportunities she missed out on when he left all those years ago—including a future with him. Can they mend broken bridges in order to have a second chance at love?

The Wedding in the Winter (Book 5): Caleb Chamberlain has spent the last five years recovering from a horrible breakup, his alcoholism that stemmed from it, and the car accident that left him hospitalized. He's finally on the right track in his life—until Holly Gray, his twin brother's ex-fiance mistakes him for Nathan. Holly's back in Gold Valley to get the required veterinarian hours to apply for her graduate program. When the herd at Horseshoe Home comes down with pneumonia, Caleb and Holly are forced to work together in close quarters. Holly's over Nathan, but she hasn't forgiven him—or the woman she believes broke up their relationship. Can Caleb and Holly navigate such a rough past to find their happily-ever-after?

The Long Way Home (Book 6): Ty Barker has been dancing through the last thirty years of his life--and he's suddenly realized he's alone. River Lee Whitely is back in Gold Valley with her two little girls after a divorce that's left deep scars. She has a job at Silver Creek that requires her to be able to ride a horse, and she nearly tramples Ty at her first lesson. That's just fine by him, because River Lee is the girl Ty has never gotten over. Ty realizes River Lee needs time to settle into her new job, her new home, her new life as a single parent, but going slow has never been his style. But for River Lee, can Ty take the necessary steps to keep her in his life?

Christmas at the Ranch (Book 7): Archer Bailey has already lost one job to Emersyn Enders, so he deliberately doesn't tell her about the cowhand job up at Horseshoe Home Ranch. Emery's temporary job is ending, but her obligations to her physically disabled sister aren't. As Archer and Emery work together, its clear that the sparks flying between them aren't all from their friendly competition over a job. Will Emery and Archer be able to navigate the ranch, their close quarters, and their individual circumstances to find love this holiday season?

The Love of a Cowboy (Book 8): Cowboy Elliott Hawthorne has just lost his best friend and cabin mate to the worst thing imaginable—marriage. When his brother calls about an accident with their father, Elliott rushes down to Gold Valley from the ranch only to be met with the most beautiful woman he's ever seen. His father's new physical therapist, London Marsh, likes the handsome face and gentle spirit she sees in Elliott too. Can Elliott and London navigate difficult family situations to find a happily-ever-after?

The Cowboy's Challenge: Brush Creek Brides Romance (Book 2): Cowboy and professional roper Justin Jackman has found solitude at Brush Creek Horse Ranch, preferring his time with the animals he trains over dating. With two failed engagements in his past, he's not really interested in getting his heart stomped on again. But when flirty and fun Renee  Martin picks him up at a church ice cream bar--on a bet, no less--he finds himself more than just a little interested. His Gen-X attitudes are attractive to her; her Millennial behaviors drive him nuts. Can Justin look past their differences and take a chance on another engagement?

A Cowboy Proposal: Brush Creek Brides Romance (Book 3): Ted Caldwell has been a retired bronc rider for years, and he thought he was perfectly happy training horses to buck at Brush Creek Ranch. He was wrong. When he meets April Nox, who comes to the ranch to hide her pregnancy from all her friends back in Jackson Hole, Ted realizes he has a huge family-shaped hole in his life. April is embarrassed, heartbroken, and trying to find her extinguished faith. She's never ridden a horse and wants nothing to do with a cowboy ever again. Can Ted and April create a family of happiness and love from a tragedy?

A New Family for the Cowboy: Brush Creek Brides Romance (Book 4): Blake Gibbons oversees all the agriculture at Brush Creek Horse Ranch, sometimes moonlighting as a general contractor. When he meets Erin Shields, new in town, at her aunt's bakery, he's instantly smitten. Erin moved to Brush Creek after a divorce that left her  penniless, homeless, and a single mother of three children under age eight. She's nowhere near ready to start dating again, but the longer Blake hangs around the bakery, the more she starts to like him. Can Blake and Erin find a way to blend their lifestyles and become a family?

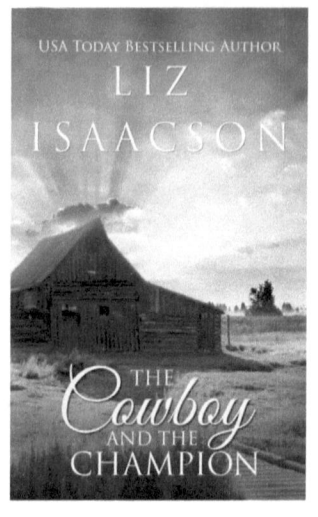

The Cowboy and the Champion: Brush Creek Brides Romance (Book 5): Emmett Graves has always had a positive outlook on life. He adores training horses to become barrel racing champions during the day and cuddling with his cat at night. Fresh off her professional rodeo retirement, Molly Brady comes to Brush Creek Horse Ranch as Emmett's protege. He's not thrilled, and she's allergic to cats. Oh, and she'd like to stay cowboy-free, thank you very much. But Emmett's about as cowboy as they come.... Can Emmett and Molly work together without falling in love?

Schooled by the Cowboy: Brush Creek Brides Romance (Book 6): Grant Ford spends his days training cattle—when he's not camped out at the elementary school hoping to catch a glimpse of his ex-girlfriend. When principal Shannon Sharpe confronts him and asks him to stay away from the school, the spark between them is instant and hot. Shan-

non's expecting a transfer very soon, but she also needs a summer outdoor coordinator—and Grant fits the bill. Just because he's handsome and everything Shannon's ever wanted in a cowboy husband means nothing. Will Grant and Shannon be able to survive the summer or will the Utah heat be too much for them to handle?

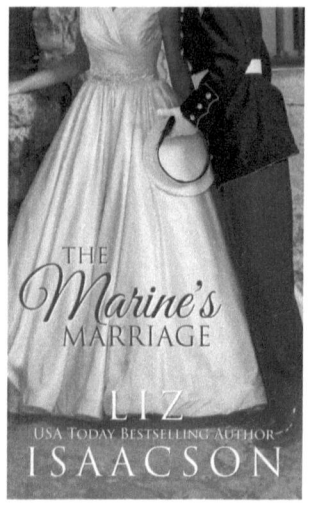

The Marine's Marriage: A Fuller Family Novel - Brush Creek Brides Romance (Book 1): Tate Benson can't believe he's come to Nowhere, Utah, to fix up a house that hasn't been inhabited in years. But he has. Because he's retired from the Marines and looking to start a life as a police officer in small-town Brush Creek. Wren Fuller has her hands full most days running her family's company. When Tate calls and demands a maid for that morning, she decides to have the calls forwarded to her cell and go help him out. She didn't know he was moving in next door, and she's completely unprepared for his handsomeness, his kind heart, and his wounded soul.Can Tate and Wren weather a relationship when they're also next-door neighbors?

The Firefighter's Fiancé: A Fuller Family Novel - Brush Creek Brides Romance (Book 2): Cora Wesley comes to Brush Creek, hoping to get some in-the-wild firefighting training as she prepares to put in her application to be a hotshot. When she meets Brennan Fuller, the spark between them is hot and instant. As they get to know  each other, her deadline is constantly looming over them, and Brennan starts to wonder if he can break ranks in the family business. He's okay mowing lawns and hanging out with his brothers, but he dreams of being able to go to college and become a landscape architect, but he's just not sure it can be done. Will Cora and Brennan be able to endure their trials to find true love?

The Trooper's Treasure: A Fuller Family Novel - Brush Creek Brides Romance (Book 3): Dawn Fuller has made some mistakes in her life, and she's not proud of the way McDermott Boyd found her off the road one day last year. She's spent a hard year wrestling with her choices and trying to fix them, glad for McDermott's acceptance and friendship. He lost his wife years ago, done his best with his daughter, and now he's ready to move on. Can McDermott help Dawn find a way past her former mistakes and down a path that leads to love, family, and happiness?

The Detective's Date: A Fuller Family Novel - Brush Creek Brides Romance (Book 4): Dahlia Reid is one of the best detectives Brush Creek and the surrounding towns has ever had. She's given up on the idea of marriage—and pleasing her mother—and has dedicated herself fully to her job. Which is great, since one of the most perplexing cases of her career

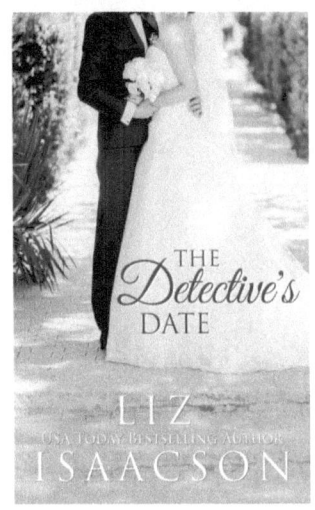

has come to town. Kyler Fuller thinks he's finally ready to move past the woman who ghosted him years ago. He's cut his hair, and he's ready to start dating. Too bad every woman he's been out with is about as interesting as a lamppost—until Dahlia. He finds her beautiful, her quick wit a breath of fresh air, and her intelligence sexy. Can Kyler and Dahlia use their faith to find a way through the obstacles threatening to keep them apart?

The Paramedic's Partner: A Fuller Family Novel - Brush Creek Brides Romance (Book 5): Jazzy Fuller has always been overshadowed by her prettier, more popular twin, Fabiana. Fabi meets paramedic Max Robinson at the park and sets a date with him only to come down with the flu. So she convinces Jazzy to cut her hair and take her place on the date. And the spark between Jazzy and Max is hot and instant...if only he knew she wasn't her sister, Fabi.

Max drives the ambulance for the town of Brush Creek with is partner Ed Moon, and neither of them have been all that lucky in love. Until Max suggests to who he thinks is Fabi that they should double with Ed and Jazzy. They do, and Fabi is smitten with the steady, strong Ed Moon. As each twin falls further and further in love with their respective paramedic, it becomes obvious they'll need to come clean about the switcheroo sooner rather than later...or risk losing their hearts.

The Chief's Catch: A Fuller Family Novel - Brush Creek Brides Romance (Book 6): Berlin Fuller has struck out with the dating scene in Brush Creek more times than she cares to admit. When she makes a deal with her friends that they can choose the next man she goes out with, she didn't dream they'd pick surly Cole Fairbanks, the new Chief of Police.

His friends call him the Beast and challenge him to complete ten dates that summer or give up his bonus check. When Berlin approaches him, stuttering about the deal with her friends and claiming they don't actually have to go out, he's intrigued. As the summer passes, Cole finds himself burning both ends of the candle to keep up with his job and his new relationship. When he unleashes the Beast one time too many, Berlin will have to decide if she can tame him or if she should walk away.

ABOUT LIZ

Liz Isaacson writes inspirational romance, usually set in Texas, or Montana, or anywhere else horses and cowboys exist. She lives in Utah, where she writes full-time, drives her daughter to her acting classes, and eats a lot of peanut butter M&Ms while writing. Find her on her website at lizisaacson.com.

www.ingramcontent.com/pod-product-compliance
Lightning Source LLC
Chambersburg PA
CBHW050610110726
47899CB00001B/51